C.A.T.

Acroname Series
By
Jack & Sue Drafahl
© 2016

Nine Lives of a Cat

One theory on the origin of this expression is that in ancient times nine was a lucky number because it is the Trinity of Trinities. As cats seem able to escape injury time and time again, this lucky number seemed suited to the cat. While in most countries, the cat is said to have nine lives, in Arab, Turkish and Brazilian proverbs poor puss has a mere seven lucky lives and in Russia, it is said to survive nine deaths.

Unknown

C. A. T.

Jack and Sue Drafahl

Published by

www.earthseapublishing.com

Copyright © 2016 by Jack and Sue Drafahl

All Rights Reserved

ISBN: 978-1-938971-00-6

10 9 8 7 6 5 4 3 2

January 2016

This book is dedicated to our good friend,
Ernie Brooks. We would like to thank him for his
never-ending support and his encouraging us to take
another path in life.

Jack and Sue

Chapter 1

June 18, 1980

"Your honor, I object. The district attorney cannot introduce the gun as evidence. The chain of evidence has inappropriate gaps that do not allow the gun to be introduced in this case." The words ran off Andrew Towers' lips smoothly, just as they had many times before.

Towers was a tall man, topping out at six feet, five inches and his slightly gray hair neatly offset his new two-thousand-dollar Armani suit. Towers took pride in looking his best in court. The buttons on the upper part of his jacket even had a custom-made thread that allowed him to easily button and unbutton the jacket as he got up to question witnesses. He casually glanced down at his patent leather shoes and then over to the jury. This case was going to be easy, and so much money would be gained from the acquittal. Andrew looked back at the judge and waited for a judgment on his call. Andrew knew he was pushing the issue a bit, but if he didn't, his client would push him a whole lot more.

His client was the son of a local drug kingpin, Constantine Santos, who called himself the "King of the Southside." His son Nikilous was up for murder one, because he was caught in the victim's apartment, with the weapon in his hand. The whole case could fall by the wayside because the crime scene investigator had been distracted long enough for a young teenager to grab the weapon out of the evidence case. A policeman nearby had run the youth down and retrieved the weapon, but it had been out of the chain of evidence for more than five minutes. Andrew could win his case on that fact alone. Nik was sticking to his story that he had stopped by to see a friend and found him dead. He had picked up the gun out of habit. It was a weak story, but with the broken chain of evidence, Andrew felt confident it was enough to

1

get him off.

The judge looked over to the prosecutor, searching for some help. From the look on his face, Andrew realized he had found a crack in the wall of justice, and pried it apart. The judge hated to rule on this one, since he knew Nik was guilty, but the law was the law. No one was in the room when the murder was allegedly committed, or had actually seen Nik fire the weapon.

The judge was ready to rule, when his court aide slipped him a message. The judge didn't care what it said, since it would provide him more time to try to figure this one out. He read the short note and smiled.

"Approach the bench, please." The two lawyers looked at each other, unsure of what was happening. The judge pulled the court microphone out of the way and looked at Andrew. "Mr. Towers, I just received a message from St. Luke's hospital. Your wife has gone into labor, and your housekeeper has taken her to the hospital. I'm going to close the proceedings for today, and get a fresh start tomorrow at 10 a.m."

Before the judge could add any more to the discussion, Andrew responded, "Your honor that's unnecessary. I can go to the hospital after we finish with this witness."

Both the judge and the prosecutor did a double take at Andrew. The smile on the judge's face quickly turned to anger. "Mr. Towers, we both live in this small town, and our wives are good friends. Mine would kill me right now if I let this case proceed any further. You go be with your wife, and I don't want to hear another word. Both of you step back."

Before anyone could react, the gavel came down, and Andrew returned to his table. He was mumbling to himself as he jammed his papers in his briefcase. Nik grabbed his hand and said, "What the hell is going on, did you sell me out?"

Andrew locked his briefcase and picked up his pen from the table. "Nik, I have to go to the hospital because my wife is having our baby. We'll reconvene again tomorrow."

2

Nik's face started to turn red. "Look, you shyster lawyer, the only family you should be concerned about is the one you're defending. You had them going. You should have objected, and we could have had an acquittal today. I could have been out by tonight, but now I have to rot in jail another day."

Andrew turned and started to walk away without saying a word, knowing he was walking a fine line. Nik had not finished ranting: "We need to talk right now and make plans for tomorrow. Your wife can wait."

Andrew kept walking as Nik yelled out, "You and your new kid will be sorry, because you picked the wrong family to cross."

Chapter 2
July 20, 1992

The squirrel sat in amazement before a very large nut. Although he had scurried by this old tree several times, he had never seen a nut so huge. He first tried to pick it up in his mouth, but found that it was too big. He carefully looked around one more time to see if any other animals were in the area. The coast was clear.

He looked back at the nut again and figured there must be a way to get this prize into the nearby tree, where he was storing his winter food supply. His instinct kicked in and he put his head down, pushing the nut toward his nut storage. Getting the nut to the storage area was easy, but getting it up into the opening was another problem. He knew he could not push it up the side of the tree. Fortunately, the opening was only a foot off the forest floor. He reached down, opened his jaw, and held the side of the nut with his right front paw. He was then able to push himself up the tree with his two back paws and remaining front paw, while maintaining his hold on the massive nut.

Curt looked over and said, "Alex, I think we might have picked too large a nut for our experiment. Look at that crazy squirrel. He's pretty smart for such a little guy."

Alex pointed to the small monitor hooked up to a cable that ran out the window of the run-down shack where they were hiding. The cable went across the forest floor, hidden under pine needles, up the back of the tree and through a small opening about four feet off the ground. "Not to worry, Curt. That little guy's stomach is bigger than his brain. It does all the thinking for him, but look, he's almost home free."

The two looked at the small video monitor as the squirrel finally pushed the nut into a dead cavity in the tree and looked around. Content that everything was safe, the squirrel lay down for a rest, unaware of the video's mechanical eye just a few feet above in another hole. The boys' small video camera was attached to a motorized chain-and-pulley system, allowing them to lower the camera remotely and not alarm the skittish squirrel.

Alex Brandon was thirteen and Curt Towers was a very old twelve. They had been friends since Curt had moved into the neighborhood at age six. They lived only four houses apart, and found each other within days of the move-in. The two hit it off right away, as both had interests in the mechanical aspects of electronics and robotics. The other kids at school classified them as somewhere between nerds and Boy Scouts.

Curt was smarter than Alex, but he was careful not to let it show, especially around Alex. Both found school to be boring, so they started to work on their own projects at home. At first, they tried working at Alex's house, but his mother objected. She ran a small babysitting service out of her home, and she did not want any projects near the little ones under her care.

Their second choice had been Curt's house, since the only other person at home was the housekeeper. Curt's sister, Kendra, was always staying at a girlfriend's house and his father, Andrew Towers, a big-time lawyer, was never home.

Curt's mother had died when he was born, so the only parent he had ever known was his father, but they didn't get along very well. Every conversation with his father was a lecture about getting good grades so that he could get into an excellent law school. Once Curt voiced an opinion about other career options, but his father firmly laid down his directive. Curt was going to be a lawyer; it was his destiny. He would take over the family business someday, and he should be thankful for the privilege. Curt hated the idea; the last thing he wanted to be was a lawyer.

Curt and Alex first began their various projects by buying small radio-controlled cars, a pulley, gears, a motorcycle battery, and a used security camera. They built the first undertaking in Curt's bedroom, but their project was doomed when Curt's father came home early one day. He had marched straight up to Curt's room, kicked in the door, and started to scream at the two boys about wasting their time on such silly projects. To reinforce his opinion, he walked over and crushed their current project with his foot.

Alex was sternly told to go home, and then Curt got a big lecture on the importance of his becoming a lawyer. Curt started to say something about his sister, but realized too late that it was a mistake. His father had no use for girls, because they couldn't carry on the family name in his business.

It was obvious to Curt that his father had been drinking more than usual that day. Little did he know that in the weeks to follow, it would become even worse. His father would make surprise visits to his room, in search of what his father called "electronic contraband." Curt and Alex realized that to satisfy their quest for knowledge, the science lab at school, and the local library was to be their only access to exploring electronic technology.

The boys still wanted to build their projects, but they had nowhere to work. Curt lived at the end of a cul-de-sac next to a small stream that gently flowed down the mountain. Natural curiosity led the boys to follow the stream back into the woods, and under an old wooden bridge, where they found a deserted fire road.

It was a steep and treacherous trail, but their young spirit urged them upward. After hiking a few miles up the overgrown road, they discovered an old mountain cabin in a sad state of disrepair. Obviously, no one had been in the cabin for years. The boys were ecstatic and staked their claim on the shack, so they could fix it up as the home base for their new projects.

Their moods at school and home took a positive change, as they were finally feeling productive again. They were careful to take different trails to the cabin, and always stopped and waited to see if anyone followed. They lied about where they went, using the excuse that they were doing homework at the library. That seemed to satisfy their families--or so they thought.

They worked diligently on their squirrel monitoring, eagerly looking forward to their daily visits. One day when they came to check the video feed from their camera, they were surprised to find a nest with five very small moving objects near the squirrel's underside. It didn't take long for them to figure out their error. At first, they were in shock, but soon they were strutting around like proud papas. For the first five days after the birth, the two boys raced each other up to the cabin to check on mama squirrel and to watch the young ones grow.

On the sixth day, Curt came home from school to find his father in a drunken stupor that topped them all. His father loudly asked him to explain, pointing to the large box in the middle of the floor. Curt cautiously looked over the edge and saw the broken remains of his experiment from the cabin. It had been smashed into thousands of pieces that only an extreme rage could have caused.

His father flailed his arms back and forth, ranting loudly before he banished Curt to his room without any meals. Anguishing about his situation, Curt listened to the noises downstairs, as his father crashed through one room at a time. Even the housekeeper had fled out the front door minutes earlier, and Curt was sure she would never return.

Things in the house eventually became an eerie quiet - not a sound. Then it came to him. What became of his squirrel? He crept down the stairs, afraid his father was going to jump out from a hiding place and grab him. He was more terrified of his father now than he had ever been, but there he was, passed out on the living room sofa, dead drunk.

Curt had to make a quick decision. He called Alex, and then ran out the front door as fast as he could. They met at the bridge and ran until they were breathless, reaching the cabin in record time. The front door was broken off its hinges, lying in the middle of the cabin. Alex looked sympathetically at Curt and was extremely thankful for his calm home life.

Curt turned abruptly and walked over to the tree where the squirrel had its nest. He was about to have Alex boost him up, so he could get a look down the upper hole when he glanced toward the ground and saw the body of their favorite pet. Curt reached down and carefully picked up the sad body coated with dried blood. A large bullet hole had ripped through the center of the small creature, and thankfully, it had died instantly.

The two quickly moved to the front of the tree and hesitantly pointed a flashlight into the lower hole in the tree. The nest was still intact, and Curt could see the baby squirrels reacting to the flashlight.

Curt's mind raced. He turned off the flashlight and looked at his best friend. "Alex, you go home. If anyone asks about me, tell them you saw me go to the library to study for an exam."

Alex turned his head slightly, shrugging at Curt. "What are you going to do?"

Curt started to run back toward the bridge. Over his shoulder, he yelled, "I'm going to save her family. My father did this and it's not fair, but I'm going to try to fix it."

"How are you going to do that?" Alex yelled, but it was too late. Curt was already out of sight.

Bonnie Sellers, age twelve, lay on her bed listening to her latest music addition, when she heard a strange sound above her headsets. She ignored it, but the sound continued. She took off her headset and realized that something was hitting her window. She walked over to open the window and to her surprise, it was Curt Towers. She liked him a lot, but he never gave her the time of day.

As a blossoming young woman, Bonnie was already

starting to attract attention from some of the boys in her classroom. She was of medium height, had long brunette hair, and a mature, yet very pretty face. She looked down at Curt and from the expression on his face; she quickly realized something was wrong - very wrong. She motioned that she would be right down. A few minutes later, they sat at the picnic table in her backyard.

Curt blurted it out as soon as they were seated. "I'm in big trouble, and I don't know who to go to for help. I remembered how you helped your brother with his hamsters, and – well -- I thought you might be able to help me."

Bonnie was totally lost as her mind raced through some possible situations. "Okay, Curt. Slow down. Start from the beginning."

Curt told her about his project with Alex and their finding the deserted shack. Then he told her about his father discovering it. When he got to the part about the dead squirrel, it still didn't make any sense as to how she could help. When she found an opening in the conversation, she put in her two cents. "Curt, I'm sorry for what your father did, but I can't bring back a dead squirrel."

Curt took a deep breath, and finally spit out the real problem. "She had five babies, and they're all going to die because of me. If I hadn't done that crazy experiment, my father would never have gone up and killed the mother. I don't know what to do. Can you help me?"

She could see from his sad eyes that there was more going on than the squirrels, but they would talk about that later. Right now, she had a challenge. Feeding baby hamsters or guinea pigs was easy. Every kid learned how to take care of pets, and feeding babies sometimes became part of the bargain. But squirrels? What do you even feed squirrels?

Bonnie looked Curt straight in the eyes, and what she saw made her like him even more. "Curt, you go home and meet me at the bridge at 8 p.m. I have to work on a solution."

Curt looked at her with unanswered questions. "Shouldn't we go right now?"

Bonnie thought about the task, knowing it wouldn't be easy. "Curt, I have to go to the library to find out how to feed a baby squirrel, and then if I'm lucky, I'll have what I need at home. If not, I'll have to go to the store. You just make sure that you meet me at 8 p.m. Bring plenty of batteries for the flashlight, OK?"

Curt was in a dazed trance before he realized Bonnie was waiting for his answer. "Okay, I'll see you at 8 p.m. ...and ...um ...thanks."

He rushed home to find his father had awakened long enough to open another bottle and down half of it. This was one time he was glad his father had passed out.

Curt called Alex, and filled him in on the plan. He knew it would be late at night before he came home, so he packed his backpack with food, water, and batteries.

He was about ready to leave, when he saw the box of broken parts. He seized the box, and headed out the front door, depositing the now unrelated junk in a large dumpster at the other end of the street. He hiked back to the bridge, arriving at 7:40, and anxiously paced back and forth waiting for something to happen. Alex arrived at 7:50 and joined in on the pacing. Before long, the two of them were agitated.

By 8:10, the two were panicking and ready to head up to the cabin, but then they heard footsteps. It was Bonnie, trudging along visibly exhausted. She leaned against the railing on the wooden bridge to rest. It gave way and she almost fell in, but Curt caught her. She picked up the sack she had just dropped and checked it to see if anything was broken.

"What took you so long?" asked Curt.

Bonnie took another deep breath. "Hey guys, give me a break. Feeding baby squirrels is not going to be easy. I had to go to the store and buy this re-hydration solution called Pedialyte. The pharmacist was not very willing to help, but then his son Bobby stepped in to lend a hand. I told them I found a baby squirrel and needed the solution to feed to it. They had never heard of such a thing, but were finally convinced when I showed them instructions I found in a book."

"You know our chances of saving them are almost nil," she said. "They wouldn't let me have a syringe, so I had to get a small eyedropper, and it may be too big."

Alex looked into the bag, and took out the bottle of Pedialyte. "Hey, why can't we just use baby formula? My mother used it to feed a baby rabbit."

Bonnie snatched the bag from Alex. "First off, if you read the instructions, you'll see that cow's milk, baby formula, and most all pet foods will kill the baby squirrels. No, we use the Pedialyte, and go slowly. OK, guys. Let's get hiking."

The journey up the hill was difficult with the setting sun casting long shadows. By the time they reached the cabin, Bonnie collapsed on the steps. Curt got out a water bottle and gave it to her.

"They're over in the base of that tree," said an exhausted Curt pointing to the squirrel's home. Alex walked over to the opening in the tree and aimed the flashlight to the side of the nest. There was immediate movement.

"They're alive," yelled Alex.

Bonnie and Curt got up and hurried over to the tree. Bonnie crouched down and looked through the opening. These were the tiniest young creatures she had ever seen. She gasped as a sudden wave of pressure came over her. It was all up to her now. They were depending on her to save them.

She reached into the bag, pulled out a hand-cleaning solution, and wiped her hands. She took a deep breath and reached into the nest, carefully picking up the first baby.

She looked at Curt and said, "Wow! The baby is so tiny;

it's only a couple of inches long. Please fill the eyedropper with solution and give it to me."

In less than a minute, she was carefully feeding the first of the five. It started to choke on the solution, which meant that it was taking the solution too fast. She stopped the feeding, rolled it over onto its stomach, and rubbed its back. Thirty seconds later the tiny patient was feeding again. She repeated the process for all five babies.

Then Bonnie pulled out a battery-powered reptile warmer she had stolen from her brother's turtle pen. She hooked it up and made a nest of shredded t-shirts to cover the top. Once it had warmed up, she gently placed all the babies into their new warm nest.

Curt was impressed and surprised at how well Bonnie was handling the situation. "Bonnie, how do you know so much about feeding squirrels?"

"An hour ago, I knew nothing about the subject. I'm just really good at finding what I want to know about in the library. You both know what the library is, right?"

She stopped to think about what she had just said. "I'm sorry guys. I didn't mean that. I'm just so tired. So where do we go from here?"

Then the real problem started to appear simultaneously in the boys' minds, but Alex was the first to voice an opinion. "Hey, my mother will never let me keep them in the house or anywhere outside. Besides, we have two cats. I could never keep these guys safe."

Bonnie and Alex both looked to Curt. "I know I'm responsible for all this, but if I take them home with me, I'll never be able to hide them. My father killed their mother, so he wouldn't hesitate to kill the babies."

There was complete silence for thirty seconds before Bonnie started collecting all the items putting them into the bag. "Okay, here's the deal and you both owe me big-time. I'll take

12

the babies home with me. Curt, I have a feeling you're going to be in big trouble for some time, so I don't expect to see you for a while."

"Alex, I expect you to come by every day and get me supplies, if I need them. The instructions indicated that I have to hand feed the babies for 8-10 weeks, so I'll have to ask my mother for help. She's a softy when it comes to animals. Don't worry, I won't tell her what really happened."

"Now I suggest that the two of you take me back to the bridge and then go home. We'll talk tomorrow at school."

The boys hung their heads low, saying nothing as they hiked down to their respective homes.

Chapter 3

20 years later

"This had better work, Curt," threatened Ross Kelly, CEO of the South Central Colorado Nuclear Power Plant.

The nuclear plant was built using a completely new design that reduced safety problems and produced less waste. It was leading the way for similar plants to be built throughout the United States, specifically in inland areas.

A few days ago, one of the main sensors sent a warning message to the diagnostic computer. Technicians inspected every inch of the system, searching for the cause of the error. Finally, the $10,000 sensor near the core was pulled and replaced, but the same error instantly appeared on the screen. They weighed the millions of dollars it would entail taking the cooling system apart, and the penalty fees for the delays would put the project way over budget. With no other options, the plant's CEO called Curt Towers, and his magical Xtreme Machines.

Over the past few years, the industrial division of Xtreme Machines had built a solid reputation for getting the job done, even under the most adverse conditions. It was now up to one of Curt's thumbnail-sized $200,000 submarines to solve the problem.

The miniaturized sub had been inserted into the cooling system at a test sample pipe, and it was maneuvering down to a larger tube that fed into the reactor core. The slow-moving current allowed the sub maneuverability, even though its large passageway dwarfed it. Minutes later, the sub came to a halt just before it approached a T-intersection. Sensor readings in the front of the sub indicated that the current in the larger passage was four times stronger than the sub could power through in a forward direction.

Peter Harden, lead scientist and the best sub operator at

Xtreme Machines looked at the controls and then back to Curt Towers. "Hang on--here we go," Peter yelled as he reached down and turned the directional control and simultaneously pressed a smaller button on the control's side panel. Microseconds later, an electronic signal triggered a grappling hook to fire out of the front of the sub and anchored itself into the far wall of the intersecting channel. As the sub maneuvered into the larger passage, Peter turned the sub around so that it could gradually work its way down the passage backward. He carefully fed out the line of the tethered grappling hook and used rear thrusters to keep the sub from being pushed down the passage into the larger chamber below.

Everyone in the control room had their fingers crossed as the sub inched its way back down the tube. Once it came to the entrance of the sensor tube, a second grappling hook was fired, anchoring itself to the channel. Peter used the take-up on the line to pull the sub inside the opening where the reactor's sensor was located.

As soon as the sub entered the smaller tube, the current dropped to almost zero. Everyone assumed that they would see the core's sensor on the video feed coming from the front of the submarine. Instead, the camera and lights were focused on a blank metal wall. Curt leaned down and looked at the screen. "So, what the hell are we looking at? That doesn't look like a sensor to me. Are we in the wrong pipe?"

The CEO's face turned red with anger. He knew what they were looking at. "I don't believe it. I just don't believe it. Damn it! I knew all those new codes we got last month were going to come back and bite us in the butt. Damn it all."

Curt and Peter continued to look at the screen, trying to figure out what the CEO knew. Peter was about to comment, but decided to let the boss handle this one. Curt proceeded by saying, "Okay, Mr. Kelly. As far as I can see, either we're in the wrong tube or the end of this one is sealed."

Kelly looked up at the ceiling and then back to the monitor. "Okay, here's the deal. A month ago, the commission that monitors our construction decided that we needed to beef up the concrete shielding around the main water line and sensor tubes. The added concrete meant that we had to extend all the sensor pipes. We had to run a pressure test before the concrete was added, and pressure caps were added to the ends of each pipe. Apparently, the workers forgot to remove the pressure cap when they added the extension piece that holds the sensor. The bottom line is that the sensor is not measuring the water temperature, but instead, the air gap between the pressure cap and the new end piece that holds the sensor array."

Frustrated, but determined, he continued his explanation. "With all the systems online, we would have to shut the entire system down to figure a way to remove the cap. If you can come up with a better idea, I'll make sure you have the contracts for all the nuclear plants."

There was total silence in the control room for almost fifteen seconds, before Peter looked up at Curt and smiled. "You want me to tell him, boss?"

Curt put his hand on Peter's shoulder and gave it a squeeze. "Be my guest. It's your baby."

Peter turned on the laser targeting system and explained. "Mr. Kelly, what we have here is Star Wars technology in the micro-world. A miniature laser is mounted on the front of the sub, capable of cutting the cap out of the tube without breaching the system. If you give me the go ahead, I can start cutting. The only problem is that the sub will be too contaminated with radiation, so it will have to be a one-way trip."

Mr. Kelly looked around at his technicians. They all nodded their heads in agreement. "Go," he said, as he leaned over Peter's shoulder.

Seconds later, the viewing screen displayed the small laser beam cutting the cap right where it joined the walls of the sensor

16

tube. From the looks of things, this was going to take some time.

Mr. Kelly leaned back and looked at Curt. "Okay, Curt. It looks like this is going to work, but I do have one question. Why do you call the sub SCRAT?"

Peter chuckled as he manipulated the controls. Curt looked around as though he was looking for an answer. "It's the acronym for Self-Contained Robotic Articulated Technologies."

Peter chuckled again.

Kelly was not satisfied. "That's a mouthful for a miniature submarine. How did you come up with that?"

"The name came first; the acronym came second," said Curt with slight sadness in his voice.

Before anyone could respond, a young technician answered, "Isn't that the name of the crazy prehistoric squirrel in the movie *Ice Age*?"

A smile came over Curt's and Peter's faces, but neither responded to the technician.

The laser continued to cut the piece out and used a third grappling hook to pull it and the sub out of the small pipe and into the larger one. Within seconds, the sub and the metal plug were swept past the core and out a small drainage port for waste collection at the bottom of the chamber.

It had been a good day for Curt and Xtreme Machines. All of his ideas were finally paying off in a big way. He glanced at his watch and saw that it was already 5:00 p.m. He needed to be home by seven for dinner, so there was just enough time to go back to the office and make a few notes for future contracts. Curt felt it was imperative to get your ideas written down before they became blurred and ineffective. This attention to detail was just one reason why Curt and his company had done so well.

17

Chapter 4

Cindy Towers sat on the couch reading the latest Nora Roberts novel, when an alarm went off on the TV control panel. Their home was not the typical family home since Curt had installed the most sophisticated encrypted communications system he could find. He had video communication at home, in the office, and on a small portable iPod-like device that his company built. Curt set up the system so that when he gave a voice command, there was instant visual communication between the home and the office.

Seconds after the alarm went off, Curt's face was on camera, and he was smiling. Cindy had not seen that big a smile on him in a long time. "Okay, what happened today? You look like you just won the lottery," she said.

Curt pressed the security system activating the video encryption. "Well, it went great today, and we got the job done. It looks like we might have a lot more SCRAT contracts coming up when the new plants come online."

Cindy closed her book and set it down next to her glass of wine. She had started to celebrate ahead of time since she knew Curt would be successful. "Curt, I'm so happy it went well, but to be perfectly honest, does Xtreme Machines really need any more work? Since you expanded to the medical and military divisions, you don't need more contracts. Either that or you're going to have to hire more people. Besides, I can see it now. Your hours will be longer, and the kids and I will see you even less." Cindy stopped. She knew she had lectured him too much and decided to table the discussion. She felt bad dampening his mood, after such a successful day.

Curt knew his wife was getting more upset with his long hours. He didn't have anything more to say, so they just continued to stare at each other on the monitor.

His mind drifted to when they were first married and how simple things were then. They were both fresh out of college. Curt had his Ph.D. in mechanical science and started up his own company. Cindy had her master's degree in education and taught junior high for the first couple of years. When the babies started to come, Cindy decided she loved raising kids more than teaching.

They were blessed with one boy and two daughters. Lisa came first, John second, and Brenda was the youngest. They were great kids; he just wasn't getting to enjoy them enough.

His daydreaming was interrupted as a small video image of Brenda appeared in the upper left corner of his monitor. "Hi, Dad, when you coming home? I have something I did in school that I want to show you."

Curt hesitated for a moment, and then pressed a button that switched the smaller video image with the larger. "Hi, honey. I'm going to be home soon, and you can show me then. I have good news too - I'll be home for the rest of the week."

Cindy was in shock because the statement had caught her completely off guard. She cut into the conversation, "Is there something wrong, Curt?"

"Yes, there is. I haven't been home for any length of time in a long while. Peter has talked me into taking some much-needed time off. It appears that I picked the right men for the VP positions of each division because they all agreed with Peter. They said I should consider even more than a week off, but I'm not so sure about that. I told them I would think about it if they agreed to keep me up-to-date every day via emails. The bottom line is that you're going to have to put up with me for at least a week."

This was a dream come true for Cindy, but she wasn't sure that it would really work. "It sounds great, Curt, but can you honestly tell me you won't be back in the office in a couple of days? The last time we had a vacation was...well I can't even

19

remember."

Curt started to pack up his briefcase and close down his laptop. "I know, I've made promises before, but the three VPs have guaranteed me that I won't be needed for a few weeks. They have cleared my docket, and will move my appointments to next month. Say good-bye now because if we talk any longer, I'll never get out of here, and just might find some reason to stay."

"Goodbye," said Cindy as she turned the communications link off. She took a sip of wine, enjoying the soft music in the background. She thought, "This is going to be a very unusual week for sure."

Chapter 5

Alex Brandon paced back and forth in his office. It was a very bad day for his company, Brandon Industries. His rival Curt Towers was successful today at the power plant, taking another bite out of the potential client base for Brandon Industries.

Alex felt that he was always one step behind Curt, but it had not always been that way. When Curt and Alex were growing up, they were best friends and equals in every way, or at least that's what Alex thought. Their friendship gradually became distant when they went their different directions in college. Alex had attended MIT while Curt had gone to Cal Tech. They kept in contact as much as possible, but as the years went by, communication between the two was reduced to holidays at home in Colorado.

Alex was sure that his top standings at MIT would make him a leader in the micro technology world, but it was not that easy. Curt was a sharp businessman with pioneering designs.

Curt tended to think outside the box, and that lessened his concentration on his required core subjects in college. Thus, his grades didn't reflect that he was a man with innovative ideas. Things turned around after graduation when he started to work for a small electronics company. Soon many of the company's clients recognized Curt's potential and encouraged him to go out on his own.

Curt struggled trying to get a fledgling company off the ground. He refused any partnerships, and that made it even more difficult. It all changed one day when he made a presentation to a bank on micro inspections in the industrial sector, and discovered the bank president had a fondness for leading-edge technology. With money for expansion, Curt found that clients started to come to Xtreme Machines in droves.

The competition between the two men changed a past friendship into competitive rivalry, which then evolved into extreme hatred and jealousy of the other's accomplishments.

Alex used a more traditional method to start his business. He had a family fortune that had been passed on to him, and he was wise enough to get a financial planner in from the start. His company paralleled Curt's in many ways, but he seemed to be losing clients to his rival because Xtreme Machines was beating them out on almost every contract. His stockholders screamed for change, and Alex was told by the board that something had better happen soon, or heads would roll.

Alex pressed the buzzer for his secretary. "Has Ross come in yet?"

There was static for a second or two, and then the answer. "Mr. Langer just came in. I've already told him that you want to see him right away."

Alex didn't respond to his secretary. He just waited. He wanted to pace some more, but decided it would be more impressive to sit behind his desk. As he sat down, the door opened and Ross Langer walked in. "You wanted to see me?"

Alex picked up the most-recent memo from his communication chief. "Ross, we're in trouble. Xtreme Machines got the contract for the power plants. We cannot lose any more contracts to them. We have to take measures that are more drastic. Are you on board for the plan we discussed earlier?"

Ross sat down in the chair in front of the desk. "Hey, I'll do whatever it takes. The key, though, is whether she's on board?"

Alex pulled out the bottom drawer on his desk and removed an encrypted phone. "Let's see, to be sure. She normally works late, and the last time I talked with her, she was going through the money we gave her as if it was growing on trees. She'll want more, but otherwise there should be no problem."

22

Alex punched in a few numbers. The phone rang three times before she finally answered, "Kathy Robinson here. What do you want, Alex?"

Chapter 6
Eight Months Later

It was like a bad dream, and each of the past few months got increasingly worse. If there was a hell, then this had to be it. Curt was still trying to figure out how he got to this point in his life, or what semblance of a life he still possessed. He was seated at the defendant's table, standing trial for the rape and murder of one of his employees, Kathy Robinson. The prosecutor had so much evidence pointing to his guilt that most of the press had written that it was going to be a slam-dunk trial.

Everyone kept telling him he needed to plead out, but he refused. He had done nothing wrong, but no one seemed to believe him. If he pleaded to a lesser charge, his life was over. Either way, he was up a creek without a paddle. His only chance was to go all the way with the jury, but the odds of that working in his favor were about one in a million.

It had all started on his second day of vacation many months ago. He was just getting comfortable with the idea of staying away from the office, when he got a frantic call from Wendy Marshall, Kathy Robinson's secretary. She was concerned about her boss because Kathy had called and said she was in trouble at a small motel in the lower side of town. She mentioned something about being beaten up by a man who worked in the shipping department.

Curt suggested calling the police, but Wendy told him Kathy didn't want the police involved. Although this seemed odd to Curt, he felt obligated to go and find out what had happened. He foolishly decided not to tell his wife Cindy about the problem, thinking he could limit damage control.

When he reached the motel, the door to the room was open, and Kathy was crouched down in a corner beside the bed.

He started to go to help her, and suddenly everything became fuzzy.

The next thing he remembered was being handcuffed and looking down at the body of Kathy Robinson. Her arms were tied behind her nude body. The bed was soaked with blood. He tried to think about what could possibly have happened, but he passed out again and when he woke up, he was in jail.

The police grilled him repeatedly, and his head was spinning; he was still in a daze. He finally regained his senses enough to ask for a lawyer, but not before some very incriminating evidence had become known.

When he was first arrested, everyone he knew stood in his support. They were all convinced that he'd been set up, or that the police had the wrong man. However, as the prosecutor introduced one piece of evidence after another, his supporters began to dwindle.

The trial had gone on for weeks, and was the highlight of the newspaper headlines throughout the state. They kept repeating the facts until the words "allegedly guilty" seemed useless.

The victim was stabbed 27 times.

The defendant's fingerprints were all over the murder weapon and on the body.

The murder weapon was found to be from the defendant's knife collection.

The defendant's seminal fluid was found inside the victim.

The defendant was found naked in the bed with the dead woman.

The defendant was seen entering the room just before the murder occurred.

His wife Cindy was strong and supportive from day one, and even brought the children to see Curt in lockup when he wasn't allowed bail. When it was brought to light that his seminal fluids were found in Kathy, Cindy stopped coming to court, and eventually cut off all contact with Curt.

Curt was lost without his family's support. He never heard anything from his father even though he was an attorney, but in truth, he never expected that he would. As the weeks progressed, only two people in his company hung onto the belief of his innocence -- his secretary, Tomas Rooney, and sub pilot, Peter Harden. They came to see him almost every day, and were the glue that helped him hold things together.

The biggest surprise of all came just a week before the trial was to end. His number-one business competitor and childhood friend, Alex Brandon, came to see him in the county lockup. Alex told him that the whole case against Curt was a frame, and that he'd never believed a word of what the prosecution had against Curt. He had told him that he would look in on Curt's family and make sure that they were all right.

Curt was in shock. He and Alex had become bitter competitors, and now Alex was stepping up to help. Maybe, there was actually one ray of hope in a very dark future for Curt. He started to wonder if he had misjudged Alex, and that he really was the same good kid he knew at age thirteen.

As Curt listened to the prosecutor make his final statements before the case went before a jury, he started to understand why all his friends and family had left him. He sounded guilty as hell, and the wimpy defense his lawyer presented only succeeded in making him look like a rich man trying to get away with murder.

As he got up to leave, his lawyer tried one last time to persuade him to plead down to a lesser charge. He refused, knowing he was innocent, but that he was going to be convicted anyway.

That evening he listened as the prisoners were taking odds on the outcome of his case. Sadly, the odds were against him 100 to 1.

Chapter 7

Curt looked out through the bars of the bus as it rolled down the narrow and winding road toward the state prison. There had been no surprises with the verdict, and the appeal's process had been just as swift. The evidence had been undeniable—Curt Towers was guilty of rape and murder. That he couldn't remember anything about the event even started to make Curt wonder about his innocence.

He overheard stories in the county lockup about life in the state prison. Even though it was a newer, state-of-the-art facility, it was still going to be hell on earth. Curt glanced around at the other inmates on the bus, and soon realized the prison social structure consisted of only two types of inmates—the strong and the weak.

Curt looked over to the man handcuffed to him and decided he was definitely part of the weaker prison structure. He was a small man, thin hair, wiry body, who didn't fit the criminal stereotype.

As Curt turned to look out the window, a mousy voice floated from the man's lips. "You don't look like a murderer, but I've been wrong before. My name is Larry Nelson."

He wasn't sure if he should respond, because this was all so new to him. Since the man seemed okay, he replied, "I'm Curt Towers. My friends sometimes call me CAT since I'm a bit like a cat with nine lives. I keep getting out of scrapes – except this one."

"Hey, you're the guy everyone is talking about, the one who stabbed that woman 27 times, right?"

Curt was about to speak, but Larry stopped him. "Before you tell me you didn't do it, let me give you a piece of advice. This is my third and final time I'm going down to state. I dabble in theft and embezzlement, but my specialty is forgery. I made a few stupid mistakes, got greedy, and got caught by the three-strikes law.

"Anyway, don't tell anyone in prison that you're not guilty. It's a sign of weakness, and that's the last thing you want to show to the rest of the prison population. Furthermore, don't brag about your crime, because those that do are generally making it up, and that's another sign of weakness. That's what prison life is all about. You can't show any weakness, because as soon as you do, you'll be dead."

Curt looked around to see if anyone else was listening. The guard gave him a dirty look, but then turned his eyes back toward the front of the bus.

Curt whispered, "So, why are you telling me all this?"

"Another part of prison life is collecting favors. You scratch my back, and I'll scratch yours. If I help you now, I may need a favor from you sometime in the future. You have to form alliances to keep the strong forces from crushing you to a pulp. Favors play an important part of these pacts."

Curt looked directly into the eyes of his new friend. "What else can you tell me? How can I survive?"

"The most important thing of all is don't piss off the warden. One word from him and you will disappear for months at a time. Try to keep it under the radar. The number-one rule in prison, though, is to never rat on another inmate--no matter what."

Curt looked out through the bars, trying to digest this new prison philosophy. The fields were going by so fast that he found his mind drifting again.

What was that movie about a fugitive? Oh yeah, Richard Kimble was framed just like me. I wonder what my chances are that this bus could run off the road, and I could escape.

He was instantly jarred back into reality when the bus came to an abrupt stop at the prison gates. A few minutes later, a guard came onto the bus, and checked his log against those inside. Satisfied that the count was correct, he whispered something to the guard in the front as he exited. The bus lurched forward, straining against the load, and stopped again once inside the prison walls. The door opened, admitting a large broad-shouldered guard.

"Okay, you scumbags. Stand up and slowly walk to the front. Stop here so I can remove your handcuffs. Any funny stuff and you'll be regretting you ever crossed me."

Twenty minutes later Curt and the other prisoners were standing in a line facing a group of six guards. As they were making their way off the bus, Larry whispered to Curt, telling him to keep his mouth shut, answer only when spoken to, and keep his head slightly down. Curt followed Larry's lead and listened intently as the lead guard laid out the prisoners' ground rules. The longer the guard spoke, the more Curt became shaken by his situation. Throughout the trial, he'd known it was going to be bad, but not until now did he realize just how bad.

The remainder of the afternoon was one procedure after another as he was processed into the prison. They took pictures, fingerprints, medical backgrounds, and finally issued cell assignments and prison clothes. Once finished, the guards escorted the newbies to their respective cells. Curt's new home was on the upper level toward the end of cellblock four. Larry was his cellmate.

As he passed by each cell, he could hear the comments that Larry had told him would come.

"Here comes some new meat.
Hey, honey. Why don't you stay with me?
Do you want to have some fun? See you later tonight."

As Curt passed by the last few cells, he noticed a huge prisoner. He had to be 300 pounds and looked like a football player with all the gear on. He said nothing, but just growled as

Curt passed by.

Curt found the next cell interesting. The man inside seemed to have everything - a small TV, books, a table, lounge chair, and other items Curt didn't think were standard prison issue. Obviously, this man acquired many privileges.

When the guard reached his cell, he yelled out the cell number, and it opened. The guard pushed him in with the butt end of a club, and told him to stand against the back wall. Minutes later, Larry was pushed into the same cell, and the door closed. Larry smiled at Curt and walked over to the two bunks.

"It's a small world. I was sort of hoping we'd get the same cell. I know you think I'll be a hindrance. However, I know plenty about how prison works, and I'll show you how to work the system. You could have done a lot worse than me."

Curt sat down on the edge of the lower bunk. "Hey, I never said a thing. Right now, you're about the only friend I seem to have, so I'll make the best of it. So, who is the big guy and the one next to him with all the goodies in his cell?"

Larry checked the mattress on the top bunk. It would do fine. "The big guy is called 'Tank.' He's in for killing three guys in a bar fight. Tank works for the fellow in the next cell. His name is Bart Tombs, and he ran a casino in Nevada before he expanded his illegal activities into Colorado. You might call him the "King of cellblock four." They got him on bribing a politician, extortion, and tax evasion. He's one man you never want to cross. When he asks you to do something, there is only one choice, unless you want to die early in this hellhole. If you can get on his good side, this place will be a cakewalk."

Curt lay back on his bunk. The way his luck was going, there was little to no chance of that happening.

Chapter 8

At 5 a.m., the guards were rattling the cells and yelling for everyone to get ready. Curt and Larry waited as each of the cell doors opened. Curt was about to walk out into the hall, when Larry pulled him back.

"No, not yet, Curt. The first day we don't eat with the population. They take us to the visitor's room where we'll get breakfast. If they dump you too fast into the population, you'll end up dead in one day. The guards look you over, so to speak this day. They'll try to push you into a fight. Don't resist. Take whatever they dish out. One other thing, breakfast is only ten minutes, so you better eat fast."

Just as Larry finished his briefing, the guard came in and told them to move along the walkway. They went down a flight of stairs, through a security door, and into a small room with tables and chairs. They were told to sit down. A few minutes later, a cook with a food table came in and set up for breakfast. Three guards remained in the room while the new inmates fed on the worst food Curt had ever tasted. He knew he needed his strength, so he downed as much as he could in the ten minutes they were given.

Just as he was about to finish his coffee, the largest guard grabbed Curt by the arm. "You're coming with me. The warden wants to talk to you. Keep your eyes straight ahead and no talking."

Curt looked up at Larry, who gave him the "I don't know what's up" look, so Curt headed off in the direction the guard had pointed to with his stick. They traversed several hallways and stairs before Curt stood before a large, ornate walnut door. The door looked valuable and featured an intricate drawing of a hunter in the woods. The guard knocked on the door, then reached down and turned the rustic door handle ushering Curt into the large office.

The warden was looking out the window toward the center courtyard. He spoke as he continued to spy on the morning conversations between the prisoners.

"I don't want any problems from you. You're somewhat of a celebrity as far as the press is concerned, and I don't want my name on page one."

The warden turned around to face Curt. He had done as Larry had told him, keeping his face at a slight downward angle, saying nothing.

"Are we straight on this, Tower?"

"Yes, Sir, I will give you no problems."

"Make sure you don't."

"You do as you're told, and I may add some privileges in a few months. Do we understand each other?"

"Yes, Sir."

"Guard, take him back to his cell, and no side trips. If I even hear that you made any detours, I will have you down in the isolation block. Understand?"

The guard did not look very happy. From what Curt could tell, he had just escaped his first contact with the stronger part of prison. "Yes, Sir, I'll take him directly back to his cell."

As the guard closed the door, he gave Curt a jab in the side, doubling him over. "Towers, you lucked out this time. The warden just gave you your first "get out of jail free" card. Next time you won't be so lucky."

Ten minutes later, Curt was back in his cell. When the guard left, Larry moved over to the bent-over Curt. "Expect a lot more of that in the next few weeks. The guards try to provoke you into a fight, and they would love for you to fight back, so don't. It would be a big mistake. Just suck it up for the next three months, and if you have a clean slate, they'll add a privilege. You'll have a choice between the exercise yard and the workshop. Both are better than sitting in the yard all day. So, what did the warden want?"

"Basically, he said what you just told me. However, I want to know one thing, Larry. Why are you helping me so much? Are you looking for more than future favors? Is there something you're not telling me?"

"Yes, there is, and someday soon I'll tell you, but for right now be thankful that you have someone like me helping you."

Chapter 9

The next day was the first day in the yard for Curt. He was the last prisoner to enter the yard, and the group made a hole in the center for him to enter. As he walked the gauntlet of dagger eyes, a foot came out tripping him. He picked himself up as the tougher-looking prisoners started to laugh. They moved closer and started to form a tighter circle around him, when one of the guards broke in and yelled for everyone to break it up. The guard looked up at the window where the warden was looking down. Curt survived another potential disaster.

Larry came over to Curt and looked around to see who was still watching. Bart Tombs and his sidekick Tank were nearby discussing something with several of the rougher looking prisoners.

Larry motioned for Curt to move out of the center of the yard. "You are one lucky son of a bitch. Those guys were going to have you for lunch. It looks like the warden doesn't want all the publicity connected with your death in prison. Right now, the only thing keeping you alive is what put you in here. I'm concerned Tank and Mr. Tombs don't consider you one of their favorite people. Make sure you don't look into their cell when the guards march us back to our hole."

By early afternoon, Curt was happy he had survived his first day in the yard. They headed back to their cell, Larry in the lead, and Curt following. As he walked by Tank's cell, he carefully looked straight ahead.

Then a voice rang out. "Towers, I want to talk to you."

The guard jabbed Curt in the back with the club, causing Curt to stop in his tracks. He looked into the cell, and Tombs moved over to the cell door. He was a fat, ugly man with a face that would have made Scarface look like an angel. Someone had gotten the better of him, and taken it out on his face. Tombs gave the guard a nod, signaling for Larry to continue ahead. It was obvious that this guard would do whatever Tombs wanted.

Tombs looked over to Tank and then back to Towers. "Okay, here's how it's going to be. I own you. I owned you as soon as you came through the prison gates. If I want to sell you to one of the other prisoners for a few days, you won't object, unless you want to end up dead. Do I make myself clear?"

Curt's good luck ended. He was about to experience the horrors of prison life he'd always heard about. The beatings, rape, and other horrific things that made him cringe. As he looked into Tomb's cell, his mind was racing. There had to be something he could find to help himself. He scanned back and forth, and then he saw a small device lying open with several scattered parts. "I can fix your MP3 player," Curt said quickly.

Curt kept his head down. Tombs looked back at the broken MP3 player. "So, you think you can buy your way out of trouble by fixing something for me? Well, I don't think that's going to work. Everyone I know with technical knowledge has tried with no success. See, the thing is that I could easily get a new one, but this one my daughter gave me when I came into this place. Therefore, it has special meaning. If you think you can fix it, be my guest. Then we'll see how you stand."

Tombs opened the cell door, and Curt walked in and looked at the broken player. It had been dropped from several feet, or was a weapon in a fight. The truth was that it was severely damaged, but with Curt's knowledge of micro devices, he might actually be able to repair it and save himself. He looked down on the counter and saw a magnifier and a set of small screwdrivers. Curt couldn't believe that the guards would allow the screwdrivers in a cell, but that only proved just how much power Tombs possessed. He looked over the broken circuit board. Three runners were broken or damaged, and a small connector was smashed. He set the unit back down.

"I can fix it, but I'll need a soldering iron, a new connector, and several jumper wires."

"Really, that's all you need? No one asked for those parts before. Why do you think you can fix it when no one else could?"

"Mr. Tombs, you already know that my company specializes in very small devices like this one. I can fix it." Curt hoped that his voice exerted more confidence than his gut was telling him.

"Okay, Towers. Tomorrow, the parts will be here. If you can fix it, I may reconsider what I want to do with you."

Magically, the guard appeared and escorted Curt back to his cell.

Larry was waiting on the upper bunk as the door closed behind Curt.

"Okay, Curt, what gives? What did Tombs want? Let me guess. He owns you, right? He made a deal and now you are his property."

Curt sat down with a blank expression on his face. "That's what he told me, but I decided to swing a postponement on my status. I told him I would fix something for him."

"Are you crazy? Whatever it is, if you don't fix it, you are in big trouble. So what is it? Does he want somebody killed?"

"He wants me to fix his MP3 player."

Larry looked down at Curt with a puzzled face. "You're going to do what?"

Chapter 10

The next morning after breakfast, Curt was escorted to Tomb's table. When Tombs waved his hand, most of the other cons quickly left. "Okay, here's the deal. The guard will take you back to my cell, but a friend of mine, Tank, will be there to watch you as you attempt to do what no one has been able to do before. You have this one chance. Screw it up and well--you're a smart man. I think you get the picture."

The guard poked Curt in the back, and they headed off to Tombs' cell. A few minutes later, the guard "gently" pushed him into the cell. On the counter lay a new soldering iron, solder, flux, and a magnifying visor. Curt was also surprised to see a small stand with two alligator clips used to hold small electronic boards. He didn't care how the tools were magically delivered; just that he had all he needed. He sat down, put on the visor, and started to work. In twenty minutes, the wires were soldered in place and the damaged connector was replaced with a new one. Everything had gone well until Curt turned it on and nothing happened. It should have worked, but it didn't.

Curt looked at Tank, who looked over to the guard. In seconds, the guard was gone and Curt feared why. Tombs was on his way back to deal with him, his newly acquired property.

Curt took the small screwdriver and started to touch the end to each of the miniaturized parts on the board. Then he saw it. A cold solder joint had broken loose from the board, just enough to lose the electrical connection. It was still attached to the board but had no connectivity. The problem now was the tip of the soldering iron was too large to re-solder the problem area, and time was running out.

He looked over the bench searching for a solution. He grabbed a small pair of pliers and broke off the end of one of the tiny screwdrivers. He wrapped a small wire around the broken end of the screwdriver and the end of the soldering iron. This added one-inch and a fine point to the soldering iron. He plugged the iron back in and waited.

The added bulk to the iron meant that it took longer to heat back up. Two minutes went by, then three. He kept trying the tip on some solder and was about to give up when it came up to temperature and the solder finally melted. He pushed the end of the jerry-rigged soldering iron onto the cold solder joint and waited. In seconds, it re-melted into a new sure-fire connection.

He could hear the guard talking to Tombs as they walked down the hallway. Tombs entered the cell and was about to speak when Curt turned on the MP3 switch. An old Elvis song *Jail House Rock* started to blare out of the small speakers. Curt took a deep breath and stepped back. Tombs walked over to the restored player and plugged his headset into the jack. For the first time since Curt had met this Mr. Evil, he saw him smile.

Tombs turned the player off and motioned to the guard, who immediately left the cell.

"Okay, you were lucky with this one, Towers. Can you put it back into the plastic case?"

For the first time in days, Curt felt that he might have avoided the alligator swamp for which he seemed destined. Then a plan came to mind. "Not a problem. In fact, I can fix a lot of things for other cons so that they would owe YOU favors."

This idea really appealed to Tombs. He loved it when everyone owed him favors. "Okay, Towers. What kind of success rate are we discussing? Can you fix five out of ten - or better? How good are you, really?"

"I think I'm pretty good. My company does very well with micro devices, and I was in on most of the technical planning. I'm confident that I can fix eight out of ten devices given to me for repair."

Tombs picked up the MP3 player parts. "Okay, here's the

deal. You put this back together, and then fix the other devices I'll get from the other cons. If this works out, there might be some better times for you in this hellhole. I'll make sure no one bothers you from this day forward. However, remember one thing, don't lie, or cross me. You'll regret it tremendously. Since you have done a good job so far, I'm granting you one special request."

Curt was hoping for this, and he didn't even have to ask for it. Tombs was a smart businessman, at least in prison. "I would like the protection you offered me to cover my cellmate Larry. It would be hard for me to work if my cellmate is constantly being beaten up or harassed."

Tombs looked over to Tank for a second. Although Curt could see no signal from the giant, he hoped that the lack of response meant yes. At least, he hoped it would be yes.

"Okay, it's a deal. Both you and Larry are under my protection. However, you must do your very best to fix anything I bring you."

Tombs put out his hand for a shake and caught Curt off guard. He squeezed Curt's hand hard, and pulled him close.

"Don't screw with me, Towers. I will only tell you once."

"I won't let you down."

"You'd better not."

The guard appeared like magic, and escorted Curt back to his cell.

Larry jumped down from the upper bunk. "So, what gives?"

"Larry, you are going to love this. I now work for Mr. Tombs, and I added you under his protection as part of the deal."

Larry's eyes got big, and then a tear formed in one eye. "I knew you were the best thing to happen to me. You're a lot smarter than the rest of these punks. How in the hell did you get on Tombs' good side so quickly?"

Curt sat down on the bed and told Larry the whole story.

Larry was very quiet for a couple of minutes, and Curt was unsure what was up. "Okay, Larry. What gives? You did me a favor by helping me when I first came in, and now I'm paying you back. Is there something I'm missing?"

Larry rubbed his forehead and looked down at the floor.

"You might as well know, but no one else can, okay? About a month before I was caught, I didn't feel very well, and went in for a doctor's appointment. I guess there's no easy way to say it; I have lung cancer and have less than a year. I think my subconscious wanted me to be caught, so that I could die in here. You see, I have a wife and three kids, and we don't have medical insurance. By being caught, I'll have my bills paid by the state. Spending the rest of my life in jail instead of with my family wasn't the best option, but it seemed the only solution."

Larry paused before continuing. "I never told my wife as I didn't want her to feel bad and try to get me out of prison. The state would have possibly dropped the charges if they had known they would have to foot the medical bills. So in a month or so I'll complain of stomach problems, and it will be the state's problem from that point on. The best part is that you got me protection for the rest of the time I'm alive. I can never thank you enough for that."

For the first time in weeks, Curt moved his concern from his own life to a prison mate. Fate was such a strange thing. He didn't know what to say to Larry. He'd never known anyone with cancer before, but now he was about to have a front-row seat. "I'm sorry, Larry. I've been so concerned about my own well-being that I never considered there might be a problem with you. Is there anything I can do?"

"Curt, you have done more than any man could ever ask."

Chapter 11

In the next few weeks, Curt repaired more than two dozen different devices ranging from hearing aids to electric shavers. It amazed him the amount of contraband floating around the prison. So far, only one item couldn't be repaired, and Tombs seemed fine with that. Curt quickly became known as Mr. Fixit in cellblock four.

The next challenge was a small TV set brought in from one of the guard stations. Tombs wanted the owed favor from the guard, so he wasn't going to take failure as an option. Curt sat at his chair, using his head magnifier to look over the circuit boards, but he was lost. This was much more complex than he had thought.

"I can't fix this without a schematic diagram of the circuit boards."

Tombs moved closer to see what Curt was looking at. "So where do we get these diagrams?"

"The internet would be my best chance, but that means I would need full library privileges. Then I could log onto the manufacturer's page and locate the data I need to fix the more complex equipment."

Tombs turned and moved to his bunk. Clearly, he was trying to work all the angles. "Well, that means I have to call in a big favor from the warden. He owes me, but I hate giving it up for your computer time. You're sure you really need access to the library to fix this stuff?"

"I can't go any further without the data."

"Alright, Towers, but it will take a couple of days. Meanwhile, work on the devices that don't need the computer. I'll put the guard off for a few days and tell him you're still working on it."

Chapter 12

A few days later Curt found himself back in the warden's office. He stood at attention as the warden gazed out the window. Without turning around, he spoke. "So, you need access to the library. What makes you think I should give you that privilege after being here only a few weeks? Most cons don't get access to that area for years. What makes you so special?"

Curt's mind was racing. What was the correct answer? Pissing off the warden at this time was not an option. He took a chance. "Mr. Tombs requested that I use the library to research repairs on equipment."

The warden turned and looked Curt directly in the eyes. "I've been hearing about your little business in cellblock four. I hear they're calling you Mr. Fixit."

The warden stopped talking for a few seconds, and Curt was not sure if he should respond. The warden continued. "So, what do you know about computers? My personal computer locked up the other day, and won't start up. It keeps telling me I have system files missing. Think you can fix that?"

Curt was ecstatic, but dared not show it. Over the years, he had grown tired of technical support working on his personal computers and making them worse than ever. Therefore, he had hired himself a computer nerd from outside the company to teach him everything he needed to know about keeping his system running smoothly. One of the first problems he was taught to correct was just what the warden had described.

"Can I take a look at it right now?"

The warden moved to the side and pointed to the laptop. "Be my guest."

Curt pressed the power on button, and sure enough he received the error about missing system files. He held the power button for five seconds, and it shut off. He pressed it again, but pressed the F8 key as it booted into Safe Mode. Now he could locate the backup system files and restore the missing drivers. He rebooted the laptop and system files appeared. Three more reboot cycles and the computer was back on line. Curt stepped away from the computer, making sure that his expression was as blank as possible. The warden moved over and entered the password, and the main screen came back on line.

He turned and looked at Curt. "Wow, I'm impressed. What happened to cause this?"

Curt had already prepared his answer making sure it appeared that he was an expert at fixing computers.

"Computers write and rewrite files every time you use them. The actual files that are rewritten to the hard disk end up in a new place each time it's written. The longer you use the computer, the smaller the useable area becomes. The solution is for the computer to break the files up into pieces and then track the location with what is called a File Allocation Table. Somewhere along the line, your system files were incorrectly written or lost in the FAT tables. The best way to correct this problem is to defrag your computer. It appears that the defrag schedule on your computer was turned off, ever since you purchased it. I can do it if you want, and back up your computer, so that if anything happens in the future, you can restore your files from the backup."

"Go ahead, Towers, but make sure it works better than before. If it does, then I'll grant you full library privileges. Can you work on network systems, or only laptops? Half the time I try to log on to our systems, they're down. Our budget can't handle using that damn outside computer repair service. If you can keep things running smoothly, then I'll consider additional privileges."

"That shouldn't be a problem since I installed all the network systems in my own house. They're extremely complex, so I'm willing to give yours a shot."

43

The warden motioned for the guard to leave. He walked over to the window as Curt opened the defrag program and crossed his fingers. He gave up a short prayer, asking that there be no viruses roaming around in the machine.

It took most of the day to finish cleaning up the warden's computer, but it was done without any problems. When he had finished, the warden told Curt he had notified the guards that his privileges had been extended to the library.

When Curt arrived at chow, Larry was full of questions about his day. As he started to fill him in, Curt looked over to Tombs. Tombs nodded his head, acknowledging that he knew Curt was now allowed in the library. This was a good day, a very good day indeed.

Chapter 13

Curt sat on his bunk looking at a hearing aid that Tombs had given him to repair. Tombs had arranged for a small table and chair for his work, but he still preferred to sit on his bunk and pull the table up to the edge.

Larry was on the top bunk reading a book.

"So, Larry, tell me about the library. What should I expect?"

Larry turned the page corner of his book and set it down. "To tell you the truth, the last time I was in here, they were tearing down the old library and moving it to a new location. I heard they had remodeled an old storage and utility room with new walls, shelves, and a few computer workstations. I understand that the room used to be the junction point for all the water, power, and security systems. Word is they covered it up and created a new access on the other side of the wall next to the library. I was out of here before it was completed."

Curt set down the hearing aid. He had repaired it in record time. "Well, I'm about to find out what the new library looks like." He banged on the bars, and the guard came to pick him up. As he followed the guard, he looked across to the opposite cell and saw one of the prisoners giving him the finger. Magically, it went down rapidly when Tombs appeared at his cell door.

"So, Towers, you have it fixed already? You're really becoming my very best asset in prison."

Tombs was about to continue when another con stopped by the cell, delivering the mail.

"Towers, I have a large piece of mail for you."

Curt was about to reach for it, when Tombs yanked it out of the con's hands.

"Let me see that," he barked.

Curt knew better than to argue with Tombs. Besides, he was not expecting anything important. Tombs bent back the prongs and pushed them through holes in the envelope. He pulled out a thick stack of 8 1/2 by 11 sheets and looked at the top sheet. "Sorry, Towers. Your day just got a lot worse. Course, it depends on how you look at it."

He handed the papers to Curt. They were divorce papers from Cindy. He quickly thumbed through them. It looked as though she had hired herself a lawyer outside the company since she wanted his 50% share of Xtreme Machines Incorporated. She pretty much wanted everything, the house, the car, and full custody of the kids. Whatever was left of his life was now going to be hers. The document indicated that she should be granted the divorce because he was in jail for the rest of his life, and could no longer use anything for which she sought possession.

He really didn't blame her, although he had hoped she would have supported him more during the trial. She was one of the first people to abandon him and assume he was guilty. He was unable to find out how the kids felt about it all, and now he might never know. He thought he knew his wife better, but sometimes it takes hard times to realize how you feel about someone. He felt no anger toward her since she needed to move on with her life.

"Got a pen?"

Tombs reached for a pen from his table. "Are you sure about this?"

"Yep, she's better off without me. Besides, I have more work to do in the library."

He finished signing the last sheet, put the stack back into the envelope, and gave it to the mail con. "You know how to get it back to her?"

The con took the envelope. "Sorry, Towers. I'll use the return address in the upper left corner. I know how you feel since

46

my wife left me soon as I was arrested."

Curt watched as he moved on to the next cell. "If you don't need me anymore, I think I'll check out the library. I've got a lot of schematics to look for if I'm going to fix that guard's TV."

Tombs motioned for Curt to go. The guard pointed the way toward Curt's new destination. The library was quite some distance from the main cellblock. He had to go through one security gate and down two levels before he found himself standing in front of a door that read, "Library – Prisoners require a permit from the warden."

He knocked, and the guard opened the door. "There's a call button on the wall if you want to go back to your cell or need to make a pit stop. We'll return to pick you up at 5 p.m. If I were you, I would make good use of your time. No computer games, because Mr. Tombs wants results."

The door closed, and Curt looked around the room. There were three aisles of books and an all-in-one printer pushed against the wall next to the oversized books. The computer terminal was at the opposite end of the wall. It appeared that the computer used a wireless connection tied directly into the printer. That made sense, since guards might need to make copies but wouldn't want to turn on a computer, and computer users could use the printer to scan and print out documents.

He sat down and looked at the machine. It was already turned on and boasted that it used Vista. He hated Vista, but at this point, he'd settle for anything. He opened the control panel to check out the specs of the machine and saw that it was a new one. It was an HP with lots of RAM, a DVD burner, and a 750 Gig main drive. He opened Internet Explorer, and started to search for any help he could get regarding the TV he had to repair. In an hour, he had exactly what he needed, so he printed out the documents for accomplishing the repair.

When he had finished, he looked around the room. There were no guards. No one was watching him. He left the schematic on the computer screen while he surveyed the room. There was new Sheetrock all the way around. He got down on the floor to check the seam at the floor. There was no trim, just a small gap at the bottom of the Sheetrock. He took a piece of printer paper, pushed it through the crack, and found that it disappeared. This showed him there was a space behind the wall. He tapped on the wall, and the hollow resonance indicated there was some depth behind.

Just then, the door started to open, and the guard came in. "Done early, Towers? Mr. Tombs will be happy to hear that. Leave the computer on. Let's go."

Curt swiftly picked up his papers and walked the long path back to his cell. He spent the rest of the day working between the schematics and the defunct TV and finally achieved success. He turned it on, and a very fuzzy picture flashed on. He yelled for the guard, and the TV was immediately whisked from his cell.

Curt lay back on his bunk and thought about the day's events. The divorce was bad news, but the library privilege was good. He started to nod off, when Larry came back from the yard.

"So, Curt, what have you been up to today?"

"I got divorce papers."

"Sorry. I know that's a low blow for the guys in prison."

"The good news is that the library has some interesting aspects that I would like to talk to you about. Can I ask you a hypothetical question?"

"I'm not sure I like where this is going."

"You will if it means a better life for your family."

"Alright, ask me your hypothetical question."

"If I could remove myself from this place, how would I make myself invisible on the outside?"

Larry's expression went from a smile to a very serious and questioning look. "Are we talking about EFP, you know: escape from prison? If so, you need to keep everything we say just between us.   No one else can know, especially Tombs.   If he thought you were trying to escape from prison, he would have a shit fit.   You are the best thing that has come along for him in years.   We need to talk later, when there's more noise in the prison.   Let's talk right after lunch tomorrow.   No more about it now, all right?"

"OK."

"Good."

"Glad that's settled," laughed Curt, as he flopped back on his bunk. He was asleep in seconds.

Chapter 14

Cindy Towers sat on the lawn chair and looked out at the rolling hills that led toward the distant snow-covered mountains. Her mind was on the divorce papers that she had finally sent to Curt a few days ago. It was probably the hardest thing she had ever done in her life.

She knew Curt was guilty, so she felt the divorce was necessary in order to move on with her life. The trial was rough on her and the kids. The media was relentless, asking one stupid question after another. She felt she had to do something to stop the merry-go-round.

A few weeks into the trial, Alex Brandon, Curt's bitter competitor, had called her and asked if he could see her. At first, she was going to refuse, but something in the back of her mind told her to keep all her options open.

A few days later, the hounding from the press lessened, giving her a moment's break, so she told Alex to stop by the house. He was supportive, insisting that he felt Curt had been framed.

During their meeting, Alex dropped a bombshell, offering his country home to Cindy and the kids, for as long as they wanted. At first, she said no, but when she thought about the mounting demands from the press, she finally accepted a tour of his home.

The house was spectacular and she immediately fell in love with it. It featured more than 10,000 square feet of endless rooms, swimming pool, horse stables, a housekeeper, and half-dozen cars. She and the children could definitely hide from the press here.

Alex was a perfect gentleman. He never stayed at the house while they were there. He would just stop by to make sure everything was all right, and then return to his home in the city. He even hired private tutors for the kids, so they would not have to endure any more ridicule from the kids at school. Each of the three kids had their own spacious bedroom equipped with computers, TVs, and the ultimate music systems.

She had trouble understanding why Alex and Curt had been such bitter enemies. Alex was so pleasant, and handsome. His wife, Cleo, even stopped by several times to help them get settled. Cleo was a smart woman, and one of the most striking Cindy had ever seen, although she didn't seem to be very happy. The two women talked a little about Alex and Curt, but Cindy didn't learn much more than she already knew.

Cindy's mind drifted back to the divorce papers and how she thought Curt would take it. A sound from the front door disrupted her thoughts.

"Sorry to barge in, Cindy, but I thought I'd stop by and see how you're doing," said Alex.

Cindy set her ice-cold cup of coffee on the coffee table. "I'm a little down today," she said. "I'm just wondering how Curt will react to the divorce papers. I know it was the right thing to do, but it hurts just the same. We had so many good years together. I just don't know what went wrong."

Alex sat down on the couch next to her and put his arm around her. This was the first time he had really made any physical contact with her since the trial. "I don't even pretend to know how you feel," he said. "You know Curt and I were bitter competitors, but before that we were friends. I don't really know how we progressed from one point to the other. It just happened."

"What you did required a tough decision," he continued, "but I really think it was the right one for you and the kids. You need to move on with your lives. It's too bad it has to be that way, but I think it's the only way. You know that you and the kids are welcome to stay here forever. I never had the time to come

51

to the country house, so consider this as a housesitting job for me. In fact, you might even consider selling your house and staying here. I just want you to know that you have that option."

Tears were now starting to run down Cindy's face. A great weight was lifted off her shoulders. "I don't know how we can ever thank you for all you've done."

Alex stood up and started to turn toward the front door. "Don't worry about it. You need a new start on life, and I'm happy to do it for you and the kids. I have to get back to some meetings. If you need anything, just give me a call."

"Thank you, for everything."

The door closed, and Cindy was alone again. She felt stronger and knew she would get through today, then tomorrow and the next - and the next.

Alex smiled as he got into his brand new red Lamborghini. Everything was going just as planned, he thought. His life and the business world were getting to look better every day. Although it might take some time, he would ultimately be the top dog of the micro world. There were just a few more pieces of the puzzle to put in place, he thought as he raced away.

Chapter 15

It was late in the day, and Curt had put in a full day of repairs for Tombs. He lay on his bunk thinking about his next move. "Larry, I have a question for you."

Larry looked down from his upper bunk. "Before you say anything, I think you need to look at my book."

Curt took the book and opened it to the paper bookmark where Larry had written: *"Before you say anything that will get you in trouble with the warden, we need to make sure we're not being monitored. Let's run a test to see what happens."*

"Hey, Larry, you're not going to believe what I found in the library today between two reference books. There was a small handgun with a half dozen rounds. I don't know who put it there, but I think I need to move it to a safer place."

Larry smiled. Curt was sharp and had picked up his cue quickly. "I don't think that's a good idea. Leave it alone. It may be a plant to see if you take it. They hardly need an excuse to put you in solitary. So which reference books hid the gun?"

Curt laughed. "They were the self-improvement. I was looking at them today and the gun just fell out."

Larry nodded at how well Curt had followed along on their deception. Now they would wait to see if anyone took the bait.

A hundred yards away in cellblock two, another man was waiting, and had been for almost 30 years. Nikilous Santos was now 58 years old and was one very pissed-off inmate. A few months ago, he had learned that the son of the man who caused his incarceration was in cellblock four. Nik blamed Curt's father for his lacking defense as his attorney, but also Curt for being born at the wrong time. He had never thought there would be a chance to get revenge, but fate had dealt him a new hand.

Nik tried to talk Tombs into a deal between cellblock kings, but Tombs was too happy with his own situation. Nik would have to figure out another way to get to the son of all his problems. He wasn't worried because he knew that time would eventually present a solution. He was just tired and felt he deserved a break. Thirty years rotting in this hellhole was bad enough, but the fact that his father had abandoned him while he was in prison was unbearable. Nik had celebrated when he heard that his father had died during a hit on the family.

Now he had just one last score to settle. Curt Towers would be dead soon. He just didn't know it yet.

Chapter 16

Several days had passed and nothing had been touched in the library to indicate their cell was bugged. They felt it was safe to talk.

Curt had just returned to his cell, and Larry was bent over the sink spitting out blood. "You okay, buddy?"

Larry turned and wiped the blood from his mouth. "I think it's time I complained about my stomach ailment. I can't seem to keep food down lately. I think this thing is going to get me much faster than I had thought."

Curt sat on the lower bunk next to him. "Larry, you need to let them know."

"Yeah, but I wanted to make sure you had everything in place first."

"What the hell are you talking about?"

"Don't kid a kidder, Curt. I know you're smart. You'll figure it out soon enough and be out of this place."

"Hey, I would love to be out of here, but I'm still not sure how."

"You know, Curt, for being as smart as you are; you haven't seen what is right in front of you."

"What the hell are you talking about?"

"The prison network router system, of course. Remember, you told me that the warden wanted you to repair it. Well fix it, but while you're doing that, create a back door with an additional port address."

Larry continued, "One skill I picked up when I was in the fake ID business was breaking into computer database systems. The last time I was in here, I ran into a computer geek who had hacked one too many computers. Luckily, he taught me everything he knew. This prison has hundreds of security cameras, and they all go through the network router system. I happen to know that all the data related to the prison is on a secure mainframe in the basement. You know the building plans, and modifications to the library, and such."

The wheels were turning inside Curt's head. Larry was correct. The solution was right in front of him. He could add a single access port to the bottom of the list and call it camera X, or whatever is the next port ID. He could then log on to the network from the library computer. When he worked on the library computer searching for schematics, he found that the security firewall coming in and out of the prison was way beyond his skill level. Nevertheless, access from one workstation to the next within the prison had almost no security.

Curt smiled at Larry. "You need to call the guard and get into the prison hospital. We can talk there when you are moved in. I don't think the warden or Tombs would object as long as I keep fixing stuff. Thanks, Larry, for being such a good friend."

Peter Harden sat at his desk and contemplated the past few months. His best friend Curt was now in prison for the rest of his life, and work was just not the same without him. The new CEO of Xtreme Machines had told everyone in an early morning meeting that business would go on as usual without Curt.

Word had come down through channels that Curt's wife, Cindy, had recently filed for divorce. She decided to stay on with the company as part of the board, eventually to become the new CEO. He liked Cindy, but she was not his good friend Curt. Peter had been told that Cindy wanted to keep him on at his present position, but with one stipulation - Peter could no longer publicly support the innocence of Curt Towers. That was tough to swallow, but he remembered that Curt had told him that pride can be both good and bad. The trick is to know when to suppress it and when to embrace it. For now, he would have to suppress it.

Chapter 17

Curt spent most of the day working on the prison networking system, concentrating mainly on the issue with the routers. The problem was easy to fix, so he started to look for the security camera ports. Best of all, if anyone came in and looked at the computer screen, it would look like computer gibberish. He could work right in plain sight, and they would be none the wiser.

He found the port, added the extra camera name, and tried to connect to the library computer. The library menu instantly came up, so he was all set. He called for the guard and headed back to his cell.

When he arrived, Larry's stuff had been removed. His first thought was that Larry might be dead, but the guard told him otherwise. "Larry was moved after you left this morning. I heard he has cancer. I'm always glad to see when things get worse for you scumbags."

Curt wanted to slug the guard, but knew that was what the guard wanted, so he restrained himself. He needed to talk to Tombs, to get permission to see Larry. He sat down on his bunk and looked up at the ceiling as the guard walked away.

Thirty minutes later, the guard returned and escorted Curt to Tombs' cell.

He continued looking at a music magazine, while Curt patiently stood in front of him. "So you lost your cellmate. How does that affect us?"

"It doesn't change anything. I'll still repair whatever you need repaired, but I do have a request; I'd like to visit Larry for an hour each day."

Tombs set the magazine down, and looked over to Tank. "It's touching to see such a concern for another inmate. I don't know why you should concern yourself about Larry; he's a dead man. However, I'm a businessman, and I know that you'll be more difficult to work with if you don't get your wish. I could have Tank adjust your attitude, but what the hell. I'll only give you a half hour, but your repairs can't be affected by these visits. Understand?"

"I understand, Mr. Tombs. I will do the same workload as before; just work it around my extra time visiting Larry. Besides, he will be dead soon; then it will no longer be a problem."

Curt hated saying what he had just said, but knew it would impress Tombs. Right now, he needed every edge he could get.

Chapter 18

Curt sat in a chair next to Larry's bed. He was fading faster than he thought possible. "Hey, buddy. How're you doing?"

"Well, for one thing, I'm dying, but that's pretty obvious about now. Curt, that's not the main problem, though. Have you started to log on to the prison's mainframe yet?"

"No, I was going to, right after I left here."

"Now listen to me. You need to cover your tracks when doing your research. First, install a second browser that no one would use but you. There is one called Opera, and another is called Chrome. Avoid Firefox, Safari, or Internet Explorer for your personal research. Anyway, make sure you install it in a weird place and call the directory 'display drivers' or something like that."

Larry coughed violently, but then continued. "Make sure to remove all the shortcuts and icons from the desktop and program menu. You'll have to start the program by going to the file manager and finding the program in the bogus directory. Do all your research using that browser and all your repair research with Internet Explorer. If anyone checks the computer after you leave the library, the cache should be hidden.

"Once you have it installed, you can just log in to www.larrystoolkit007.com as 'Larry.' The password will be the previous date backward, starting with the two-digit year, month and day. The nerd I told you about taught me how to set it up. Now, once you are logged in, run the stealth drive program from the list. It will create a stealth drive on the library computer. When the drive is completed, it will ask if there are any programs or data files you want to move on the drive. Move the new browser you installed. Keep in mind that this will keep the information hidden from the guards and other computer users. If any kind of computer geek gets into your system, it will only be a matter of time before they see that something looks a little fishy."

Larry coughed again and spit up blood. Curt handed the water glass to him and said, "Do you really think it's necessary for all this secrecy?"

Larry took a sip and set the glass down. "Look, if you want out of here, you need to cover all your bases. What if there is some kind of computer check? They do that sometimes, and without any notice. Make sure you save all your documents to the stealth drive. Any time you want to open the drive, just use the password I gave you. If you have to get out fast, hit the escape key. The drive will go into a stealth mode."

He took a deep breath and said, "I'm getting tired, so let's talk again later. I'll need to talk to you about creating fake documents from my website. You'll also need to know how to stay hidden once you're out. Plus, one other thing--my family, but we'll talk later."

Curt got up and squeezed Larry's hand. "See you tomorrow. I have some computing to do."

Two hours later Curt had completed all the tasks that Larry had assigned. In a way, it was scary that he could hide so much information right in front of their eyes. He then logged on to the prison's mainframe and did a search for construction projects.

After refining his search, he found the construction project section for the prison. Unfortunately, the blueprints were in an unknown random order. It became obvious that the warden or someone had a key or index to the construction projects in the prison.

Word among the cons was that the warden had taken kickbacks on some of the projects and kept construction accounting books in his office safe. Curt assumed that the key to the list of projects was locked away in that safe too.

He was struggling since most of the blueprints looked the

same. It was hard to tell if a blueprint was of the kitchen or the medical lab. He was having trouble concentrating on the pages, for fear that the guard would come back and check on him and see a blueprint on the screen.

He started looking for something unique to the library that he could match up to one of the blueprints. There were over 500 blueprints in the records, so it was going to take a very long time. He pulled up the first one and started scanning the diagrams.

An hour later, he heard the guard opening the door, so he hit the escape key. The screen jumped to Internet Explorer showing a list of instruction manuals for an old CD player.

"Okay, Towers. The warden wants to see you."

Curt started to panic, but only on the inside. He wondered if the warden had seen him log on to the construction section of the archives. The guard pushed him in the back with his billy club.

"Come on, Towers. Don't keep the warden waiting."

A few minutes later Curt was standing in a familiar spot that he seemed to be visiting often.

"Towers, you've been doing very well here. You listened to me, and the guards tell me that you don't fight back, which is good. I don't want any trouble from you."

He cleared his throat and said, "Before you go, take a look at my daughter's laptop. It seems she was careless, and now it's loaded with viruses. Fix it and your privileges will be extended to the exercise yard. Just make very sure you don't make me sorry I extended this privilege."

Curt picked up the fancy quad core, dual operating system that had to cost more than five grand. "Can I work on it in the library? I may have to download some virus fixes from Norton, before I can start fixing it."

The warden frowned, and then waved to the guard. "Do whatever you have to, Towers. I just want my daughter off my back and out of my hair."

Chapter 19

Cindy Towers sat in the living room, overlooking the sprawling grass valley in front of the house. A special delivery service had dropped off a legal document. She was afraid to open it. She knew it had to be the divorce papers.

Brenda Towers came into the room with her homework in hand.

"Mom, can you help with some of these math problems? They are driving me crazy."

Cindy looked up at her daughter and then back down to the document envelope. "Sorry, Honey. I need some time to think. Can we do it later tonight?"

"Sure, Mom. Can I go over to the mall to meet some of my friends?"

Cindy was lost again in thought, when she realized her daughter was waiting for an answer.

"Go ahead. We can work on the math problems later. Maybe Alex will be here tonight, and he can help. He's better at math than I am."

A tear formed in the corner of Cindy's eye. She tried to hide it from Brenda.

"Mom, is there something wrong?"

"No, Honey. I'm fine. You go along."

Brenda knew her mom was lying, and that parents were no better at lying than kids. She wanted to go to the mall, but she was a long way from getting her homework done. "Oh well," she thought as she grabbed her purse and was out the front door.

Minutes later, Cindy heard a car pull up and a door slam. The front door opened and there was Alex, smiling as though he had just been handed the keys to the kingdom.

"Hi, Cindy, how was your day? My day was incredible. We

picked up several new contracts, and my company is now on the way into the black."

Alex stopped his conversation abruptly when he saw the manila envelope in Cindy's hand. He came over and sat on the couch next to her.

"Is that what I think it is?"

"It arrived a few minutes ago. I'm afraid to open it."

Alex slowly took the envelope from her hand.

"You want me to open it for you?"

"Would you?"

Alex undid the clips and pulled out the papers. He turned over the pages, looking for those that required signatures, and then put the papers back in the envelope.

"He signed all of them. It looks like he signed them the same day as he got them. There's a log showing the received date, and it's the same as his signature date. There's no note, nothing else, just his signature."

Emotions were going crazy inside Cindy. She was happy and terribly sad at the same time.

Alex set the envelope on the coffee table and took her hand in his.

"You knew this was coming. It's the best for you and the kids. My lawyer has been reviewing Curt's case and tells me there's no way that any further appeals will ever gain any momentum. I'm so sorry, Cindy. I know how much you loved Curt. Is there anything I can do for you?"

She replied, "Please, hold me."

Chapter 20

The last few weeks had been a juggling act that was starting to take its toll. Between the repair work, blueprint research, and visiting Larry, there was little or no time left in a day. At first, Curt had decided to skip the offer to use the exercise yard, but Larry told him that he should bulk up as much as possible. The exercise yard had just about every muscle-building device known. He would need that extra strength and agility when he broke out and was on the run, that is, if he ever figured out the blueprints. He was halfway through the drawings, and nothing so far resembled the library. He told him several times that he thought it was a lost cause, but Larry wouldn't let him quit.

Larry seemed to be doing better with chemotherapy, but was still very weak. Tombs had cut his time visiting Larry down even further, saying Curt was spending too much time with a dead man. Apparently, the "fixit services" had increased, and Tombs didn't like Curt's slower pace.

Surprisingly, Tombs didn't seem to mind the time Curt spent in the exercise yard. At first, he hated the exercise and was exhausted after just an hour of working out. After a week of continual exercise, things changed and he started becoming addicted to the exercise yard. This was a new feeling for him, since he was never much of an exercise guy. About the most exercise he had ever gotten was on the handball or tennis court. The muscles in his forearm were starting to get tighter, and he noticed that his chest muscles were starting to feel different too.

Curt had been busy today, and his last stop was to visit Larry. As the guard escorted him into the room, he instantly noticed that the bed was empty. A dreadful fear came over his body. He relied on Larry so much to help him get from day to day. Was he now gone?

"Hey, your buddy will be back in a few minutes," the guard said. "He's just finishing his chemo session. What a waste of money. He should just die and save the state some money."

Curt wanted to turn around and slam the guard in the face, but instead he took a deep breath. Larry had told him to keep his cool, no matter what happened, to focus on getting out: nothing else mattered.

He sat on the edge of Larry's bed as the guard closed the door and left. He took this time alone to look around the room. From what Larry had told him, all the infirmary beds were full when they brought him in for treatment, so they had stashed him in one of the day surgery bays.

He looked around to see if any of the guards were looking through the window in the door. The coast was clear, so he started looking through all the cabinets and drawers. The first drawer contained bandages and a heart monitor. The next had various instruments labeled "clamps," "sutures," and "IV packages." He moved the assortment to the side, and at the bottom of the drawer found a package labeled "#11 blades." Inside was a long, sharp surgical knife. It had to have been left there by mistake, but Curt wasn't going to overlook this stroke of good fortune. He decided it would make quick work of cutting Sheetrock, so he picked up the package and stuffed it in the bottom of his shoe. He closed the drawer, just as the medical attendant escorted Larry into the room.

Larry's treatment had taken its toll, and he was out for the count. Curt turned to the guard. "It looks like he won't be doing much talking today. Can you drop me by the library before I go back to my cell? I have to check on a couple of schematics to fix the razor that Tombs just got."

The guard was in no mood for any detours.

"No way, Towers, you are heading straight back to your cell."

Curt knew he was pushing it with the guard, but he had too much to risk.

"I don't think Tombs would be happy to hear that you prevented me from getting the information I need to fix his razor."

Curt already had the information, but he needed an excuse to get back into the library. The guard hesitated a second in the hallway, and thought about what Curt had said. The guards were afraid of Tombs, not just the warden.

"Okay, Towers. I'll give you fifteen minutes and no more."

They worked their way back to the library, and Curt logged on to the manufacturer's page for the razor. He started to scan down through the pages, and eventually the guard became bored and left. As soon as the door closed, Curt took out a paper clip and used it to remove the side panel of the computer. He slid the #11 blade under the hard drive, and taped it into place so that it wasn't visible, even with the side panel off. He closed the panel, and shut the computer down. He signaled for the guard and they headed back to Curt's cell.

Another piece of the escape puzzle was in place. Now if he could just find the damn blueprint to the library.

Chapter 21

The morning had started an hour earlier than normal when the guard came to Curt's cell and banged on the bars with his stick.

"Towers, we have something new in store for you today. The warden has decided to let you out of prison, but there's a catch. You still have to come back at the end of the day. It seems as though you've been chosen for a National Parks project today. A friend of yours will be there, too. Let's see. What was his name? Oh, yes, it was Nikilous Santos. Have you ever met the man? He seemed to know you, and even mentioned something about your dad. This must be your lucky day."

The guard smiled and pushed him down the hall. Curt rapidly tried to figure out what was going on. He racked his brain for the connection between his dad and Nikilous Santos. Then it came to him. His dad had been the gangster's lawyer, and Nik had blamed his father for losing the case. This couldn't be good for him. He'd been set up again and this time it looked like the warden instigated it.

The bus ride into the mountains was Curt's first trip outside the prison since he had been sentenced. He concentrated on the countryside as it passed by the side of the bus. He memorized the road intersections, large trees, barns, bridges, and small towns. His mind was racing as he tried to cram as much information as possible in such a short time.

He had been one of the last prisoners on the bus, so he didn't see Nik. He never turned around to see if the old gangster was nearby. That would happen soon enough.

When the bus finally stopped, the cons were escorted off the bus, one at a time. A new guard whom Curt had never seen before stood before them. He was huge and looked like some kind of super soldier.

As Curt stood in line, he watched Nikilous Santos step off the bus. Their eyes met, and Curt looked into the deep dark eyes filled with hatred. Nikilous was definitely looking for payback. All those years in prison caused his soul to fester into something wicked and evil. Nikilous looked to his side as he got in line. A couple of the other cons smiled at Nik, and Curt knew his problems had become even worse.

The guard looked down at the thick tablet he was holding, and barked out orders.

"Here is how the day is going to go," he snarled. "We have a half-mile of trails to repair today, and we'll do it in record time, or else. Don't even think about running away. We have vicious dogs in the guard truck, and they would love to track you down. You'll make it back to the prison alive if you just do your work. One fight and all of you will spend a week in solitary confinement."

He stepped back, and a second guard started listing the names of the cons and detailed where they would work along the trail. Curt was given a rake to level out the areas that the other cons had dug up, so they could insert wooden steps. Curt looked over and saw that he and Nikilous were at opposite ends of the work crew.

The morning went without a hitch, and his work in the exercise yard was definitely paying off today. The lunch break came and passed, and the crew was fifty yards ahead of schedule. Curt started to relax, thinking that maybe all his fears about Nikilous were unfounded.

His mind drifted toward the soothing sounds of the birds and the fresh smell of the forest. This was so much better than prison life. Curt reached down to pick up a small branch that had fallen across the trail, when he noticed a shadow appear from the side. A sharp pain slammed into the side of his head, and he fell to the ground. He cringed in pain as Nikilous jammed a boot into his ribs. Curt looked up just as Nik was taking a second swing with the shovel, and used his arm to block the attack. The shovel blade glanced off his arm, but not before creating a deep gash.

Nik was about to take another swing when Curt heard the guard shriek, "What's going on here?"

By the time the guard reached the scene, Nik had dropped the shovel, and was looking down at him. Curt looked up at the guard as he stood towering over him. His mind was racing, and his head hurt like hell. What should he say? Then Larry's voice crept into his mind, reminding him about the con's code.

"Sorry, I tripped and fell. Nik came to help me up," Curt said weakly.

Nik continued to glare down at him as the rest of the cons gathered around. Curt could hear the guard say something about getting the first-aid kit out of the truck. He tried to focus on the faces in the group, but then everything went from gray to black.

Chapter 22

Curt tried unsuccessfully to focus his eyes on the bright ceiling lights. He could hear a voice, but it was muted. As he continued to refocus, a figure came into view.

"Towers, can you see me? Blink your eyes three times if you understand."

The medical technician was rapidly moving a small flashlight back and forth in front of Curt's eyes. He could vaguely see the facial features and recognized the man who had been taking care of Larry. He blinked his eyes three times and then cautiously turned his head toward Larry.

"What the hell happened to you, Curt?" asked Larry, smiling with relief. "We all thought you were a goner. Who the hell hit you in the head?" He ended his sentence with a deep hacking cough.

Curt was finally able to sharply focus on Larry. "Well, it seems that someone higher up tried to schedule a final meeting with me and the devil. Someone thought I should pay for the sins of my father, and they almost succeeded."

The technician continued to check his vitals as Curt expanded on the day's events. Eventually, the technician was satisfied with his condition and left the room. No doubt, his poker game was interrupted by Curt's appearance.

Larry sat up in his bed and looked toward the door. The coast was clear.

"Curt, you need to find a way out of here soon, or you'll go out in a body bag. You may have Tombs protecting you now, but that will end soon since you're running out of things to repair. I bet anything the warden would love you gone too. With Nikilous now added to the equation, you may only have days before you die here."

"So, tell me more about the problem with the blueprints. Maybe I can help," Larry muttered.

Curt took a sip of water from the glass at the edge of the bed.

"All the blueprints look the same to me. I thought it would be easy, but they're all keyed to an index that isn't on the system. I've been through 400 of the 500 blueprints with no luck, and I'm not even sure that I haven't already passed the one I need."

Larry swallowed and tried to clear his voice. He was failing fast. "Well, you're running out of time, and so am I, so listen to what I have to tell you. You'll find the right blueprint soon; just keep searching for an anomaly in the library construction."

For the next hour they talked, took breaks, and then talked some more. Larry was a wealth of information, and Curt hoped he could remember it all. Larry faded and fell asleep for an hour. They continued their discussion during dinner and then finally called it a night.

Curt didn't want to admit it, but sadly, his friend had only a few days left before he would be leaving prison for good.

Chapter 23

Curt was released from the infirmary in the late afternoon the next day and taken directly to Tombs' cell.

"Okay, Mr. Fixit. I don't know who you pissed off or why," Tombs growled. "Your problems are yours, but now you've lost several days of repairs, so that makes it my problem, too. One of the guards has a microwave that keeps shutting down as soon as it starts. I want him to owe me a favor, so get the damn thing fixed by tomorrow. No excuses, or I'll find out who beat you up and send you back for another round. Have I made myself loud and clear?"

Curt nodded. He was then escorted to the guards' eating area. He took a quick look at the troublesome microwave and informed the guard that he would need access to the library. At first, the guard balked, but one of the other guards whispered into his ear, and magically he agreed to take him to the library.

A few minutes later Curt was booting up the system and doing a search for the ancient microwave. As soon as the guard was out of sight, Curt pressed the hot keys to the stealth drive and pulled up the last blueprint he had reviewed. He clicked "Next," and was in total shock. The blueprint he was looking for had been the subsequent one in the queue. He hastily saved it to the stealth drive, and glanced at the library door to make sure the guard wasn't returning. Convinced he was safe; Curt looked back at the blueprint that would be his ticket out of prison.

As he scanned the blueprint, he noticed that it was one of four library blueprints. He logged back on to the server and found the remaining three blueprints, which showed the utilities connections. This was better than Curt could have ever imagined. Finally, something had gone right.

Larry had been right about the library. Because of all the

utilities, the library Sheetrock wall was set 36 inches away from the original concrete wall. Most of the space between the two walls was taken up with power and water lines, but there was a dead space area--not a lot, but hopefully enough for a man to crawl through. It was like a maze, with all the different pipes joining up with the main line.

Curt looked around again to see if anyone was watching. He continued ahead to the second and third blueprints. They showed a 36-inch diameter conduit within the walls that ran to a utility shed 200 yards outside the prison barriers. The shed housed the main power substation for the entire prison. It was fully automated, so there were no guards in the building.

The fourth blueprint showed a smaller 24-inch drainpipe exiting from the middle of the prison. It too had an access panel within the shed. This pipe then followed a small gully, which eventually led to the river that flowed below the prison. Curt grinned. He found his way out.

Larry had told him that time was short for both of them and if an opportunity presented itself, Curt should seize it. The guard had stated that he would be back in a few hours. Curt wasn't going to be able to fix the microwave because of its age and his limited skill level. When Tombs found out, he could easily lose his library privileges and who knows what else. He looked at the door and decided to make the biggest decision of his life.

He opened the side of the computer, removed the #11 surgical blade, and pulled the chair out from under the computer desk. He had to work fast. The blade on the surgical knife was sharp, but thin and fragile. It was not designed to cut Sheetrock, but it would have to do.

He looked up to the screen one last time to make sure he had memorized the blueprints. He hit the "Escape" key, and then started slowly cutting the wall. The knife blade was sharp, but getting dull rapidly. By the time he reached the fourth side, it was barely cutting, but finally finished. He lifted the Sheetrock out and looked into the dark metal cavern. Ready or not, he was committed.

He reached into the desk drawer and pulled out a roll of tape. He cut off several strips and used the adhesive to gather all the dust that had accumulated from his rough cutting. He tossed the tape into the passageway and looked into the desk drawer again.

He found a box of rubber bands, which he tied together and fastened to make a long stretchable cord. He punched a small hole in the center of the Sheetrock and pulled the end of the rubber band cord through the hole. Curt then attached a paper clip to the end and covered the paper clip with white 3M tape he had found in the back of the drawer. He added additional white tape to the four edges of sheet rock. It was a rough cover up job and if anyone looked closely, the tape would be seen. His only hope was that it wouldn't be discovered until they had exhausted all other search options.

His final act in the library was to write a note, stating that he left to make a pit stop. He placed it on the keyboard, and pulled up the microwave schematic on the screen. Curt took one last glance around the room and then crawled into the opening under the desk. Then he reached out and pulled the desk chair under the desk.

The area between the pipes and the walls was much smaller than he had anticipated, so this was not going to be easy. He pulled the Sheetrock into position like a puzzle piece. He grasped the rubber band rope, and pulled it tight, allowing the sheet rock to fall back into place. He looped the stretchy material around the pipes, and it seemed to hold the Sheetrock in place. It was scary to think that his escape relied on rubber bands, tape, and paper clips.

Thirty minutes later, he had gone only 50 feet. Squeezing between the pipes was difficult, especially in total darkness. He was constantly reviewing the blueprints etched in his mind. The one thing Larry had told him was to get as much distance between him and the prison in the shortest time. Larry wouldn't be impressed with his progress.

He reached his hand up to find the next obstacle in the long path to freedom. He felt something furry and then he felt a sharp pain. Curt was about to scream, but then stopped himself. Damn, a rat almost caused him to give away his position. He ripped off part of his prison shirt and wrapped it around his hand before continuing through the tunnel.

Forty-five minutes into his escape, he could see a small light, in the distance. He moved closer, so the light silhouettes and shadows could make his progress easier. As he crawled along the concrete floor, he noticed that it started to slope downwards and was picking up water. He remembered that the blueprints had shown a slight angle as it moved toward the shed.

An hour had passed, and water was now filling half the tunnel. The tunnel abruptly made a 90-degree turn up to a large door in the floor of the shed. He prayed that it would not be locked. He pushed, and it resisted. The door was locked. Now was the time for all those exercise workouts to pay off.

He inverted himself so that his feet were against the door, and then held on to the ladder attached to the wall. He pulled back his feet and with as much force as he could muster, slammed them against the door. To his surprise, it shot up into the room, and bright light entered the shaft. Curt popped his head up to see if the area in the shed was clear. "Good news," he muttered as there was no one in sight.

He was about to look for the smaller drainage pipe access, when the prison escape alarm siren started blaring. Larry had told him when that happened, he would have only minutes before the prison would be in full lock down.

He searched for the drainage pipe, and discovered dozens of electrical panels, several pressure valves, and lockers. He looked through the lockers until he found one that contained two uniforms. He slipped one on. It was a tight fit, but it would have to do. He took it off and donned his prison clothes.

As the sirens continued to blast into the night, he continued his search. He located a utility closet containing several trash bags. He wrapped the work uniform in one bag, then enclosed it into a second bag, and put the package under his arm. He spotted a flashlight and started to pick it up, but then stopped. If the guards searched the shed, they would miss the flashlight right away. He couldn't chance it; he just hoped they wouldn't notice the second uniform missing.

He used the broom to sweep away any sign that he had been in the room. When the access door was back in place, he arranged the lock so it appeared to be undamaged.

In the corner, he found the access door to the drainage pipe. It was heavy but still manageable. Once he entered the pipe, he pulled the cover in place and headed down the ladder. At the bottom, he found the smaller pipe was covered with two to three inches of mud. He reached into the mud and started to smear it over his shoulders and legs. He hoped this added lubricant would help him slip through the pipe easier.

He inched his way along and found the pipe sloped down, as he got closer to the end. It became apparent that the oozing mud and water would soon fill more than three-quarters of the pipe. He took several deep breaths and pushed ahead as hard as he could, praying that the end of the pipe would be nearby.

However, something was terribly wrong. He had not even considered the possibility that the pipe could be blocked. Curt was about to gasp for a nonexistent breath of air when he gave one last lunge that flung him out of the pipe and ten feet down to the river below.

As he fell, he lost his grip on the garbage bag. The water was so cold that he felt as though he'd been hit with a jolt from a car battery. While he shook his head back and forth trying to clean off the mud, the plastic bag hit him in the face. He snatched it and untied the outer bag. He blew into it, filling it with as much air as he could before tying it off. He could now use this buoyant bag to help keep him afloat.

The time that it took to complete this process had already carried him a few hundred yards downstream. His best shot at escape was to stay in the river as long as possible, but it was 40-degree mountain water, and hypothermia would be his enemy in minutes.

Thankfully, the moon was on the other side of the Earth, so the night was black. Curt focused on the dark shapes along the shoreline as he floated midstream, holding tight to the garbage bag.

Larry sat in his bed smiling. His good buddy Curt had made his escape. He sure hoped he remembered everything he had told him. The alarm had gone off more than an hour ago, and was still blaring away, so that was a good sign. The warden and guards had come to see him about twenty minutes after Curt's escape. It was obvious that they had no clue where he'd gone. The warden had even threatened him, but Larry played his sick-and-dying card.

Chaos was everywhere and everyone scurried, trying to discover the escapee.

Curt's guard was called to the warden's office and now stood front and center. He explained that he had seen the sign on the keyboard about Curt going to the head, and assumed it for fact. When he came back a few minutes later, the sign was still there, but Curt was nowhere. The guard continued to explain that he was the one who pressed the prison escapee button, and that a full search of the library disclosed no possible escape route.

"So, you left Towers alone for more than an hour?" barked the warden.

"Yes, Sir, but that has been the norm, since you gave him

library privileges."

"You idiot, he had privileges to use the library, but not to be left unattended. What the hell were you thinking? Never mind, it's obvious you lack the ability to think. I want you out of my prison right now. Do you understand? Immediately, and without severance pay, or I will personally file charges against you for negligence."

The guard nodded as he left the room with his head hanging low.

The warden walked over to his window overlooking the main compound.

"I want a cell-by-cell search. Take this prison apart. I have not had an escapee in years. The governor will be pissed when he hears about this. Do you understand how important it is that you find Towers? Use whatever means you have to find him. He must have had help, so grill every guard. Assume that anyone could have helped him. You understand what I'm saying?"

"Done, Sir," said his assistant, as he walked out the door and closed it behind him.

The expression on the warden's face was that of a man facing his worse fears.

"Damn you, Towers. How could you do this to me? Another few days and you would've been out of here in a pine box. Damn you to hell. We'll find you, no matter how well you hide. Mark my words, we'll find you."

The room was empty except for the warden, so no one was there to respond to his comments. He sat in his chair and started to punch in the number to the governor's office, then stopped. He scrolled through his phone index, and dialed the private number not connected with the prison system.

"Mr. Brandon, this is Warden Parker. We may have a problem."

Chapter 24

He climbed on logs in order to rest and reduce his exposure to the cold water, but Curt had been in the water for more than two hours and hypothermia was starting to win out. He was now thankful for all the time he'd spent in the exercise yard.

In the distance, ahead he could see the rotating lights of a police car. He kept in the center of the river as the lights became stronger. As the silhouette of a large highway bridge came into view, it became obvious there was a roadblock at the end of the bridge.

His mind started going a mile a minute, trying to come up with his new strategy for maintaining his escape. Suddenly, he had a crazy idea. This was an old-fashioned bridge with crisscrossed beams between two large arches. Tall trucks would often clip the bridge when entering, because they were too close to the side of the road.

Curt moved to the opposite side of the river and climbed up the bank, trying not to leave any footprints. He didn't have much time to spare, but he had to wait for just the right moment to make his move.

Several cars arrived, were inspected, and they proceeded ahead. Then the ride he had been waiting for appeared in the distance. An eighteen-wheeler full of new pickup trucks was approaching the bridge. Curt looked from side to side and then climbed up the small access ladder attached to the side of the bridge.

He hoped the cop was thorough with his inspection, in order to give him enough time to get to the front arch of the bridge. With less than ten feet to go, he heard the diesel engines start to pull the heavy load across the bridge. Curt had done some crazy things in his life, but this was stupid, and his timing had to be perfect. Jumping from a bridge onto a moving truck in total darkness was something only stuntmen in a Hollywood movie would do, but he had no choice.

Curt hoped that the cop was looking in the opposite direction when the truck passed through the bridge. The truck driver was taking his time getting the rig up to speed. Luckily, he stayed in the center of the bridge to avoid hitting anything. If Curt truly had nine lives, now would be the time to use one.

The smoke from the diesel engine shot up through the beams as the cab passed underneath. Curt waited for the cab of the first pickup truck to come into view before he jumped into the darkness. He hit hard, and the momentum rolled him toward the tailgate of the new truck. The eighteen-wheeler slowed, as if the driver had heard the crash of bones and flesh against metal. This hesitation lasted only a second before the monster vehicle gained speed and advanced down the long stretch of road. Curt was content that he was safely heading to a newfound freedom, so he curled up and went to sleep, using the garbage bag as a pillow.

Five hours later, the morning sunlight crept over the western mountain range and filtered over the truck tailgate. Curt woke and discovered the truck was slowing to a halt. He heard a truck door slam and several truckers talking about the road conditions between Denver and Las Vegas. They slapped each other on the shoulders and walked toward the truck stop for breakfast.

Curt was thrilled because he was in the mountains far away from the prison, but he still had on his prison clothes. He carefully glanced over the edge of the pickup truck to see what was in the area. It was a small truck stop with only two trucks taking their early break.

He stripped down to his shorts and opened the garbage bag to remove the maintenance clothes. He used the driest and cleanest part of the prison uniform to clean any remaining mud off his face and arms. Once he donned the maintenance outfit, he put his prison uniform in the garbage bag. He took one last look over the edge of the pickup truck to see if anyone was around. He threw the bag as hard as he could into the field on the opposite side of the road. Luckily, no one saw the toss.

He then lay back and tried to design a plan. Up to this point, he had been winging it, and had been very lucky. As he was formulating a plan, he heard voices approaching the truck. The two truckers were talking about the good old days and how hard it was today being on the road.

Then fear struck. The driver of his eighteen-wheeler was checking the pickup trucks on the carrier. He was climbing up on the back, so it would be just seconds before Curt would be found. Then a voice came over the radio from an angry dispatcher. It seemed that the trucker had spent too much time at the stop and was behind schedule. The driver immediately jumped down and a few choice words were exchanged between the two before the truck's diesel engine fired up.

Curt debated whether to get off now and take a chance, or go another five-six hours away from the prison. Larry told him that every hour Curt put between himself and the prison increased his chances by 5-10%. Curt figured his chances were about 50-50 at this point, but his concern was the next stop would be in a larger city, like Las Vegas. He couldn't afford to sleep anymore. He would have to keep his eyes alert and be ready to make a quick exit if necessary.

Chapter 25

Alex Brandon gazed out the office window in his home, enjoying the sun's rays as they highlighted the meadow. Ross Langer was late, and Alex had no patience for such a practice. Alex was about to pick up the phone to make a second call to Ross, but set it down when Ross hurried through the door.

"Ross, when I call you and tell you that it's important, I want you here in the blink of an eye. We have a real mess, and I need you to clean it up. Towers broke out of prison, and he has a good nine-hour start on the police. They don't have a clue where he is."

"Sorry, Sir, but I heard about the escape an hour ago, and wanted to check with our man on the inside. You were right not to trust the warden completely. His assistant was a great choice."

Ross put his hand to his ear and carefully listened to one of his operatives.

"Sir, I just got a call. They found a piece of Sheetrock in the library with a hole in it. They followed the trail, and it ends in the river next to the prison. They put the dogs on the trail but no luck so far. It's as though he never came out of the river. Who knows, maybe we got lucky, and he drowned. He just might show up as a floater in a couple of days."

Alex broke his pencil in half and threw it in the trash. "Not a chance. I really do believe that Towers has the nine lives of a cat. No, I know he's alive, and that somehow he got away."

"Now listen to me carefully," instructed Alex. "I don't want the police to find him; that's your job. Use whatever resources you need, and there's no budget limit. I want Towers found dead somewhere--anywhere. He can drown, be run over by a truck, or fall from a cliff. I don't care, just make sure it's an accident, and I want it to happen today. Do you understand?"

"Okay, Mr. Brandon, I'll put my best men on it."

Langer hesitated for a second. There was something else on his mind, and Alex could see that he was unsure about pursuing the next question.

"Okay, out with it, Langer. What else is on your mind?"

"Sir, what do we want to tell your wife, and Cindy Towers? They both will find out soon since it will be all over the news."

Alex smiled and looked out the window. "My wife does as she's told. If I tell her it's none of her business, she will happily go shopping with her friends. As for Cindy Towers, I'll wait and see how she reacts to the news. The bugs you installed throughout the house are working great. I'll be able to judge how to discuss the escape with her. You know, supportive, yet concerned. She won't be a problem. Now, get out there and find Towers and don't come back until you do."

Langer didn't answer, but made a hasty exit through the side door.

Cleo Brandon stood in the entryway down the hall and shook her head in disbelief and pure fear. What she had just overheard had shaken her marriage to the core. Now she prayed that her husband wouldn't discover her eavesdropping. Luckily, Alex walked down the hall toward the kitchen and Cleo scurried back to her bedroom, where she was safe. Alex rarely came into her room, only when he was desperate for sex.

Her mind was racing with thoughts of where to go from here. Her life with Alex hadn't been a Hallmark marriage. When she first met Alex, he was gallant and sophisticated. He'd swept her off her feet, and they dated for less than two months before they were married. Her friends kept telling her that he was after the millions that her parents were worth. She adamantly told them he didn't need her money, that he was already a wealthy man.

She soon realized that his vice was power, and that he

loved it more than sex or money. The more money he made, the more power he achieved, and he was a greedy man. In his quest for more power, Cleo always felt she might be dumped for another woman, and that feeling was becoming stronger each day.

Most upsetting was Alex's recent attention to Curt's wife, Cindy. Although she really liked Cindy, she prayed that she wouldn't be the instrument in her divorce. The more she thought about it, she realized she wasn't worried about the divorce, but more about what would happen to Cindy and the kids. Cleo knew how persuasive Alex could be, so she decided she must find a way to talk to Cindy. She had to warn her, and soon.

Curt looked over the edge of the truck bed. The wind was cutting his face, making it hard to focus on the large green state sign. As it got closer, he realized it read "Las Vegas 110 miles." There was not much time to make a new plan. There seemed to be only two choices – disembark from the truck in downtown Vegas or jump from the truck when it slowed. He decided to take his chances downtown.

The signs kept flying by, and now it was only ten miles to the bright lights. The truck slowed down and headed into another truck stop. This one was larger than the other was, but it would be darker than the bright lights of Vegas. Therefore, he changed his mind and prepared to get off here.

The truck stopped, a door slammed, and lively conversation between two drivers could be heard. Curt waited to make his move until the men headed off to the restaurant laughing. When he felt sure it was safe, he started to crawl down from the truck. His legs were stiff and cramped, but the urge to get away from the truck compelled him on. As soon as his feet hit the ground, a gruff voice came from behind.

"Put your hands in the air and turn around slowly."

Curt did as he was told and turned to meet a Nevada State

Trooper. The gun in his hand told Curt that this cop was not taking any chances.

The cop motioned his gun slightly at Curt.

"Who are you and what are you doing around that truck? I know the driver of this rig, and you're not him."

Curt hesitated for a few seconds, trying to think.

"Sorry Sir, I was just hoping to get a ride into town. I'm down on my luck and meant no harm."

The cop looked Curt up and down. He wasn't buying the story.

"That story isn't going to fly. You're going downtown with me, and we're going to find out just who you are."

He wasn't looking to fight his way out like Steven Seagal, so he would just try to pass himself off as another homeless person. Curt was so close to freedom and now this bad luck.

A distant siren caught the cop's attention. He looked beyond Curt and lost his responsiveness for the moment. The siren got louder, and then a bright-red sports car flew by, followed by the source of the siren.

The cop looked back at Curt.

"This is your lucky day. I want you to get as far away from this truck stop as you can. I'll notify the truck owner and tell him you were out here. Now get lost and I don't want to see you around here ever again."

The cop holstered his gun and jumped into his car. The tires spun gravel, and in seconds, Curt had regained his freedom.

He had to get off the main highway and travel side roads from this point on. After walking about a half mile, he found a dark narrow side road sure to take him away from potential exposure to the Nevada Law.

After five miles through the outskirts of town, he came upon a small community northeast of Vegas. He walked the dimly lit streets, looking for a telephone booth. Larry's instructions were clear: change your appearance as soon as you can. Fifteen minutes later, he found a booth near an abandoned gas station. He skimmed the yellow pages for clothing donation centers. He saw Salvation Army, a few churches, but found nothing close by. He set the phone book down feeling discouraged.

He looked around and saw several sheets of paper tacked to a nearby telephone pole. One item caught his eye. It was a clothing drive for the homeless, and the center was only a few blocks away. He tore the notice off the pole and headed out.

The morning was early enough that few people were in the area. When he got to the drop box, he seized a large sack of clothing and backed away to sort through the bag. Nothing he could use in this sack. He moved back to the box and removed clothes until he found a set that would work, including a baseball cap.

He walked off into a field and changed into the new clothes. He carefully removed the two hundred dollars Larry had given him a few weeks prior and then headed back to the edge of the road and started walking.

Thirty minutes later, he found himself at a local market, where he purchased everything he needed for a clean shave. The bill was thirty dollars, but well worth it. He was careful to keep his head down, to avoid any cameras recording his purchases.

His next stop was a nearby gas station where he locked the bathroom door, shaved off his beard and then gave himself a military crew cut. The resulting reflection from the mirror wasn't great, but would have to do.

He walked out into the warm sunlight feeling like a new man. Traffic was picking up, so more people were now walking the streets. Curt laughed to himself for the first time in days and thought his luck was greatly improving. Of all the places to land, Las Vegas was the best. It was a place where you could easily lose yourself.

Since Larry spent most of his time in Nevada and California, he had picked San Francisco, Las Vegas, and Los

Angeles to maintain his emergency stashes of ID equipment and money. From what Curt could remember, the storage area he needed to find was on the other side of town. Larry had told him not to take taxis because the drivers seemed to remember everyone, and kept exact pickup records. Several blocks away, he found a bus stop, and determined the route he needed to take.

Chapter 26

Alex Brandon paced back and forth in his office. Curt was still on the loose. The longer Curt was out, the greater the odds were that something would go wrong with his plan. He couldn't figure out how so many people could screw things up. The warden had called several times in the past few hours, indicating they had no leads. Alex was about to pick up the phone, when Langer burst into his office.

"Good news. A Nevada state trooper remembers seeing Curt getting off a truck just outside Las Vegas. He would be in jail except that a little red sports car took the trooper in another direction."

Alex pulled up a map of Vegas and looked at the area where Curt had been spotted. "Ross, take a dozen men and find him. Use whatever company resources you need. I want him found before the authorities do."

Langer's phone rang, and he flipped it open. He listened for a few seconds, and the look on his face turned to extreme concern. He closed the phone, and slipped it back into his pocket.

"Mr. Brandon, that phone call was from one of my men, and it seems we have another serious problem. He got a call from our security company about a security video of your home. They are sending it to your screen as we speak."

Alex and Ross watched the video as one of their worst fears unfolded in front of them. They watched the entire sequence of his wife eavesdropping. They replayed it a second time, confirming there was no mistaking what they had seen.

Alex closed the file and turned to Langer. "I'm sorry to give you this one, but I want you to take care of it personally. No one else must know. Do you understand?"

Langer swallowed with a slight hint of hesitation. "Is there no other way, Sir? That seems so extreme."

Alex glared at Langer. "Don't ever question my orders.
The whole thing could fall apart because of this. Just take care of
it and the sooner, the better."

Curt reached his destination with no problem, enjoying the
bus ride as it gave him time to assess the area. The small storage
facility rented huge containers and various-sized postal-type boxes
for extended periods. Larry had rented a box two feet wide by
one foot high for 20 years, and it was perfect for hiding his
escape materials.

Box number 666 was easy to remember, but the seven-
digit code might be a little more difficult. Larry used the number
1235813, which is derived from the sum of the two proceeding
numbers. He added 1 plus 2 to get 3, 2 plus 3 to equal 5, 3 plus
5 to get 8, and 5 plus 8 for the final number 13.

Curt found the box in the back of the first hallway, about
halfway down the wall. The area was deserted, but even so, he
covered the keypad with his left hand, as he entered the code
with his right. The door opened and inside was a large briefcase.
He grabbed the briefcase, closed the locker, and headed toward
the front door.

Once outside he looked for a quiet area to explore inside
the case. A nearby park seemed a good choice, so he sat down
on a lone park bench, and slowly opened the case. Inside were
six large packs of twenty-dollar bills. He jammed one pack into
his pocket. He looked around again, but no one seemed to be
paying him any attention.

Larry had mentioned several nearby hotels, so ten minutes
later he was checked in. He closed the door and sat down on the
bed. He was so tired. He flopped back on the bed and was
asleep in less than a minute.

An hour later, a siren woke him from his deep sleep. He
was not out of the woods yet, and he still had a couple more

tasks to accomplish. He opened the briefcase again and looked at its contents. In addition to fifty thousand dollars in cash, there was a stack of passports, driver's licenses, and a small makeup kit.

He sat down and looked at himself in the mirror. Curt took a small vial from the kit and started to smear it on his cheeks and under his chin. In less than an hour, his cheeks and chin bloated into a new shape. Larry had told Curt that his secret concoction would last for a few days, before he would have to re-apply the solution. He had enough in the bottle for a month's worth of masking. The worst part was that it stung, but better to endure pain than jail.

Satisfied with his new look, he closed the briefcase and headed back to the storage area. Larry told him never to leave the case in the room or carry it around town. Larry had many rules, and Curt planned to adhere to them all, especially the tips for staying out of sight.

Once the briefcase was secure in its hiding place, his next stop was the local clothing store. Curt selected a simple shirt and pants, nothing flashy. He paid the salesclerk in cash and headed to the park bathroom to change into his new outfit.

He walked two more blocks to a second clothing store specializing in suits and ties. Curt looked over several before selecting an outfit priced somewhere in the midrange. He again paid in cash, and then headed to the restaurant next door. He asked for a table at the back and sat back to enjoy his first decent meal in months.

When he had finished, he paid the bill in cash and left a decent tip on the table for the waiter. He headed for the restroom and changed into the new suit, depositing his previously purchased clothes in the trash. He waited until he was sure that his waiter was at the other end of the restaurant and then exited.

His next stop was a local computer store, where he picked up a laptop computer, a small high-quality color printer, and four

16-gig thumb drives. Curt paid cash and made a quick exit from the store, heading in a direction away from the storage area. He circled around the block and came back to the storage area to pick up the briefcase.

Briefcase also in hand, Curt headed for a second hotel where he again checked in under a different name and paid cash for a week's stay. Once he was settled in the room, he checked the locks and ordered room service. Dressed in the complimentary bathrobe, he tipped the waiter who brought his burger, beer, and fries.

Curt sat down, opened the beer, and turned on the TV. As he took his first bite out of the burger, he watched the reporter describing the daring escape of this dangerous killer. He hoped the cloak-and-dagger stuff had kept him below the radar, but no, there he was in living HD color. As the reporter repeated the story of Curt's arrest and imprisonment, he set the half-eaten burger on the nightstand. He suddenly lost his appetite.

Chapter 27

When Alex reached his country home, Cindy Towers ran out to meet him. Alex was surprised when Cindy put her arms around him and held him close. They broke apart and walked into the house. Alex set his coat and briefcase inside the door of his office and headed for the living room. He poured two stiff drinks and handed one to Cindy. He looked around the room.

"Where are the kids? Are they alright?"

Cindy took a sip from the glass. "I sent them over to Curt's sister Kendra. I told her to take the kids somewhere where the press couldn't find them, and then to call me. She's upstate in a fancy hotel, and although the kids don't like it, I didn't give them a choice. Have you heard any more about Curt?"

"Not much. He had to have had some help inside the prison, but that's water under the bridge right now. The police lost his trail just outside Las Vegas. If he calls, I think we should try to persuade him to turn himself in to the authorities. If he doesn't, his chances aren't very good. I'm so sorry that you and the kids had to be dragged through this mess."

"Alex, it's not your fault. You have been such a gentleman throughout it all. The way you took care of the kids and me is more than most would have done. We all thank you so much. I just hope Curt doesn't do something stupid. I don't know what he was thinking."

Tears started to form as she tried to be strong. Alex took the opportunity and put his arms around her. Soon Cindy and her husband's fortune would all be his. He had never loved Cleo, and had always had a thing for Cindy. She was a knockout; smart, sexy and he was green with envy of Curt. He smiled and thought; "Now she'll be mine."

They sat for the next hour as Cindy talked of the times

before Curt had gone to jail. Alex was getting tired of hearing it, but knew he must endure for a bit longer.

His cell phone rang, and he flipped it open as he got up off the couch. He listened without saying a word and then folded it up and looked at Cindy.

"My men have heard nothing from the police. It looks like Curt dropped off the face of the earth. We will have to wait until tomorrow before we have any further news. I think you should take a sleeping pill and get to bed early. I have a feeling that tomorrow will be a long day."

Cindy took the last sip and tried to stand. She'd had a bit too much to drink, so that a sleeping pill wouldn't be necessary. Alex told her he would stay at the house tonight, in case she had any problems. He then helped her to her room, took off her shoes, and bid her good night.

Alex went downstairs to watch the updates on the prison escape. Most of it was just a repeat, and already becoming old news. By tomorrow, the media would be exposing a politician who had cheated on his wife or had taken kickbacks. There was always something new. He had bribed his share of bigwigs, but the difference was that he would never be caught doing it. That's why he had underlings.

Chapter 28

Alex woke to a strong smell of coffee, eggs, and bacon. He quickly dressed and ambled into the kitchen. To his surprise, Cindy was laying out an elaborate breakfast for two. She motioned for him to sit down and placed a plate of food in front of him. She filled his coffee cup, adding his special creamer.

He looked down at this great meal. "So, what's gotten into you?"

"I don't know what I did last night. I hope I didn't do or say anything stupid. All I know is that I woke up more rested than I have in a week. I need to let Curt do his thing and get caught. It will be hell with the press once more, but I just need to focus on getting my life back together, for the sake of the kids."

Alex took a bite of the bacon. It was perfect, and the eggs were even better. Cindy was a great cook. Things were getting better by the moment. His mind started wandering, and he mused about if she were good in bed?

He looked at the paper lying on the edge of the table. Curt was still on page one. "This breakfast is incredible. You really didn't have to do all this. I don't want you to take this the wrong way, but Curt was a lucky man to have you. You're smart, beautiful, and even a great cook. Yes, he was lucky indeed."

Alex thought Cindy was going to sit down, but instead she came over to the side of the table next to Alex. She leaned over and kissed him on the cheek.

"Thanks for the compliment. I could say the same about you. Cleo is a very lucky woman."

Alex was about to respond, when his cell phone rang. He got up and walked out onto the patio. Cindy watched through the glass doors as he talked for about five minutes. She saw Alex's face transformed from a cheery smile to sadness she'd never seen before. Alex closed the phone and sat down at the table. He pushed his breakfast away, indicating that he had lost his appetite.

"That was my assistant, Ross Langer. He just got some terrible news. My wife and my son were killed in an automobile accident. Ross told me the police thought she lost control on a curve and ran down the canyon."

Cindy came over to Alex, put her arms around him, and pulled him close.

"I'm so sorry, Alex. I really liked Cleo and Eric. You've done so much for me. Now it's my turn. What do you need me to do?"

"I appreciate the offer, but I'm going to need some time to sort this out. I'm sorry to leave, but I have to take care of things."

Cindy sat down in the chair across from Alex. "I'm so sorry, Alex. You do what you have to. I understand, and I'll help wherever you need me. Go."

Alex got up from his chair and looked across to Cindy with a pale look on his face. He walked to his office, grabbed his briefcase, and headed out the front door.

While driving down the long driveway, his face transformed into a big smile. He was almost there. If they could only find Curt, and make certain he was dead. His first act was to stop by the police station, and then off to the funeral home to take care of the final episode in his present marriage.

Curt spent the last twelve hours in a dead sleep. He woke to the sound of a police siren; he jumped up and ran over to the window. The police car passed and headed down the street, the siren no longer an irritation to his ears. He sat down in the desk chair and opened the briefcase. He thoroughly looked through the contents and then pushed it to the side. Curt withdrew the laptop, booted it up, and installed the Norton Security that he had purchased with the laptop.

Once that was completed, he logged on to Larry's website to see if it was still functional. He used the previous date backward, starting with the two-digit year, month, and day as the password. It worked just as Larry had said and in a few seconds, Curt was ready to go.

He connected the printer, installed the inks, and then made a test print. Following Larry's instructions, Curt positioned the computer's webcam and took a couple of portraits. The background and lighting were wrong, so he turned the laptop toward a window and put his back against a white wall. It only took a few more shots, and he had what he needed.

He downloaded Larry's special software to create a variety of fake documents. He first made an Oregon driver's license and then a US passport. Larry thought of everything, including adding several stolen passports and driver's licenses for comparison. He also added a UV device similar to the one US Customs agents use to spot fake passports.

Curt had some basic experience using Adobe Photoshop, so he quickly set to work. He used the software's facial recognition feature to adjust and size the photo to match the stolen passport. He ran the first print of his attempt through a special 4x6 scanner that had been included in the briefcase, but the comparison images weren't close enough to sneak by Customs. Fortunately, Larry's software used the comparison to make corrections in the printer profile. The next print was a perfect match. After making all the passport adjustments, printing the driver's license was easy.

Finally, Curt took a small toolbox out of the briefcase to help him complete his task. These tools allowed him to put the passport together and create the plastic-coated driver's license. He looked at his two masterpieces and deemed them perfect.

Now he needed to put them to the ultimate test. He

packed up the briefcase and headed out the hotel lobby, and then down the street to a bank. He hesitated when he saw a guard standing inside the door. The guard saw Curt and walked toward him. He opened the door and welcomed him inside.

Curt walked up to the new customer desk and filled out the forms to open an account. The clerk seemed very helpful, especially when he gave him $4000 for a deposit. Once the transaction was completed, Curt shook the clerk's hand and exited the bank as quickly as possible.

His next stop was a car rental facility five blocks down the street. He picked a midrange-sized car and told the clerk he was on a one-way trip to San Diego. He had to pay extra, but that was just fine with Curt. A few minutes later, he was on his way, determined to get as far away as possible from the prison.

Later that night, he checked into a small hotel on the beach in Santa Barbara. He sat back on the dingy bedspread watching the nightly news and saw he was becoming old news. His escape had been reduced to a 15-second clip that followed the two major stories of the night. Larry had told him that the press would give up, as soon as he had pulled his disappearance act. A few more days, and he would be old news. That sounded good to Curt.

Chapter 29

Curt stopped at the US Bank on State Street and made a transfer of $3000 to the savings account of Larry's wife, and replenished his own account with another $4000. The clerk looked up Curt's account and wanted documentation showing where he had acquired the cash. Larry had warned him this might happen, so he had provided several bills of sale for old cars that were probably under mounds of drifting sand in the Nevada desert. Again, Larry's foresight saved the day.

He repeated the task at a local US Bank three hours later in Los Angeles. This second deposit was a bit risky, but Curt wanted to help Larry's wife since his friend had done so much to help him get out of prison.

The next task was the riskiest. Curt drove around and looked at several used-car lots before he found one that looked a bit shady and might not be in business long. He selected one of the most expensive cars and offered cash. At first, the dealer hesitated, but when he was about ready to walk, the manager took the cash and gave him the pink slip. Curt asked the dealer if someone could drive his purchase over to the car rental yard so that he could return his rental car. Aiming to please, the dealer told Curt he would return the car for him. Curt tossed him the keys and headed on his way to San Diego.

Once in San Diego, he stopped at a car dealer specializing in purchasing used cars. He haggled with the dealer for cash, finally taking a 35 percent loss. Now that he had safely laundered the money Larry had given him, Curt was ready to go back to yet another US Bank and make a large deposit. This time the clerk told him they would have to put a hold on the money until the bill of sale had been verified. Curt agreed and walked out of the bank.

His final stop was a storage facility much like the one in Las Vegas. He placed the briefcase and everything else but his driver's license, passport, and $2000 inside the storage unit. He paid the manager for five years storage in advance and ordered a cab that would take him across the Mexican border. He'd never heard of such a service before, but Larry assured him the option was available--for a price. It was a necessary service provided to executives who conducted trade along the border. Certain cab drivers had permission from the border guards on both sides to transport passengers back and forth.

Curt's biggest concern was the passport. He was about to find out just how well he had used Larry's special equipment for forgery. His cellmate had told Curt the best time to cross the border was when the guards were ready to get off their shift.

The guard motioned for him to roll down the window, and he looked at the passport. He asked Curt what his business was in Mexico, and he told the guard that he was looking for deals on used cars. The guard was about ready to take the passport back into the office but then looked down at his watch. He handed it back to Curt and told him to have a good day.

The Mexican guard barely looked at the cab drivers' passport before waving them through. Curt directed the cabbie to drop him off at one of the better hotels. He gave the cabbie a tip that wouldn't raise any red flags and then booked a hotel room for a week. Once in the room, he locked the door and flopped down on the bed.

"I'm free, really free," he thought. With that warm feeling of safety, he drifted into a deep peaceful sleep.

Chapter 30

Alex Brandon was pissed. There had been no news on Curt in the past several days. Langer had put every man he could on the trail, but all had come up cold. They had nothing, and his men had no direction to turn. It was as if Curt had done a Houdini disappearing act, and it was really starting to get on Alex's nerves.

He knew from their experiences that Curt was not the type of person to hide well from his father or the police, so he had to have had help. Alex asked the warden to talk again to Curt's cellmate, Larry. The warden informed him that Larry was near death and unable to talk to anyone.

Alex stood up and looked out the window. A fall storm passed through; dumping several inches of rain, but the weather was now in the process of clearing. He clenched his fist and was about to hit something on his desk when Langer came bursting through the door.

"Good news, Boss. One of our agents on the police force just got word that Curt showed up on a bank camera. For some strange reason, he seems to be buying and selling cars and depositing the profits in several bank accounts. So far, we have a visual record of him in Santa Barbara, and then in Los Angeles. It appears that he's heading south, so I assume he's heading for Mexico. I've already sent men to the border, and they should be reporting back to me later today."

Several scenarios whirled through Alex's head. This might be a good thing since people disappear in Mexico all the time.

"Okay, let's assume that's where he's headed. Assemble a team and head down there to find him. I don't want to hear any excuses. When you do find him, make sure he gets lost in the open wasteland desert down there."

"Langer, there's one more thing. If you know that I'm with Cindy, wait until I'm alone before you update me. Just tell me that you have an update on the new weapons project. She's a smart cookie, and can see through any cons. Now go and get your team together. I want them in Mexico by tonight. Understood?"

Curt lay on the pool chair drinking a margarita and reading the LA Times. There was nothing written about his escape. This was the first day since his escape that lacked news on Curt Towers. "No news is my best news yet," he thought.

The past few days had been so relaxing. He spent most of his time trying to figure out a new plan. Going back to the States was now out of the question. He had no way of proving that he was innocent, so nothing had changed. Even if he could get a new trial, they would now add prison escape to the charges. With all the evidence stacked against him, if he were on the jury, he'd even vote guilty.

He missed his wife and family, but knew that the police would be monitoring any communication. Larry told him that although Curt dearly wanted to talk to his wife, it was something that should never ever happen. He had to move on for the sake of his family. It was just so hard to realize that he'd lost more than his freedom. He had lost his family. It was as though they had been killed in a car accident, never to be seen again.

He was feeling sad and sorry for himself, when a shapely leg stopped by his side. He reached up and pretended to massage his eyes to wipe his tears away. He panned up to see the beautiful blonde standing next to him. She could easily be a supermodel and the subject of most men's dreams.

"Hi, my name is Cindy. Are you on holiday?"

"I wish. No I'm Curt," he said, immediately regretting using his own name. "I'm down on business. I buy and sell used cars. So, how about you?" he asked.

101

"I'm recovering from my divorce. This holiday is part of the settlement."

She pulled up a pool lounger and lay down next to Curt. It was hard for him to keep his eyes off her body, and she knew it. She rolled over so her back faced the sun.

"Do you mind? I can't reach back there," she requested.

At first, Curt wasn't sure what she was talking about, but then it slowly sank in. Nevertheless, he wanted to make sure they were on the same page.

"Trying to get rid of the tan lines?"

"You got that right."

Curt slowly undid the back clasp on her small bikini top. He dropped the two straps to the sides of her gorgeous body. The sides of her breasts were now visible. She turned slightly toward Curt, giving him an even better view.

"Could you put some of the suntan lotion on my back? It's on the ground next to me."

She turned again toward Curt to make sure he saw her breasts. She smiled, and then turned back to lie on the lounger.

Curt picked up the lotion and started to apply it to her back. Although he had been out of circulation for a while, there was no doubt in his mind that she was trying to pick him up. She obviously wanted to get some sack time to make up for whatever had or had not transpired in her marriage.

His mind started to drift to what she would be like in bed. The idea that he was the chosen one turned him on. The whole idea that she was looking to pick him up had made his day. Then paranoia set in as he thought that maybe he was the only man of choice in the area. Nope, there were several other men in the area, and they were definitely better looking. "Whoa, what a stupid thought comparing yourself to other men. Get a grip, man," he thought.

He continued to put the lotion on her back, but his mind started to drift back to the other Cindy in his life. His good life

102

with his wife was gone forever and now here he was in Mexico with another Cindy, running for his life. He abruptly stopped putting the lotion on her back. What was wrong with him? He felt like he was cheating on his wife, even though they might never see each other again. His mind became instantly clearer, so he got up, and used the newspaper to help cover his quickly deflating erection.

"Sorry, Cindy, but I have to go to an appointment. It was a pleasure meeting you. Have an enjoyable vacation."

As Curt walked away from the pool edge, Cindy rolled to her side and followed him with her eyes. In a low voice, she started to talk to herself. "Well, that was a first for me. Either I'm losing it, or the man has to be gay. Just you wait because I'm not done with you yet Mr. Car Dealer, or whoever you really are."

Once Curt closed the door to his room, he stripped off his trunks and headed for a cold shower. As he stood under the spray, his mind kept going back and forth between his wife and this new acquaintance." I must be crazy," he thought. "That woman was mine to be had, and I passed it up. Most guys would think I'm out of my mind—no; ALL guys would think I'm crazy."

He sat down on the shower floor with the water running full force and cried for the first time in years. Life was not fair. He did nothing wrong. He had always been faithful to his wife. He had just proven it again, even though his marriage was over. Nevertheless, his mind kept going back to the blonde-haired woman at the pool. He had to get out of here, fast.

He dried off; packed up the few clothes he had purchased, and headed down to the hotel lobby. He immediately noticed a woman from the bell desk talking to an older couple. Curt listened in as they were inquiring about travel to Loreto, a large town located on the Pacific side of the Baja Peninsula. The bus was scheduled to leave at noon and would arrive later that night. The more he listened, the better this new idea sounded.

When the couple left, he walked up to the woman, and asked if there was still space on the bus. She asked for his credit card, but Curt told her he was paying with cash. A few minutes later and a few dollars less, he had a ticket going south.

As he sat in the chair waiting for the bus, Cindy from the pool strolled by and stopped when she saw him.

"Leaving so soon?"

"Yep, I'm going down to Loreto to look at some old cars."

Then Curt realized his error. He had just given out too much information. He wasn't thinking straight. She was so tempting; he just knew he needed to get away from her quickly, before he did something stupid.

"Enjoy your time around the pool."

Curt thought about what he had just said. It was so stupid, and he had made it sound like she was a shark looking for a kill. Well, in a way she was.

"Sorry, I meant to say--well sorry. You have to understand; I just lost my wife."

The words came out before Curt could think why he said such a thing. Then he realized that it was what he should have said in the beginning.

Cindy's demeanor immediately changed when she heard his words. All of a sudden, the sexy poses and the flirting stopped.

"Sorry. I should have known something was wrong. Look, I'm sorry I came on so strong."

Curt got up as the bus arrived at the front door.

"That's all right, Cindy. I never said anything, so you had no way of knowing. It's been nice knowing you."

The two shook hands, and Curt picked up his baggage and headed to the front door. The bus was about half full with three couples, a few younger men, three children, a dog, and a crate of chickens. That combination would be strange for a bus ride in the States, but it was the norm for Mexico.

Curt was the only American on the bus, so as he sat down, everyone focused his or her eyes on him. He pulled out a book he had purchased for the journey, and everyone went back to what they were doing. A few minutes later, the driver took his seat and closed the door. He said a few words in Spanish, which Curt could determine as the travel time to their destination. He sat back for his ten-hour ride to Loreto.

The driver started the engine and was about to put it into reverse when there was a pounding sound on the front door of the bus. The driver opened the door, and Cindy stepped up, handing her ticket to the driver. She worked her way down the aisle and sat down next to Curt. He was in shock. He did not know if he was happy to see her or upset. He was about to ask her what she was doing, but she beat him to it.

"Sorry, Curt, but I had to get out of there too. The trip to Loreto sounded like the new adventure I needed. I'm sorry I came on strong to you before; it was somewhat childish. So, what was your wife's name?"

"Cindy."

"Wow, was it spelled the same way...C I N D Y?"

"Yes, spelled the same. Look, I accept your apology, but don't take this the wrong way. I'm not interested in a lengthy conversation right now. I just want to get to Loreto in peace and quiet."

Cindy smiled. "No problem, Curt. I have my book to read. Is it all right, if I sit next to you? I promise not to bug you anymore."

Curt thought for a second. He'd been a jerk, and now she was the one trying to make amends.

"I'd be happy to have you sit next to me. In fact, I'd be crazy not to let such a beautiful woman be my traveling companion. Sorry I was so short; it's just been a hell of a week."

Cindy opened her book, and the two of them started reading almost in tandem. The next three hours went by quickly.

The bus started to slow, and Curt assumed they were stopping for a pit stop and gas. He looked out the window and saw nothing but open desert in all directions. He saw a horse out of the corner of his eye and then a second. The driver opened the door and got out. Curt could hear him talking with someone outside. By the tone of his voice, the driver knew the person who had stopped the bus.

He was about to settle back into his book, when a large man boarded the bus. This member of the Mexican Federal Police had crossed ammo belts and a huge pistol. He looked as though he had stepped out of some Hollywood movie.

When he spoke, his English was very clear. "Americanos get outside right now."

He ambled back to where Curt was sitting. "You two gringos get out right now. Bring all your belongings with you too. Now, I said!"

Before Curt could even stand up, the Mexican seized Cindy and began dragging her toward the front of the bus. Curt made a feeble attempt to stop him and was rewarded for his efforts with a blow from the Mexican's pistol. Curt fell to the floor and a second Mexican Federal dragged him from the bus. The driver closed the door and waited, making no effort to help them.

Curt and Cindy were stripped of all their belongings, especially the money that Curt had hidden in his pocket. The Mexican knocked on the bus door and handed the driver a small portion of the proceeds. Then the bus engine started up and continued down the road towards Loreto, less two passengers.

As soon as the bus was out of sight, the second Mexican grabbed Cindy again. Curt stepped up and tried to stop him, but was hit across the face with the butt end of the gun. He fell to the ground, and Cindy ran over to help him. She held him close as though Curt was her child.

"Look, you got your money. Leave us alone. We don't have any more to give you."

He leaned down and looked at her through a smile of broken and rotten teeth.

"You are right about one thing. The American you are holding is of no further use to us. We will see that he dies quickly. You, on the other hand, have much more to offer us-- much, much more," he snickered.

Curt tried to focus through the blood running down his forehead and into his eyes. The leader had assumed that Curt was incapacitated, so he had returned his attention to Cindy. He waited until the leader put his gun away so that he could put both his hands on Cindy. Curt seized this opportunity to grab the gun, pull back the hammer, and shoot the leader in the leg.

As the leader was falling, the second in command was trying to ascertain what had just happened. In the confusion, Curt started to shoot in the air and yell, "Run, Cindy. Run as fast and far as you can. Run until you drop. Go now, or you will die. Run."

As Cindy ran into the sagebrush, the second in command raised his gun to fire, but Curt's gun was already leveled at the man's head.

"That's not a good idea. This time I'll shoot you in the head, not in the leg. I'm getting sick and tired of your crap, so drop the gun now, or you are dead."

The second Federal stopped and dropped his gun to the ground. He started saying something in Spanish, but Curt was unfamiliar with the words. The leader was still lying on the ground, yelling about being shot in the leg, and demanding restitution. He wanted his second in command to sacrifice himself in an attempt to get Curt's gun.

Curt thought about shooting the two banditos and walking away. No one would be the wiser, but Curt wasn't a killer. Although they had just tried to kill him, he didn't have what it took to kill in cold blood.

The three were at a standstill, when the unexpected

happened. The leader had a smaller hidden gun that he retrieved when Curt looked away. Curt heard the hammer pull back, followed by a loud explosion next to his head. He reached up to his right temple, and drew back his hand covered with blood. His vision started to blur, and then he fell to the ground.

The commander ripped off a section of his pants and tied it around the flesh wound on his leg. He yelled out several profanities to the other man before attempting to stand. He snatched the gun from Curt's limp hand and pointed it at his bungling companion. He smiled for a few seconds and then released the hammer. The second man relaxed as he had been given a second chance.

The two argued about what to do about the woman before deciding to head back to camp and take care of the leader's injury. They tied a rope around Curt's legs and then mounted their horses, slowly working their way deep into the desert. After a mile of dragging Curt's body behind the horses, they realized it would be too slow a process. Instead, they hoisted Curt over the back of one of the horses, and the two men rode together on the other horse.

A few hours later, they felt they were far enough from the road to bury the body. They got out a small shovel from their saddlebag and started to dig a hole. The digging was harder than they had anticipated, so they stopped with just a shallow grave. They figured the buzzards would eventually finish the job.

They rolled Curt into the shallow pit and the leader put a bullet into his chest. They covered the dead man, and got onto their horses heading back to their families, rehearsing their cover story along the way.

Chapter 31

Alex Brandon returned to his country home, hoping to sort things out in his mind. It was a welcome feeling to see Cindy when he arrived. She had been helping Alex with his family's funeral arrangements, so the two went over all the details before calling it a night. Alex was surprised to see how much Cindy had become involved in his life. She was really starting to grow on him. Curt had indeed been a very lucky fellow to have her, but now it was his turn.

In the morning, he came downstairs and discovered Cindy had prepared a full breakfast, complete with a newspaper propped next to his plate. Before sitting down he thought about his new situation, determining just how he could best manipulate it to his benefit. He decided the time was right, so he moved over and gently put his arms around her.

"Thanks so much for helping me through these difficult times. I don't know what I would have done without you."

The embrace was short. It was just long enough to show appreciation, without implying more. The response from Cindy indicated it had been right on target.

"Glad to be of help. You helped me through some difficult times. Now I can return the favor. Is there anything else I can do for you?"

Alex had several ideas, but all were inappropriate at this time. Maybe later they would be on his agenda, but for right now he would have to be patient. So much was riding on how he handled the situation. Langer's research had shown that Curt's company was worth more than 500 million dollars. Adding that to his company's value, he could eventually realize his dream to become a billionaire. Curt had been such an idealist, and now he was nothing because of it. Alex wanted it all – power, wealth, and Cindy.

"No, you've done so much for me already. I don't know what I would have done without your help. I still don't understand how she ran off the road since the road conditions were perfect. It just does not make any sense."

Cindy poured a second cup of coffee for Alex.

"I wondered about that, too. I just don't understand why life has been treating both of us so badly. We need to stick together to get through this and move on."

Cindy reached from behind and gave him a hug for a few seconds. Alex wanted to turn and return the favor, but realized that it would be inappropriate for a grieving father and husband.

"Thanks for all your support. Yes, we'll get through this-- together."

A dirty hand extended up through the shallow surface of the grave. A second hand then pierced the surface of the desert sand. Curt rose out of the sand like a character out of a Hollywood horror movie. He was alive. How was that possible? It looked as though Curt had used up another one of his nine lives.

He tried to make sense of it all. He had been shot in the head and chest and buried alive. He put his hand to his temple and found that the bullet had glanced off the side of his skull. There was more blood than wound.

The second bullet was the one that did most of the damage. The Mexican used reloaded ammo but cut back on the amount of powder to get more loads. The effect was that the bullet had the sound of a real round being fired but very little impact on the target. The bullet in fact, had hit a rib in Curt's chest and stopped. No vital organs had been hit, but there had been a considerable amount of bleeding from both wounds.

The one thing that saved his life was that when the Mexicans dumped his body into the shallow grave, his arm had fallen across his face creating a small air pocket. Not long after the bandits had left the scene, the loose sand had filtered down around Curt's face creating an open space for him to breathe. In addition, the light layer of sand over Curt's body had kept him warm during the freezing nighttime temperature.

As Curt sat up in the shallow grave, he tried to get his bearings. The loss of blood made him dizzy. It was already getting hot, so shade was first on his agenda. He scanned the area and saw nothing but flat open desert. He started to get up, but passed out.

Four hours later, Curt woke again, but now the temperatures had become extreme. He tried to stand up, but fell to the ground yet again. After several tries, he was finally able to stand long enough to get a better view of his surroundings. He spotted a large Saguaro cactus, but it was some distance away. After an hour of struggling, he stood beneath the shade of the gigantic cactus.

On the ground were a couple of smaller cacti that he had never seen before. He looked around for a rock in preparation for the task. Slowly, he started to strike the smaller cacti with the rock until small pieces fell off. As he struck harder, some of the glancing blows resulted in large cacti needles being lodged in his hand. Each time he had to stop and pull them out before continuing.

Eventually, he reached the meat of the cacti and pulled out a piece, which he squeezed until a few drops of liquid fell into his mouth. He continued chopping and squeezing the cacti meat for fluid, but realized it was not enough. He took a bite of the meat, and although it tasted awful, he continued to eat and drink the cacti meat. The sun was getting hotter and hotter. He may have survived the gunshots, but this desert heat could finish him off. He stood up again and passed out.

Alex spent most of the day sorting through business

contracts he had recently acquired. When Curt had been convicted of the murder, Xtreme Machines had taken a big hit in the stock market. There was an exodus of clients, many of whom migrated to Alex's company. Business was starting to look promising.

Now if he could just fix this final problem, he could move on with his new life with Cindy. Where in the hell was Curt? How was it that he could disappear so well?

As the day wore on, his temper worsened. By late afternoon, most of his assistants worked to avoid contact with him. Then his day improved as Langer came into the office.

"Good news, Mr. Brandon. Curt was spotted crossing the border a few days ago. We tracked him to a hotel, and then to a bus headed to Loreto. The strange thing is that he never arrived. He and an American woman were no-shows. Our men asked the driver about them, and he immediately clammed up. When we offered him a pile of money, he came clean. It seems that Curt flashed his cash around at the hotel, and the driver passed the information on to a couple of corrupt Mexican policemen. Curt and the woman were taken off the bus and never seen again."

He continued with his story. "We have no way of confirming the story until we find the two Mexicans or Curt and his new-found girlfriend. It seems the two were traveling together. The strangest thing of all is that the woman's name is Cindy. Anyway, I have my men checking out the situation, and I'll get back to you, as soon as we know more."

This was good news. Alex knew of the corruption in some of the districts in Mexico since he had dealt with them before. He knew a little money could buy a lot in Mexico. He just hoped the men who took Curt and this new Cindy were evil enough to kill for money. Then the Curt portion of his life would be finally over.

"Okay, Langer, good job. Take whatever cash you need to buy off everyone to get to Curt. I need confirmation that he is dead, so make sure the authorities discover his body. I want this

112

chapter of Xtreme Machines closed. When you have news, wake me any time, day, or night."

Chapter 32

Curt woke again. He was still very weak, but he gradually stood up. The night was black with no moon, but the skies were clear and the stars vivid. It was cold, and he was freezing. It was unbearably hot in the day and frigid at night. He wondered to himself, "How could such a place exist?"

He visually scanned the surrounding area and didn't see anything. Then he saw it—a small light in the distance. He thought he might be imagining it as it would appear for a few seconds and then disappear. He realized that the light was not changing, but it was his impaired vision. Curt tried to focus again since it was his only chance. Yes, there was a light, but it might be the campfire of the two Mexicans. Without any further options, he would have to chance it, so he headed off in the direction of the light.

He fell, and then woke a few minutes later to start once more. Curt struggled for a few hundred yards further before falling again. He was rapidly losing his remaining strength and with this amount of progress, there was no way he was going to make it.

As the next couple of hours melded together, he couldn't even remember what he was doing. He just knew his legs kept getting him up and walking, but he could hardly feel them moving. He was becoming a half-dead zombie walking in the desert.

Almost three hours later, he reached the point where he could see the source of the light. It was a campfire outside a small hut or house. It was too hard to determine more, but he decided it was worth finding out. He got up one more time and started to walk, but instead he took his final step and collapsed on the desert floor. A dog howled in the distance.

Alex paced the office like an expectant father. The morning hours had produced no news, but shortly after lunch, Langer had called saying that he had an important update. Alex decided it would be quicker if he went to Langer's office in the basement of the building. No one in the company knew of the offices on the lower level. Only Alex and Langer's men were allowed on this floor. This was where all of Alex's black ops were conceived and executed. Once he reached the B3 level, Langer greeted Alex.

Before saying anything, Alex looked around to confirm they were alone.

"So what do we have today? Tell me that this is finally over and Curt is dead."

"Well, there is a pretty good chance that is the case. A woman was picked up a few hours after she, and Curt were taken from the bus. We have a copy of the interview taken by the Mexican police. It appears that the two Mexican policemen who took Curt, and this woman off the bus hit Curt very hard on the side of the head. When the two men tried to attack her, Curt grabbed one of the guns and shot one of the robbers. Curt yelled for her to run, and she did. She ran for miles, and eventually got picked up by a passing motorist."

Langer scanned the pages before proceeding. "From what we can tell, the Mexican police are not happy that some of their own were so bold with the robbery. The Mexican police force has developed a poor reputation over the past few years, so they've been trying to clean up their act. This episode didn't help their image any."

Alex listened intently as Langer continued with his report.

"After the interview, the police let her go, and one of my men intercepted her. We told her that we worked for Curt, and we're trying to find him. She was very grateful and gave our man a piece of her blood-soaked blouse for DNA comparison. We obtained pictures from someone we have inside their police force, and she picked out the two culprits right away."

Langer closed the folder and smiled. "We then had no trouble locating the twosome. One had a wounded leg that confirmed her story. Now here's the good part. After we produced a large pile of money, they told our man, they had shot and killed Curt. They said they took his body out into the desert and buried him before returning home. I asked if they were certain that he was dead. They said they were positive he was deceased. All we need now is the DNA confirmation, and we're done."

Alex rubbed his hands across his face. His skin was crawling as though a bug was on it. He sensed that something was not right. This was all too good to be true. He knew from experience that Curt had nine lives. That was how he got the nickname CAT, besides the fact those were his initials. No, something was definitely not right, but what?

"No, Langer. We're not done yet. You are right on one count. We do need to confirm the DNA, but we also need the body. Until we have the body, Curt should still be considered alive. Do you understand? So, what happened with the two policemen?"

Langer hesitated for a second as he composed his answer. He hoped it would be the correct response.

"Well, I felt the two had not earned the cash we gave them, so we took it back— of course after they told us where they buried Curt's body."

Alex smiled. "How did they respond?"

"They couldn't because of the holes in their heads and chests. No, they won't be a problem for us at all. It will take some time for their boss to find their bodies, maybe never."

Langer smirked and said, "It will take some time to find Curt's body, but without those two around, we can take our time. According to the directions, they buried Curt about five miles east of the main highway. I rented several small planes to check out the area. Hopefully, we should find the body by tomorrow."

Curt opened his eyes to discover a bright out-of-focus light hanging over his head. As he assessed his surroundings, he realized he was lying in a bed. Then he was startled by a wet object with bristles touching his face.

"Digger, leave him be," came a voice from somewhere across the room.

"Sorry about my dog. He loves it when new people come a callin'. If it hadn't been for him barking, I never woulda found you. You owe your life to that mutt and so do I. I'm guessing that means he now has two men owin' him. My name is Henry. Henry Farnsworth. You know, you're one lucky man. It looks like somebody wanted you dead bad. Are you on the run?"

There was quiet for a few seconds. Curt was still trying to get his bearings. He felt his head. He had a large bandage around his head and another on his chest. They both hurt like hell. He tried to focus on the voice, but couldn't. He tried again and then he saw an old man sitting on the chair across the room. He looked to be about a hundred and ten years old. Curt knew that was probably not the case; it was just the results of a life in the desert.

"My name is Cirrrrrrrrrrrr, Cris Blumfield. I was robbed by a couple of Mexican police. They tried to kill me and rape the American woman who was with me. Did you find her?"

"You were the only one out there. Digger would have found her, too, if she were anywhere close. I have a feeling that's not yer name, but that's fine by me. I know those two police fellas who bushwhacked you. They tried the same thing on me once. They're like the Mexican version of dumb and dumber. There aren't enough brains between the two to take a piss without dribblin' all over themselves. Never figured out how they became part of the police force. They must have someone high

117

up that owes them. How did you get away from 'em?"

Curt had to make a major decision right now. This man had saved his life, so he had to trust him, completely. He also knew that the old codger would see through any lies right away.

"First, you are right. My name is Curt Towers. I escaped from a prison in Colorado a few days back, and I'm on the run right now. Those two Mexican police officers shot me and thought they had killed me. The only reason I know this is that I woke up in a shallow grave the next day. The woman who was with me ran away near the road where we were kidnapped. I hope she got a ride from someone. If she did, that's both good and bad news."

The old-timer passed him a cup of water, which Curt sipped slowly. He then passed a rock-hard biscuit to Curt.

"I understand the good news about her being found, but what's the bad?"

"Well, it won't take long for the authorities to figure out who was with her. My blood was all over the woman's blouse, and I think she'll be able to pick me out from newspaper clippings of my trial, even though I changed my looks a bit. At first, I thought Cindy was the typical dumb blonde, but now I realize she was, in fact, very smart and was just playing the part. Anyway, once they figure who was with her, they'll be out in force looking for me. When they find the open grave, they'll come looking in this direction. I'm sorry; I didn't mean to bring all this on you."

The old timer reached out and patted Digger. He smiled widely, exposing his missing teeth.

"You're in luck since you aren't the first fella those two have bushwhacked. A few months ago I found a grave somewhat in that same direction. It was an Americano just like you, but shot three times. It appeared this fella died after they buried him alive, 'cause, I found signs of diggin'. These guys are worthless; you'd think if they blasted him three times, they could have hit at least one spot to do the job."

118

Henry laughed and continued, "We can go dig the poor guy up and move him to where they buried you. We'll open up the grave a little and let the vultures do the rest. They'll pick his bones clean, or at least what's left of him. If the police get those two numbskulls to show them where they buried you, everyone will guess the bones are yours. Yeah, down the road they'll figure different, but it'll give us time to get lost down south."

Curt tried to clear his head a bit since this was a lot of information to process after being shot twice.

"Why are you helping me," he questioned, "and how long do we have before they get here?"

"Hey, you seem like a nice person, only with really bad luck. I don't care what they said you did; you just don't seem the type. I'm a pretty decent judge of character, and my gut tells me you're one of us good guys."

Henry stood up and stretched taking a few seconds to organize his thoughts. "Well, I would say that the woman has already ID'd the bumbling Federales. Although those two are stupid, I don't think they're dumb enough to let their boss know what they did. They might talk to somebody else though, if they waved around enough money. I think they'll hold out for several days before they cave in or maybe lead everyone on a wild goose chase. I'd say we have two days max. You work on getting your get-up-and-go back today, and tomorrow we'll do the body switch. I have an old donkey that we can use to haul the body. Just rest now and I'll get everything ready."

Chapter 33

"Curt, wake up. We don't have as much time as I thought. I have everything ready to go."

Curt rolled over on the cot, but grimaced as his whole body ached. Digger was at his side trying to lick his face. Curt reached down and gave the dog a quick pat.

"What happened?"

"I heard a plane off to the North this morning. They're doing a search pattern with a small plane. It was about two or three hours for each trip, so they could be here by afternoon. We have to act fast. You can eat a biscuit on the way."

Curt almost fell over as he tried to walk for the first time in 24 hours. After a few more minutes, he was doing better. His two wounds still hurt like hell, but he would have to deal with that later.

Henry was a great tracker and had no trouble backtracking to where Curt had been buried. The other body was only three-quarters of a mile away, so the body swap took less time than they thought.

After digging up the body, Henry opened a bag that had been strapped to the donkey and pulled out some bloody rags. He poured dirty desert sand over the rags and then wrapped the body's wounds with the rags. This made it look as though the victim had tried to treat himself before he died. The rags had been the ones used on Curt's wounds when he first came to the cabin. Although it was a lame attempt, it might give them the extra time they needed. Curt was again amazed at the ingenuity of the old-timer.

They could hear the plane moving off into the distance. The vultures were already circling the area. Curt looked down at the body and decided this idea would never work. The body had decomposed a lot more than it would have in just a few days. No one with crime scene technology would buy this scene. What the hell, any time they acquired would put them that much closer to safety.

Alex couldn't stand the tension anymore and decided to feign a business trip to Mexico. Langer picked him up in San Diego, and once they crossed the border, handed Alex a file.

Langer briefed his boss saying, "We have narrowed the search area down to a few hours south of the border. According to our two recently deceased policemen, Curt should be somewhere within the circle. Our biggest problem is that the police couldn't find our two missing police friends and went to talk with the bus driver. He was quite talkative, so now they're concentrating their search efforts south of where our search plane started."

While keeping his eyes on the road, Langer continued his report. "The locals didn't approve of our pilots in the area and ordered them to leave or be forced down," he said. "It seems that they want to clean up their own internal problems and want no outside interference. All we can do is wait to see what they find. Unfortunately, they operate on a much slower timetable than we do, so it may be days before they reach the area where we think Curt is buried."

Langer drove about a mile before speaking again. "Now here's the really bad news. Somebody in their main headquarters took a sample of the blood from the woman's blouse before they released her. Our man on the inside never even knew about it. Anyway, they ran the DNA and found out that it belonged to Curt, so that's why they clamped down on the investigation. No one is to get near the area; not even our inside guy knows what's going on."

Alex listened intently and then slammed his fists against the dashboard.

Curt and Henry finished the grisly task and headed back to the cabin by noon. When they arrived, Digger started to jump up and down looking for something. Henry went inside the cabin and came out with a bowl of dog food. The dog dived into the bowl, and his food was gone in seconds.

Henry put his hands on his hips and stared at the cabin. "This place has been good to me the last two years and I kind of hate to see it go. Oh well, let me grab a few things, and we can head out."

Curt was amazed. A man, who had saved his life, barely knew him and yet was now ready to abandon his home.

"You really don't have to do this, Henry. You can tell them I held you at gunpoint. You've done so much for me. I don't know how I could ever repay you."

"Curt, I've been here for two great years. In the past few weeks, I've been thinking about moving on. You just sped up the process."

Henry scratched his beard and said, "We'll have to be extra careful traveling this afternoon. If we hear a plane, we'll need to find somewhere to hide our shadows fast. It may mean moving from one big cactus to the next until nightfall. Then we can move about. There's a small village south of here that we could reach by first light, if we really push it."

Curt stood by the donkey while Henry went inside one last time.

"I need just a few more things from the cabin, and I'll be ready to go," he yelled back.

Five minutes later, he came out with a sad look on his face.

"Sorry, Curt. There are many memories in there. I hate to burn it down."

Curt thought about the planes overhead and felt sure a large fire would draw them in.

"Are you sure that's a good idea, Henry? It would be like sending up a flare."

"Actually, Curt, I set it up with a delayed fuse, so to speak. I had a couple of old candles that I put next to a dynamite fuse. The candles should take two to four hours to burn down and light the fuse. The cabin will be blown to bits; that is, if that old dynamite is still good. Just in case, I put some paper next to the dynamite so that if it's a dud, the paper will set the cabin on fire. Either way, the cabin will be toast by nightfall. That'll draw the search teams away from us."

Curt nodded and agreed the plan was a good one. He really didn't have much choice since he realized his life was in Henry's hands.

The next three hours they traveled south through gently rolling hills, sagebrush, and small gullies. The further they went, the rougher the terrain became. They kept looking back every half hour expecting smoke or a muffled explosion. Curt was starting to worry that maybe the candles had gone out. Had he left anything behind that would indicate he was still alive? He could think of nothing.

As the sun dropped below the horizon, and the dark sky pulled its cover over the desert, the two stopped for a break. Curt looked back in the direction they had come from.

"Looks like your candles didn't..."

A bright flash of light and a muffled explosion came from the north. The fuse had worked, and it was a brilliant display. Curt looked up at the sky that was now producing a new crop of stars.

He sat down on a rock while Henry pulled out some jerky to share. Sadness came over his face.

"What's on your mind, Curt? I can see something is buggin' you."

"I've been thinking for the past few hours about my perspective on life. I've always thought I was a good judge of

123

character. Now I'm convinced I don't have a clue. When I was CEO of Xtreme Machines, I would evaluate people based on their backgrounds, experience, and their personal interaction. After going through everything I have for the last few months, I'm just not so sure about anything anymore. A few months ago, I would have never dreamed that my best friend was a con, and sadly, I might not have given you a second glance. I guess I'm starting to look at people differently now."

Henry took a sip of water from the canteen and handed it to Curt.

"The difference is that you are now judgin' folks with your gut. I'll bet anything; you used to read reports about a body before you even met that person. Am I right?"

"Guilty as charged."

"You seem to get along with me, and you don't know nothing' 'bout me. That's 'cuz you used your gut first, and you haven't even asked who I am yet. When you were the head honcho of your company, would you have had anything to do with me if you knew I had a double manslaughter charge against me?"

He waited a minute to let that news settle in before proceeding. "So now that I've told you about it, how do you feel about me?"

"Henry, you should have been my company advisor. You are right on both counts. I don't care what you've done in your past because I now know the real you. I guess what really bothers me is that my lousy judge of character may be what got me into this mess. I have run the trial repeatedly in my mind, and I just can't figure it out. Someone framed me, and they had to be right in front of me."

Henry processed Curt's thoughts for a few moments before he commented.

"Maybe you're looking at the problem from the front when you should be looking from the side. Let me try to explain what I mean. You need to group people you knew before, during, and

124

after the trial. List the folks that would have the most to gain by having you out of the picture or in prison. You need to include everyone: your wife, kids, friends, anyone in your will, and even competitors. Now make a list of everyone who supported you durin' the trial and while you were in jail. The third list should include those who turned against you."

Henry paused to let Curt think about what he just told him.

"It appears that whoever framed you is a smart whippersnapper, and wouldn't do nothin' to call attention to themselves. All you have to do is cross the lists of those who backed you all the way, with those who had the most to gain. Those people should be at the top of your list. Does anybody come to mind?"

Curt continued to focus on the blackness of the desert sky. He hadn't really thought much about the trial lately, but now his mind was spinning. He searched for names to cross-reference, but only two names kept appearing on the list.

"It's impossible. I can't believe it. Only two people fit the bill, and I can't believe either one had anything to do with it," he said with sad confusion.

Henry focused his eyes directly on Curt.

"Now you have names. Don't try to second-guess yourself, just use your gut. What does it tell you?"

"The first name is Cindy, my wife. My gut says no way. I knew my wife very well. She didn't have any hidden ambitions. I'm sure of it."

"The other name puzzles me, though. It's my competitor, Alex Brandon. We grew up together and were best friends. When we became competitors, we drifted apart and haven't spoken to each other in years. When the trial began, Alex showed up in my support. It was a total shock. After all those years, he told me he believed I was innocent."

Henry put the cap back on the canteen.

"What does your gut tell you about that?"

125

"Holy shit, you mean to tell me that Alex was responsible? How could I have been so stupid? It was right in front of me. Now it all fits. He'll get everything, including my wife."

"I'm sorry Curt, but greed is the oldest reason on the Earth for man to be dishonest. It's been our pitfall since the first bite of the apple. Don't assume that Alex was the bad guy; just put him on the top of the list. The important thing is that you are now a little more street smart than before."

"Henry, you don't have to answer me, but can you tell me about the manslaughter charges? It won't make a difference; it just might help me better understand."

Henry started to pack up the campsite as he began his story.

"About two years ago, I worked in a dive shop in Loreto. The owner was always out chasing women, so I ended up runnin' the shop. A local dive club got some money to buy a small Navy ship to sink so they could dive on it. Once the ship was anchored in the right spot, it had to be cut and welded to make it safe for divers. A storm came up before all the work could be done, and the ship sank. Now it wasn't safe for diving because of all the dangerous spots and sharp metal. The dive club didn't have money to pay to make the ship safe, so they just put up underwater signs."

Henry sighed and continued, "A couple of hotshot American businessmen came into our shop and wanted to dive the wreck. We told them it wasn't safe to go inside the wreck, but they said they were "experts." I took 'em out on the boat, but they never came back up. We found 'em both at the end of a long passageway, with no air in their tanks. It looked like one of 'em pulled a knife on the other, trying to steal his air. It didn't do him no good 'cause he used up all the air before getting out."

"Anyway, hotshot lawyers for both men came after my boss with guns blazing. They blamed me for not warning the two gringos. It didn't matter what I said, they all said I was the one

126

who caused 'em to die. I know different, but it didn't do me no good. My boss knew the truth too and told me to get lost quick. I heard later that his shop was closed up tight for a month. In the end, everyone pointed the finger at me, and I had to high-tail it into the desert."

He sighed and then continued, "A lot of time has passed, so I think it's safe we can go see him without raisin' any red flags."

Curt got up, brushed off his pants, and helped put the last of the supplies on the donkey.

"What you told me doesn't change my opinion of you. My gut tells me you are a good man. Thank you for trusting me with your story. So, who do you know in the village where we're headed?"

"My brother had a place in the village, but he kicked the bucket a few years ago. When he died, I sold it to his good friends. They'll help us get to Loreto."

Chapter 34

It was a busy day for the crime scene investigators in Mexico. A local police officer had seen the explosion the night before, and an investigation team had been sent out at sunrise. Not long after that, a more advanced team from Mexico City had arrived to process the scene. Everything from Curt's gravesite and the cabin was moved to the more sophisticated autopsy office in the main city.

When the initial results came in, the entire case was closed down to everyone except a few people higher up in the Mexican Police Department. When they realized that the body did not belong to Curt Towers, a decision was made to cover up the whole affair. Their two rogue policemen had been a big embarrassment to their country, and cleanup was the order of the day. If it had been announced that Curt Towers' body was somewhere in the desert, they would have every newspaper in the US down nosing throughout their countryside. Their biggest concern was that those investigations would turn up even more bodies, and send their image further into the toilet.

A decision by the hierarchy was to cremate the body, but the bloody rags were processed and stored in the evidence room. If anyone ran any tests on the rags, their falsified story would be confirmed. An announcement was made later that the body of Curt Towers had been found in the desert inside an old miner's cabin. Somehow, Towers took shelter and accidentally blew himself up with several sticks of dynamite.

There was concern that there might be a leak of their falsified story, so only four people knew the truth - the medical examiner, the technician who did the DNA tests, the captain of the Mexican Police Department, and the president of Mexico. Everyone else in the department was fed the same fabricated story as the press.

On his return to his office in Denver, Alex Brandon immediately turned on his TV to watch the 6 o'clock news. The top news story was that Curt Towers had been killed in a freak accident in the Mexican desert. The news commentator showed scenes from his trial, the daring escape, and then his final death in the desert. Several of the TV stations had tried to contact Cindy Towers, but she was not available for comment. Luckily, she was stashed in his country home, and his security force had strict orders to maintain her secrecy. So far, it worked.

As he continued to watch another news story, Langer came in with an update. When he saw his boss intently watching the news, he waited until a commercial filled the wide-screen TV.

"Our man inside the Mexican police force is getting the same story as the media. It sounds solid enough. Initial tests show that the body was burned beyond recognition. The only thing they could test was a couple of bloody bandages thrown from the body during the blast. There was just one body, and the DNA from the bandages matched Towers. I know you wanted a physical body, but for some stupid reason they cremated the body. When our man inside asked why, they commented that no wife should ever see their loved one in that condition. It sounds pretty weak to me, but that's all we've got."

Alex clicked off the TV. He stared out his office window for a minute before responding to Langer.

"I agree that the story could be a sham, so we need to get our own confirmation. Get our man on the inside to get a piece of that bandage, so that we can run our own private tests. Have him poke around a little more to make sure everything matches. If anyone has a different spin on the story, I want to hear about it. Assuming all DNA matches, we'll have to assume he really is dead."

He gave a huge sigh before continuing. "My wife's funeral

129

is the day after tomorrow. I'll talk to Cindy and see if we can schedule a funeral for Curt a week later. Once we get past that, we can proceed under the assumption that Curt is no longer a thorn in our side."

Alex got up and paced. "I'm still not totally convinced that he's dead, so I want your men to continue searching for the next six months. I know it will cost a lot, but if he does show up, we can make him disappear again and blame the Mexican government. I would have preferred a solid solution with a 100 percent confirmation that he is dead, but this alternative seems workable. Keep me in the loop if you hear anything."

Chapter 35

When Alex came back to the country home, he found Cindy surfing from one newscast to the next, totally absorbed in the news commentary on Curt's death. He tried to talk her into turning off the set, but she refused.

He left her alone for an hour. When he returned, her eyes were red. Cindy told him that she had started to come to grips with the idea that Curt was gone forever. Alex gave her space, but made sure she knew he was there if she needed a shoulder to cry on.

The kids actually took Curt's death harder than Cindy did, and Alex wasn't sure what to make of that. He told his staff to do whatever Cindy or her kids requested. If they wanted something, get it. Make their grieving process as bearable as possible.

The day of the funeral, the rain was coming down so hard you could barely hear the preacher speak the words over Curt's grave. Cindy and her children stood huddled under two large umbrellas attempting to keep dry. The funeral was short, only attended by a handful of people. Alex recognized a few people from Xtreme Machines, including Peter Harden, who now worked in the industrial division. Curt's sister, Kendra, and her family were there and said a few words to Cindy before the service began. Alex did not hear what she said, but the two hugged, and Cindy seemed to be better afterward.

When the funeral was over, Cindy and the kids piled into Alex's long limousine and headed back to the country home. The press met the car at the cemetery gate and tried to follow. Alex was one step ahead of them, and had asked assistance from the local police to control the press. The press was relentless, and even had their helicopters in force.

He knew that his effort was in vain, and they would soon publish that Cindy was staying at his country home. His biggest concern was that someone might try to connect his family's deaths to that of Curt's. He didn't need a conspiracy theory rising up making page-one news.

By late afternoon, he had settled Cindy and the kids at the home and headed back to his office to make a press announcement at five o'clock. He would beat the press to any foregone conclusions. His limo pulled up in front of the main building, and he stepped out. The rain had stopped, but the clouds were still threatening.

Alex waited until most of the press had their microphones set up in front of him before proceeding.

"This week has been a tragedy for both Cindy Towers and me. We both have suffered great losses and are trying to cope as best we can. Curt Towers and I were close boyhood friends. It's true that we became business competitors over the years, but deep down, we were always good friends."

With a somber face, he continued. "I have known Cindy Towers since she married Curt, and thought they were a perfect match for each other. I never believed the murder charges against Curt. I still contend he was framed. I have even asked the district attorney to reopen the case and prove that I'm right."

He let those words sink in before saying, "Now the press may read something into the fact that Cindy Towers has been staying at my summer home, but please don't. The only way I could help protect her from the press's prying eyes was to hide her at my place. This allowed her the peace to come to grips with Curt's escape and eventual death. If you want to make something more out of it, be my guest. Cindy is the wife of my best friend. If I hear of a story that says any more, I will be suing your publication. I guarantee you; I have more lawyers than any of you, and I would love to get a piece of one of your publications. Freedom of the press is one thing, but lies won't be tolerated. I won't take any questions, but thank you for your time."

Langer opened the car door, and Alex ducked inside, escaping the press. Seconds later the car was out of sight, and the press was busily doing follow up narrations in preparation for the six o'clock news.

Curt sat in front of the old TV set, his eyes glued to the press conference. He had been hiding out at a friend of Henry's since they left the cabin in the desert. The man and wife had set Henry up on a cot and Curt in a small closet converted to a sleeping area. Henry had persuaded Curt that they should lie low until the investigation into his death had settled down. There were many Mexican police in the area, and traveling to Loreto at this time would be risky. He was fine with the idea and was comfortable, for the time being.

The TV could only pick up one station, but it was enough for Curt to see what was going on. He looked at the newscaster, and then back to Henry, becoming more and more confused.

"Henry, I just don't understand. Alex was never my friend after we grew up. We hated each other as competitors. During the trial, he told me he would take care of my family, but it looks like there's more to it. You told me to trust my gut, and I'm telling you that something doesn't smell right. I see his little speech as a cover for something else. Alex is beginning to look more guilty by the minute, but I don't have a clue how I could prove it."

Henry was about to respond when the news jumped to the funeral coverage. Curt held up his hand to keep Henry silent. Curt was surprised at the lack of people at his funeral. He saw images of his sister, and her family and then Peter Harden. Seeing Cindy and the kids huddled under the umbrella made him want to cry.

He reached for the remote and turned the TV off. He'd

seen enough. He wasn't sure which was worse, being in prison for a crime he didn't commit, or watching those in his former life move on without him.

Henry opened two cold beers and handed one to Curt. He took a sip and looked out the window into the darkness that shrouded the desert.

"Okay, Henry. Where do we go from here? I mean no disrespect to your friends since they have graciously helped us, but I feel locked up."

Henry took a long swig from his bottle and smiled.

"You need to relax, Curt. We have all the time in the world. We'll stay here for a few more weeks until the heat from the local police drops off. Then we can skedaddle to Loreto."

He rubbed his burly hand over his face. "You need to face the fact that you can never go back. You need to start over. It may never be the same life, but it's better than prison. My friend who runs that dive shop is always looking for good help. After I left, I heard that he tried to run it himself, but couldn't keep up. He went through more than a dozen locals trying to help around the shop, but most left after a few weeks. Anyway, you would be perfect for the job. You have a sharp mind, and are a quick learner. I'll put in a good word for you. Besides, he owes me for taking the fall for him."

Henry looked over at Curt to see that he had fallen asleep during the dialog. When Curt woke, he would go over this speech again. They now had a plan— not much of one, but it was a plan. All they had to do was stay here and lie low for a few weeks.

Chapter 36

Curt looked at the repair shelf. He had two more regulators to fix, and he would be done for the day. It had been six weeks since he, and Henry had arrived at the Diver's Den in Loreto. The owner, Buck Henderson, had greeted Henry with some reluctance, but after a brief private conversation, Buck was pleased to see his old buddy.

Initially, Buck was cold to Curt because he had heard about him on the news and wasn't sure what to make of the situation. After he heard the real story from Curt and Henry, his opinion started to change.

Curt had noticed a lot of broken dive equipment in a storage locker and asked about it. Buck's response was that he had no one to fix the gear, and couldn't afford to send the items off for repair. It was easier to find other used equipment on eBay or at the local pawnshop, but the gear would break down as fast as it was acquired.

Buck was definitely not a businessman, but somehow had survived in business. Curt decided to help him and asked if he could take a shot at fixing the defective gear. Buck gladly gave him the key to the storage locker, and Curt set off discovering a new line of work.

After all his web searching while in the prison, it was easy for Curt to log on to several of the dive manufacturers' websites and download the necessary technical manuals. Within a few days, Curt mastered the basics of regulator repair. He found that many of the overhauls were simple, and took only a few minutes to repair. Even the more complicated repairs were within his quickly learned expertise, except one. He made the challenge of trying to fix it part of his daily routine, as he wasn't willing to let it get the upper hand. It really bugged him, so again he grabbed his visor, snatched the hex tool, and started to work.

Alex sat in the back of his limo as it wormed its way through Denver's traffic. Langer was sitting next to him, bringing him up to date on the events of the last two months. He opened the folder and started to give the verbal version to his boss.

"So far, my men have found nothing to conflict with the Mexican authorities' story of Curt's death. I'm starting to think that his death is a secret that belongs to the Mexican desert. Four weeks ago, the locals pulled out of the area, but my men continue to go over the area with the best equipment made. So far, they have found nothing to contradict the story. Our man on the inside confirms the same."

He closed the folder and said, "They don't have a clue where Curt is, but they're pretty sure he's dead somewhere in the desert. There's an order to report any bodies found in the desert to the chief of police immediately. We can assume that once Curt's body does show up, the locals will cover it up as quickly as possible. We'll just have to wait."

Alex looked out as the wet snow slid down his window. He was still not convinced.

"I'm not so sure. You have to remember why we called him CAT. True, those are his initials - Curt Allen Towers, but that's not why we called him CAT. It was because he had the knack of getting out of the worst situations, kind of like a cat with nine lives. I can't tell you how many times he's fallen out of trees, tumbled down steep hills, and was involved in a couple of nasty car accidents during college. Every time, he walked away with just a few scratches. Most people would have died in some of those situations, but not Curt. No, I'm not counting him out yet. There's still a chance he's out there alive and kicking."

He continued, "I want you to assume he's still alive. Make sure you monitor everyone in his family. I have a feeling he'll try to come back into the States and contact a friend or family member."

He waved a hand and said, "Ever since Curt left Xtreme Machines our business has improved greatly. Let's use some of that profit to ensure that we can keep it. Use whatever resources you need, but remember, if you find him, make sure he disappears without a trace. I don't mean being buried or dumped at sea, just cremate his ass. I want it to be dust to dust, just like in the Bible. The only way I can rest is when that task is accomplished."

As the limo stopped, Langer put the folder in his briefcase and started to exit. He leaned back into the car one last time.

"Not to worry, Sir. If Curt is alive, we'll find him. If we find his body, we'll confirm it for sure, then cremate it, and scatter the ashes over the desert. No one will ever know what happened to him."

Langer closed the door and trudged through the three inches of freshly deposited snow. Right now, he wished he was back in Mexico with his men since it was a hell of a lot warmer than in Denver.

Cindy Towers looked out the living room window. The snow was almost a foot deep. The staff was busy clearing the walkways, and the gardener was on a large snowblower machine clearing the driveway.

She thought back to the past few months, thinking just how crazy things had been. For the weeks following Curt's funeral, she and Alex enjoyed several long conversations. Alex had continually been supportive, listening to everything she said and always being a perfect gentleman. He arranged for the kids to attend a school nearby. They seemed to adjust and quickly made new friends. Every time she called the school or met with a teacher, they seemed to go beyond the norm to be cooperative. She wasn't sure how Alex did it, but she didn't care, as long as her kids were moving on with their lives.

The reality of Curt's death was starting to sink in, and she was slowly beginning to accept it. Last week, she even agreed to join Alex for a dinner appointment in Denver with some business associates.

Her mind drifted back to that evening, and a smile crossed her face. When they had arrived, Alex received a call that the business friends had an emergency and wouldn't be able to join them for dinner. Although it sounded a bit like a setup to her, she really didn't care at this point, because they were having a good time. She found herself laughing for the first time since Curt had been convicted.

She really had enjoyed that evening and when they arrived back at the house, she kissed Alex on the cheek. She had wanted to kiss him on the lips, but something in the back of her mind caused her to refrain. She knew that if she kissed him, their relationship would forever change. The idea had excited *her and yet scared her half to death at the same time. Was she in love again, or was it a rebound?

Her thoughts were broken as Alex drove up to the front of the house. The back door of the car opened, and all three kids bounced out. Brenda and Lisa headed toward the house while John reached down and made a snowball. He packed it tight and threw it at Brenda. The two girls turned and immediately returned fire. Alex had just gotten out of the car and was hit midsection by a second shot from John. Cindy laughed, then grabbed her coat and ran out the front door to join in. Soon all five were engulfed in a massive snowball fight. Cindy smiled. Her family was healing.

Chapter 37

Curt woke with a start. He didn't sleep well. His head was filled with dreams of past Christmas holidays with his family, and it hurt to realize that it was never to happen again. He looked up to see the ugly smiling faces of Henry and Buck as they stood there holding out two large presents. Curt sat up and looked at the twosome in bewilderment.

Henry pushed his smaller package into Curt's hands and cried, "Merry Christmas, Curt. Buck and I knew you'd be upset today, missing your family Christmas and all. So, we decided to have our own Christmas. Hurry, you have to open my present first."

Curt tried to wipe the sleep from his eyes as he tore the wrappings from the box. Inside was a brand-new scuba facemask. It was not one of the cheap ones that Buck kept in his shop, but an expensive one from Oceanic. It had a digital readout showing dive pressure, time, decompression limits, water temperature, depth, and several other cool features. He looked up at Henry.

"Henry, this wasn't necessary. This has to cost at least a thousand dollars. You can't afford to give me this. It's way too much," said Curt as he started to give the mask back to Henry.

Henry smiled and pushed the mask back into Curt's hands.

"Curt, you don't know everything. I have a lot more money than you think. Remember my brother's place. I still get money for it, and Buck pays me. Don't worry, I can afford it. Now open Buck's present."

Curt tore into the larger box. The words Oceanic again appeared on the boxes. As he opened each part, he found a regulator, dive fins, and a buoyancy compensator. He was about to say something, but Buck held up his hand.

"Hey, you deserve it. All the equipment you have fixed far exceeds the cost of this gear. The only thing you need now is a wetsuit and some diving lessons. I don't want to hear anything about you wanting to give this stuff back. I'm not about to put it in rental because it would walk away in a second, never to be seen again. No, you just enjoy it. Between Henry and me, we'll get you officially certified. Now let's sit back and watch some football."

Curt was about to say something in response, but realized these gifts were genuine. They were given without expecting anything in return. These two grizzly old guys were true friends. He vowed to make them proud by becoming the best damn diver in the region. Just then, the volume on the TV increased, and the pre-game show began.

Cindy and Alex sat at the kitchen table sipping hot chocolate. The kitchen staff had the day off, and the only other people on the property were the security staff that Alex insisted always be on alert. The fireplace was roaring, and the Christmas music gently flowed from room to room. The kids had been up since dawn, and had eagerly opened all the presents. They were now in the snow trying out some of their new expensive gifts. The two girls were sporting the latest in designer coats while John was riding around in the snow on an ATV.

The laughter from outside could be heard as Cindy and Alex looked out the window. Cindy turned back to Alex, and grabbed his hands with hers.

"Alex, I don't how we can repay you for everything you've done. You've been so good to us. The kids love it here, and seem to be adjusting better than I could have ever imagined."

Alex looked away from the window, and directly into her eyes. He smiled and then walked a few feet to one side.

"I wouldn't have it any other way. You deserve the best. I would do anything to help you and the kids, but there's one thing you can do for me."

"What's that?" she hesitated, not understanding the question.

"Move back this way four feet," he said. "Stand right here in front of me."

Cindy moved back the four feet and looked up to the mistletoe directly above Alex. At first, she hesitated, but then gave in. She really wanted things to move to the next level. Alex had made his move, so why shouldn't she? She deserved to live her life too.

She moved over to Alex, but said nothing. She reached up and pressed her lips to his. The kiss lasted much longer than it should have for just a mistletoe kiss. It felt so good to Cindy, and yet it was so wrong. The longer the kiss lasted, the more the good outweighed the bad.

When they finally separated, she blushed. "Thank you, Alex for everything and--oh yes, the kiss too."

"No. Thank you, Cindy for trusting me."

As they sat back down on the couch, Cindy realized feelings she hadn't had in more than a year started to resurface. She really enjoyed his kiss. Cindy liked Alex, or was it more? Before Alex could pick up his hot chocolate, Cindy leaned over and pressed her lips against his again. This time the kiss went even longer and with even more feeling.

As she pulled away, she explained. "Alex, I'm not sure where I'm going with this, but I've wanted to kiss you for some time, but hesitated. I have strong feelings for you, but don't know where to take it. I hope you understand."

"I feel the same way," Alex replied, "but I didn't want to destroy the memory of your husband. I respect your right to take life one day at a time. Just know that my feelings for you are strong, and that I'll always be here when you're ready. I realize it isn't very masculine, but I'll let you be in the driver's seat with respect to our new relationship."

He hesitated before continuing. "It may seem cold to you that I don't miss my wife as much as you miss Curt, but Cleo and I weren't doing well for the last couple of years. I had the feeling she was going to file for a divorce soon."

He brushed a lock of hair from her face and said, "Cindy, you make me feel like a young buck on his first date. Don't be afraid to pursue a relationship with me, because I'm very open to the idea."

Cindy wasn't sure how to respond, but she was warming to the idea. She did not expect such an outflowing of emotion from Alex. She was about to say something in return when the front door burst open and John came running in, yelling about being chased by the girls. Well, so much for their quiet time together.

Chapter 38

"This is a crazy time to be diving," said Curt as he attached the last snap on his buoyancy compensator or BC in diving lingo.

Buck looked over his gear, and then Curt's. He pressed Curt's safe second regulator before he responded.

"Hey, we rarely get new divers trying to bring in the new year underwater as most are out celebrating. You did great the past few days in the pool, so we decided you're ready for your first dive. All you have to remember is to breathe. Your fancy-ass equipment will do the rest--kind of like on autopilot. Just make sure you watch the numbers on decompression and the air pressure. You're a natural at this, and I have a feeling you'll be better than me in a few days."

"That wouldn't be too hard," boomed the voice from behind them. Henry just had to get in his two cents worth.

"Curt, just use that technical brain of yours to stay safe. Have fun and Happy New Year."

As the hour of the new year approached, Alex looked over to Cindy. She was in a beautiful evening gown, sipping a glass of very expensive wine. Alex had considered inviting friends over for a New Year's party, but opted for something a little more private. Luckily, a neighbor organized a sleepover party for the kids in a nearby home. They had a large video room and several HD movies, guaranteed to entertain the kids until morning.

Alex left strict instructions with the staff that the two of them not be disturbed. They finally had the house to themselves. Alex picked up the remote to the music system, and selected some quiet music he knew Cindy enjoyed. He adjusted the volume and sat back on the couch feeling more relaxed than he had in ages.

They drank wine, relaxed, and listened to music for more than an hour. Cindy abruptly set her glass down, and Alex followed suit, as he knew the sign. Their bodies met and intertwined. The embrace became passionate and his hands around her back felt so good, that his mind was whirling.

Cindy knew the wine was going to her head, but really didn't care. She unexpectedly interrupted the kiss, and Alex looked at her with a worried expression. He was about to say something when she gently put her fingers to his lips and then spoke words he had been praying to hear.

"The couch is nice, but I think your bed would be much more comfortable."

Those were the only words spoken for the next few hours as the two made passionate love.

Chapter 39

Fifty-eight-year-old Lloyd Becker sat at his desk, sorting through the last of the boxes. More than two dozen were collected during the Curt Towers murder conviction. He was glad it was over, but for some strange reason he felt uneasy.

Becker had been with the Denver Police Department for more than 35 years, the last 18 as a detective. Dirty Harry he was not. Rather, he was short, overweight, out of shape, and too slow to catch the bad guys. He had worked his way up in the department, and it looked as though he would retire soon with a nice pension.

Becker had been slow to adapt to electronic technology, and many new computer requirements continued to put his career in jeopardy. The only things he had going for him were that he had so many years on the force, and that he knew where the hierarchy had hidden skeletons.

Year after year, Lloyd Becker was demoted to a job title that demanded lesser responsibilities. In a way that was all right with him; he just didn't have the spirit to do it anymore. Sometimes he wished one of the bullets that had passed through his body had been more accurate. Then he could have been enjoying disability, kicking back, and taking life easy on a fishing boat.

The only thing that had kept him going was this Towers case. Near the end of the trial, his captain asked him to go back over the evidence, to make sure the defense lawyer couldn't pull a rabbit out of his hat. Everything had to be near perfect in this very high-profile case.

At first, everything seemed in place, but as Lloyd read more and sorted through the evidence, something seemed very wrong. From what he could tell, Curt Towers was a highly intelligent man who would never make so many sloppy mistakes. Lloyd had seen his share of dumb criminals who make one mistake after another, but Towers seemed different. The more he read, the less sense the reports made. It appeared to be a slam-dunk, perfect case, and this sparked his interest.

Although it looked as though Curt had committed judicial suicide, he professed his innocence, saying that he was framed. The main evidence against Towers was his DNA, fingerprints, and semen. They were tough facts to argue against, but still Becker doubted a murder case could be perfectly executed.

Nowadays, there are so many detective and CSI shows on TV; it expands the possibility of proclaimed innocence. Becker loved these shows and often put credence in their findings. He knew that the shows were a delicate balance of CSI experts and writers who took creative liberties with the storyline. Still, he saw firsthand some of the bizarre things that can happen to the chain of evidence.

Lloyd put the lid on the last box and stacked it onto the large moving cart. He supposed none of it really mattered at this point, since Curt was deceased, and the case was closed. At least, they were sure that Curt was dead, even though the Mexican police CSI had given them reason to doubt his death.

As Lloyd closed his desk drawer, he noticed one folder that had been missed. Someone had put it on his desk a few weeks back, and he hadn't filed it away. In fact, he totally forgot about it. This follow up report made by some thirty-year-old rookie was supposed to tie up all the loose ends in the case.

He was about to toss the folder in the box, but decided to take a closer look, since he had nothing better to do. His wife had divorced him ten years ago, so he was a loner and hated to go home to a quiet house. He sat back and started to read.

The first part of the report was about the botched-up handling of Towers' death. Why would the Mexicans cremate the body of a very important fugitive, before ID could be confirmed?

Something was definitely wrong here.

The second part of the report was even stranger. It mentioned the death of the wife and child of Towers' direct competitor. It seemed the two had died in a single car accident, just days before Towers' death was announced.

Then, there was another report on the death of the warden at the prison where Towers had escaped. A few weeks following Tower's escape, the warden also died in a single car accident.

Lloyd kept looking back and forth between the reports. Had no one even considered a connection between these deaths? Three people all associated, in one way or another, with Curt Towers, had all died in mysterious deaths. This was too much of a coincidence.

Lloyd knew the best thing he could do was to put the folder in the box and move on. That's what his idiot captain would tell him, but Lloyd's problem was that he rarely did what he was told. That's why he was delegated to perform this lowly task. However, this case kept nagging at him, so he decided to do something about it.

Over the past few years, he had accumulated enough vacation and sick time to take off two to three months. He needed a change, so tomorrow he would put in for an extended vacation. The captain had told him that if he didn't start taking the time off, he would order him to do it, so getting his approval would be a cinch.

Best of all, his captain couldn't care less where Lloyd was going. That was critical, since his destination was Mexico. His next-door neighbor was a travel agent, so he headed home to talk with her and set his plan in motion. "What the hell," he thought, "Life is too short." He was going on vacation, and maybe he'd do a little detective work on the side. There had to be someone down in Mexico that really knew what happened to Curt Towers. Two months away from this place was just what he needed.

Chapter 40

Curt swam along the edge of the increasingly familiar shipwreck. He had been spending his after-work hours underwater, welding off areas of the shipwreck that were unsafe to divers. Once a local welder had given him a few lessons, he modified this technique to apply undersea. After a few practice tries in the harbor, he moved his efforts to the wreck.

Henry was operating the boat and generator from above, and Curt's welding work was going smoothly. In the past two weeks, Curt welded more than half of the most threatening areas shut to allow for safer wreck penetration. The remaining few dangerous spots required pieces of metal larger than he could handle alone.

As he finished the last weld for the opening he was attempting, he began to formulate a temporary safety plan for the rest of the wreck until the remaining metal plates were in place. Putting up signs or stringing wire was not a good solution, but he was running out of ideas.

He swam back and looked at the problem from a different perspective. "Wow," he thought. "It might be a crazy idea, but it just might work." He decided to talk with Buck and Henry about it when he got back that afternoon.

"I love you," said Cindy as she hung up the phone with Alex. It was hard to believe that so much had happened since their relationship took a dramatic change on New Year's Eve. As their affection increased daily, she could now imagine herself married to Alex. He was so good to her, and she loved him very much, almost as much as she had loved Curt. She knew it would get better in time, but for now, it would have to do.

Even the kids started to accept Alex in their lives. She

knew in part that their approval was because Alex was spoiling them rotten. He rarely said no, and bought them whatever they wanted. She was eventually going to have to put an end to that trick.

She worried about how they would handle it if Alex were to become their new father. John seemed all right with it, but Brenda and Lisa usually changed the subject when she mentioned the possibility. It would take time, but once the kids were on board, she would broach the subject of marriage with Alex.

Every so often, her mind would drift back to the good times she had with Curt. Those thoughts were interrupted by the memory of the prosecutor stating that Curt had also raped the murder victim. How could she have been so wrong about him? It made no sense. No, she would be much better off with Alex.

Curt and Henry were back in the dive shop busily putting away the dive gear, when Buck came into the room.

He looked at the two with a grin and said, "So, how much did you get done today? Can I start putting divers back on the wreck soon?"

Curt was about to respond, but Henry had already put together a correct response.

"Didn't you learn from the last time? We can't send divers down on that wreck until it's good and safe. We need larger metal plates and another diver to help. Until then, it's unsafe."

"But other shops are running dives out there," responded Buck, doubting Henry's statement. "I'm losing a lot of clients because we don't dive that wreck. What can I do to help?"

This time Curt stepped into the conversation.

"Henry's right. The wreck is still very unsafe, even for experienced divers. There are some areas I wouldn't want to venture into without additional tanks and backup gear."

Buck ran his hand across his face. He knew what was coming. Curt wanted more equipment and things he really

149

couldn't afford.

"Hey, I understand, but I don't have enough extra tanks or regulators. We use them all for diving off the house reef and on the pinnacles. What you are asking will take the gear out of our rental stock permanently."

"I understand," said Curt, "although I do have a temporary solution. You have a bunch of tanks that are out of hydro, and several regulators you can no longer rent because they're too flaky. The tanks are fine, and I can beef up the regulators, so they can work in a pinch. I want to store several sets of dive gear deep in the wreck. Put them in places where divers could get themselves into trouble. We can remove the backup gear once we get some helping hands to get enough metal in place to finish the project."

Excitedly he continued. "There are even several air pockets in the areas I'm considering. I can put the gear in those areas, so they're not constantly in the water, and I'll personally check the equipment once a week. It isn't the best solution, but it's better than more divers dying. What do you think?"

Both Buck and Henry looked at each in surprise. It was obvious that neither had considered Curt's idea. Henry sat down while Buck analyzed Curt's proposition.

"Curt, the idea sounds good," said an excited Buck. "How long would it take you to put it in place, so I can put divers on the wreck?"

Curt shook his head from side to side. He didn't like where this was going.

"You misunderstood me. I want the safety gear for myself while I work on the wreck. It wouldn't be a good idea to put divers in those areas with the idea that the backup gear would make it safe for them. Please don't book any diving groups on the stern of the wreck. Just get me another diver and larger pieces of metal. With help, it will only take a few weeks."

150

Chapter 41

Curt, Henry, and Jose, a local diver, worked around the clock for the past ten days trying to get the last plates welded on the wreck. They were down to five openings, but they were the most dangerous points in the ship. Several corridors crisscrossed the wreck, connecting crew quarters with the rest of the ship. Curt had stored two backup systems at the ends of the longer passageways, just in case things went awry during one of the repair sessions.

Curt and Jose decided to surface for new tanks and a two-hour surface interval. As they surfaced, Henry was yelling that they all had to return to the shop immediately. While they took off their gear, Henry removed the mooring line. He explained that one of Jose's children had been hurt at school, and he was needed at home. When they reached the shop, they learned that Jose and his injured boy would have to leave for a larger hospital and wouldn't be back for several weeks.

Curt sighed, disgusted that they had been so close to making the wreck safe. It was decided he should go back the next day and install signs in the five unsafe areas. Although it wasn't enough, it would have to do for now.

Cindy Towers sat restless trying to read a book, waiting for the kids to come home from school. She had decided to talk to all three as a group, and she was as nervous as a mother hen was.

When they came bursting through the front door, she asked them to sit on the couch because she wanted to talk. It was difficult for John to sit still at his age, but even he realized this conversation was going to be serious.

Cindy started to stand to make her speech, but then stopped. It would look too domineering if she remained standing, so she sat down on the couch. "First, I want you to know that Alex and I both love you very much. You have done nothing wrong. I just wanted to talk with you about Alex and me. You know that we have become more than friends, and I want to be totally honest with you. How would you feel if Alex and I got married? That would make him your stepfather. He hasn't asked me yet, but I would consider it if he did. What do you think?"

Before anyone could answer, Brenda shot out of the room. John looked at Lisa and then to his mother.

"I'm fine with it, Mom, but I don't think Brenda will ever be. I wouldn't let that bother you though. Go for it, Mom."

"Is that what you really want, Mom?" said Lisa. "It seems so soon to get remarried. I don't know if I can look at Alex as my dad, even as a stepdad. I had a real dad, and I miss him. If we said no, would you still get married?"

Cindy had really stepped into it. Now she had one child for it, one on the fence, and one definitely against it. Not the response she desired.

"Remember, I said Alex hasn't even asked me yet. I was just trying to get a feel for how you would react to our getting married. Do either of you know what Brenda has against Alex?"

Both John and Lisa were quiet. They knew the answer, but neither was about to break a sibling's trust. They both got up and left, leaving Cindy speechless.

Alex sat in his chair talking to a military liaison about a new contract that would bring millions into his company. As he hung up, Langer came in with a folder in his hand.

"Sir, we just got word that several more bodies have shown up in the Mexican desert. It appears that the two rogue cops were more corrupt than we initially thought. The bodies' decomposition ranges from a few years to just a few months. Our man on the inside is getting samples from each body to check against Curt's DNA. If he is one of the bodies, we'll snatch it and then spread the ashes across the desert. We should know more in a couple of days."

Langer continued, "How's it going with Cindy?"

Alex didn't like the tone of his last statement, even though he understood that Langer meant no harm by it.

"I'm still not convinced he's dead. Not until a body matches Curt's DNA will I be satisfied that he's out of our hair."

With a stern voice, he proceeded. "Langer, in the future, you will never mention Cindy. What goes on between the two of us is *MY* business. Things are going well, but we cannot be too careful. Remember what happened to my wife."

Langer nodded. He understood completely.

"I'm sorry, Sir. I'll never mention it again. I'll get back to you when I hear further regarding the bodies in the desert."

Chapter 42

Grif Wiler sat idly in a local coffee shop in Loreto. He had been traveling from town to town almost four weeks now, looking for someone who was supposed to be dead. His boss, Ross Langer, had told him that he was sure Curt Allen Towers was deceased, but Langer's boss, Alex Brandon, wasn't convinced. Wiler was certain he was just going through the motions looking for a ghost, but it was a paying job, so what the heck.

As he turned the page of the local newspaper, he noticed a large American enter the shop. The man walked up and talked to the young woman behind the counter. They seemed to know each other, so he assumed that the American must be a local.

Wiler pulled out his picture of Towers and slid the photo up inside the newspaper. He took a quick look and then glanced back to the stranger. He returned his gaze to his newspaper so that he wouldn't attract attention. Although the man had a beard and mustache, there was no doubt in Wiler's mind that this was Towers.

His status in Brandon Industries had just moved several steps up the ladder. He slid the photo back into his pocket and continued to read his newspaper until the American was gone. He then headed back to his room and made the call.

Alex had just finished lunch in his office when Langer burst in without knocking. Alex assumed that whatever he had to say was critical. In his gut, he knew it was about Curt, and that he was alive.

"Sir, we just got word from one of our men in Loreto who has spotted a man he thinks is Curt. He says he has a beard, but he's still sure about the ID. He took a digital picture from a distance, but I told him not to do anything else until we decided

154

how to handle it."

Langer hesitated for a second. "It appears that Curt is working at a dive shop called 'The Divers Den'. I have two men who are very experienced divers, that I can send down to take care of the problem."

Alex stood up from his desk and slammed his fist down hard.

"I knew it. That bastard is still alive. I don't know how he did it, but now he's aware that someone is after him. He's going to be cautious, so make sure to tell your men that Curt isn't an amateur. He has to be treated as a professional, and they can't assume anything. I want reports every hour, even if there's nothing to report. You tell these men that if they don't succeed, it will be their last assignment, and someone will be sent to eliminate them. I won't tolerate failure. Do you understand?"

Langer stood at attention and said, "My men fully understand the importance of this mission. They should be in place by tomorrow afternoon. Their plan is to go to the dive shop the next morning posing as Americans looking to dive the local area. Don't worry because they understand the importance of completing their mission, yet not being discovered."

Langer was about to continue when his beeper went off. Alex waved his hand to dismiss Langer allowing him the freedom to set up the hit on Curt Allen Towers.

Chapter 43

Mel Linker and Stan Walker stepped into the dark and musty dive shop that had previously served as a local brothel. The two men chatted together about their past diving adventures and seemed excited about diving in this area. As they headed to the back counter, Buck Henderson looked them over.

"Are you two Americans looking for some diving in the area? We have two dives in the morning and one in the afternoon. There are some nice wall dives, a great house reef, and even a new wreck."

This information seemed to perk Mel up as he looked at the display of facemasks.

"Tell us about the wreck. How big is it and how deep? We would love a wreck dive."

Buck thought about all the things Curt had told him about the unsafe wreck, but these two just reeked of money. They sported fancy shoes, expensive watches, and shirts that cost more than Buck could earn in weeks in this shop. He didn't want to lose this moneymaker, even if he had to take a chance.

"Yes we do have a wreck dive, but the stern is still not safe. You can dive from the midsection to the bow with no problems. I can take you, or my repairman, Jim Farber, is a certified divemaster. Jim, come out here for a second."

A few seconds later, Curt wandered through the piles of old dive gear to greet the new customers. Both Mel and Stan realized they had found their target since Curt Towers was standing right in front of them. Langer would be thrilled.

Mel, the voice of the two contract killers, would make the arrangements. He shoved out his hand to Curt. "It's nice to meet you, Jim. I'm Mel, and this is Stan. We've done wreck diving before, so we understand the need for caution. We want to dive the bow of the wreck. What do think about diving tomorrow morning? We can go through the rental gear today, so that we'll be ready."

Curt was impressed by the two. They looked to be in very good physical shape, and didn't seem to act irresponsibly. When told that the stern was unsafe, they seemed fine to dive on the bow. Most wreck divers would want to know why it was dangerous, but these two seemed to understand the danger. That would make his job as divemaster easier. Curt walked over to the BC rental area and picked up one of the more expensive units he thought would fit Mel.

"Let's start with the BCs," said Curt as he undid the snaps and held it up so Mel could try it on. "We should be able to outfit the two of you in 20 minutes. So, how many dives do you each have under your weight belt? Knowing this information helps me judge what kind of dive we'll do."

Mel pulled on the BC and snapped it into place. "I have 3000 dives and Stan here is a newbie with only 2000 dives. We both have done more than a dozen wrecks and understand the dangers involved. We'll be back at 7:30 a.m. for the dive. Do you take US dollars?"

As Mel pulled out crisp one-hundred-dollar bills, Buck wrote out a receipt and handed it to Mel.

"See you boys tomorrow."

"You can count on it," was the response.

By late afternoon, Alex was a nervous wreck. He desperately wanted to call Langer, but knew it would be unprofessional. The man was good at his job, and Alex just had to trust him. He was about to stand up and look out the window when Langer walked through the door.

"Good news, Sir. My men have arranged a dive with Towers. He has no clue and thinks my men are just Americans looking for a good dive on a wreck. My men are proficient at diving wrecks from their Navy SEAL days. One of the reasons they got court-martialed is that they killed a man on a wreck dive, so this is right up their alley. Curt seems to have learned to dive at the local shop, and is an amateur compared to my men. The dive is scheduled for tomorrow morning."

Alex sat back in his chair and turned it toward the skyline. He loved to give commands from this position. He felt that it gave him more power.

"I'll go back to the country house tomorrow. If you get any word, call me. Just don't say anything that might be intercepted. Tell me there has been a development with a client. I'll ask the questions, and you answer yes or no. Do you understand?"

Langer gave his affirmative answer and was out the door.

Chapter 44

Curt entered the local coffee shop, and picked up five cups of coffee. Buck insisted that he bring enough coffee for everyone in the dive shop, including these new clients. Buck's coffee was bad, and everyone knew it.

When Curt arrived at the shop, he was greeted by the two men he was to take diving on the wreck. They gratefully accepted the coffee, and Curt went over the dive profile with these knowledgeable divers. Buck double-checked the equipment list, and everyone helped load the gear into the truck. There was no such thing as being too careful when scuba diving.

By eight-thirty, the truck was at the harbor dock down the coast, and the gear loaded. The thirty-minute trip out to the wreck took them well out of mainstream boat traffic. In fact, the closest beach to the wreck was a nasty shoreline covered with sharp rocks and massive waves.

As Curt suited up, he watched the other two don their gear. He was impressed by their professionalism. They were very good, almost too good for sport divers.

The two had been quiet and Curt decided to break the ice. "So, where have you two done most of your diving? You said you've dived a few wrecks, so I was curious as to where. I'm not trying to be nosy, just cautious."

"That's alright, Jim. Most of our dives have been in Truk Lagoon. The depth of the wrecks ranged from 60 to 180 feet down, but we did a few with mixed gas at 250-300. Those were some great dives, but damn dangerous. That's why we're happy to go on your wreck because it sounds like something a little less risky."

Curt didn't respond at first. So far, everything had seemed great with these two, but now something in his gut was bothering him. He remembered that Henry said to trust your gut, but it was too late since the two divers were all suited up and ready to go. He dismissed his concerns and started his final dive briefing.

"The boat is moored to a line that is attached to the bow. Just follow the line down, and then we'll work from the bow to the mid-section and back. We always ask that you do a five-minute safety stop at fifteen feet before surfacing. I know you normally need only three minutes, but we like to play it safe when diving on the wreck. Are there any last-minute questions?"

Each diver shook his head in acknowledgment before taking a giant stride over the side. Curt waited a few seconds and then followed. As he checked his systems, he looked at the divers and saw they were doing everything by the book. He thought maybe this dive was going to be easy after all, but then his gut started to hurt.

Two minutes into the dive, the three were on the bow of the submerged ship. As he looked around to see what kind of fish were in the area, he saw the others use a strange sign language. He'd seen that hand language before but couldn't place it. His gut began to ache.

The larger of the two divers quickly swam over the port side of the bow and went out of sight. Something was not right, so Curt also dropped over the edge of the wreck, scaring a large grouper and himself in the process. Curt returned his focus to the missing diver and saw him heading toward the stern. He motioned to the other diver to join him, but the dive buddy refused.

Curt looked back just in time to see the scuba diver enter one of the openings in the stern that had not yet been secured. Curt now knew that this dive was doomed. The men had conned him and Buck because their intentions had always been to dive the stern.

Curt put power to his fins, kicking as hard as he could to reach the opening in the stern. When he did, there was no sign

160

of the diver; only a small amount of debris pushed aside, indicating the diver penetrated the wreck. Curt reached for an emergency buoy he carried and tied its line to a rail on the side of the wreck. He filled it with air and let it head toward the surface, marking their position.

Now there was no sign of either diver, so Curt had a decision to make. Should he go inside the wreck or go for help? If he went for help, the odds were that it would come too late to save the divers inside the wreck, and the shop would be in trouble again. That meant that Curt would have to exit Loreto, and be on the run once more. That was all it took to convince him.

He kicked his way inside the wreck, but still saw no sign of any divers. Curt began checking each passageway that split off the main corridor. He was down about three doorways, when his regulator was suddenly ripped from his mouth. Then his mask was pulled off, and a large finned foot pushed him deeper into the wreck. As he turned, he could see a blurred image of two divers and the reflection off a knife blade. The larger of the two divers was swimming toward him with the knife extended.

Instinctively, Curt unbuckled his BC, swung it around in front of himself, and pushed it between him and the charging diver. The knife cut the high-pressure hose in the struggle. He hoped the air from the hose would create a screen of bubbles to mask his exit. He inhaled deeply from the severed hose and headed off. Curt had a long way to swim, and he wasn't sure that he could even make it, assuming the other divers didn't catch him.

Thankfully, he had been diving a lot in the last month, so he could hold his breath a long time, but would it be enough? He had to go along a passageway, turn right, down two doors, and then take a sharp left. Curt made sure he kicked up the sediment in the corridor in an effort to blind the other divers.

As he reached the last turn, he started to get light-headed. He reached the small closet, where he knew there was about six cubic feet of trapped air. He hadn't tested the air when he placed the emergency dive gear on the top shelf, but now was not the time to doubt the odds. He took a desperate breath. The air was rotten and stale, but breathable. He turned on the stored scuba tank's air, took a breath out of the regulator, and found it worked.

Now he had two new choices: he could stay, or swim for it. He was sure that he couldn't out swim the two divers. No, he needed to play dead. He pulled his legs and fins up in a tight ball at the top of the closet, in hopes that the divers glancing in the opening might not look up. He looked at the gauge and wished he had overfilled the scuba tank. At the most, he had 40 minutes of air.

As Curt floated in the top of the closet, he started to figure out what had gone wrong. For some reason, these men were trying to kill him. He had never seen them before, but they knew him, so it had to do with his murder trial. Whoever framed him-- no, rather the men who worked for Alex Brandon--were now in the process of cleaning up his mess.

One thing was for sure; he had to have a plan. He couldn't go back to the shop or see anyone he met in Loreto. He wouldn't even be able to say good-bye. He would just have to leave town. Curt was starting to get really pissed, causing him to breathe harder. When he realized what he was doing, he slowed his breathing to a pace where he needed to inhale less often.

There was no sign of the other divers. Every so often, he would hear a loud tapping on the side of the wreck. Curt assumed they were trying to spook him. Thankfully, they didn't know about his emergency tanks inside the wreck. They might get that information out of Buck when they went back to the shop, but by that time, Curt would be gone.

Thirty minutes had gone by and no pounding had occurred for the last ten minutes. He had about ten minutes of air left, and a considerable distance to go. His only chance was to head for the rocky shoreline. It was now or never.

He backtracked his way down the passageways toward the

light at the opening. The water had settled, so visibility was better and he was able to make good time. When he reached the opening, he heard the engine on his boat start up and motor off into the distance, but then it stopped. Those two would be waiting with binoculars for him to surface. No doubt, they had more weapons in their gear.

As Curt swam toward the bow of the wreck, he moved his hand over his head every time he exhaled. This broke the bubbles with his hand, so that when they reached the surface, they would be minimal.

When he reached the bow, he looked toward shore. If he swam very hard, it would still take five to seven minutes. It was going to be close. Each breath became precious, so he would take a breath just before he felt the urge to pass out. He looked back, and that friendly grouper was chasing him. It was better that than the two other divers.

He was starting to doubt his direction, when he felt a huge wave and sharp rocks appeared directly in front of him. He swam to the right and then the left, trying to dodge boulders while looking for a small crack or cave for escape. Curt was about to give up, when he saw a black opening under one of the rocks. He could see water moving in and out of the hole. He had to try it because the air in the tank was almost at zero.

As he swam through the opening, the wave action pushed him hard. He looked up to see a large outcropping dead ahead. He hastily turned and pushed his dead scuba tank against the rock and was propelled beyond its jagged edges. Curt looked up to see beams of light hitting the water. He took one last kick and broke the surface. He found himself inside a large room that had eroded under the shoreline. Although there was little light, Curt could see a small ledge along one side. He swam over to the shelf, and slowly crawled onto this narrow safe haven.

He looked up at the light and thought to himself, "Well, Curt old boy; you just used up another life. Now what are you going to do?" The answer was simple. He passed out from exhaustion.

On the surface, one diver scanned the shoreline with the powerful binoculars, while the other waited with a high-powered rifle. The job hadn't gone as planned because Curt pulled an escape act, and they had lost him. There was no way he could have survived, but their boss had warned them that Curt could survive some of the worst possible situations. They could afford to wait about four hours before Buck back in the dive shop would become suspicious.

If Curt had surfaced, their plan had been to shoot him and then dump his weighted body in a deep-water trench. Obviously, the plan hadn't worked, but the killers were adaptable. They must get their prey, because their reputations depended on it.

By late afternoon, they were running out of time and needed a new plan. Their orders were clear--they had to have a confirmed kill with a body. If they went back to the dive shop, they would have to answer many questions, so plan B was about to come into play. They pulled the mooring line and headed farther down the coast, which was less populated. They would then wait until dark before proceeding.

Curt woke and found himself shivering from the cold of the cave. He looked up at the ceiling and saw a small crack in the top. It was debatable whether he could make it through the crack, even if he could reach it. The ocean below him was churning. He doubted that he could make it back out through the cave entrance and survive the surf.

He picked himself up and started the tedious climb up the sharp rocky wall. He slipped several times and almost fell back into the surging waters below. His hand-over-hand efforts resulted in blood-and-mud-caked fingers. Several feet below the opening, he saw a tree root extending down, so he grasped it and pulled himself up the rest of the way. The opening was almost too small for him to pass through, but he forced himself by twisting, turning, and squeezing as his flesh cut on the sharp rocks.

When he finally stuck his head above the surface, Curt could tell that the sun had just set and darkness was flowing over the coast. The brush around the opening was very thick, so Curt didn't have a clear view of the ocean. When his foot cleared the hole, he collapsed on the ground. Curt was so thirsty, but he suspected there wasn't any water nearby. He figured the two men would still be searching the ocean, rather than the brush, so he crawled up next to a tree and promptly fell asleep.

The cell phone kept ringing, and the killers knew who was on the other end. They still had unfinished business to deal with before reporting in. They went a few miles off the coast where the water was deep, and loosened the main seal on the engine shaft. In just a few hours, the dive boat would be on the bottom, never to be seen again. The two planned to use the small dinghy to navigate down the coastline, where they intended to pick up a stash of guns, money, and their passports. Once they were clear of the sinking dive boat, they made the call to their boss.

Langer was going crazy. He called his men several times with no answer. This was not like them, and he sensed something had gone wrong. This whole thing with Curt Towers was putting them all on edge. He was about to call Alex and update him when his encrypted cell phone rang.

"Mr. Langer," Mel said, "We ran into some problems with the hit. Towers got away inside the wreck. We disabled his dive gear and blocked his way, but he never came out of the wreck. We watched the surface for more than four hours, but saw nothing. No one could have survived inside that wreck. Therefore, we sank the dive boat and went to our backup plan.

What do you want us to do now?"

This was not good. Alex would not settle for this incomplete solution.

"You two get out of there. Take a long trip as far away from there as you can. I'll bring in a second team, and they'll snoop around to see what happened."

The response was immediate. "What about our money?"

Langer's response was even faster. "Hey guys, you know how it works. You won't be paid until the kill is confirmed. Now just stay out of sight, and I'll stay in contact at the second number I gave you. Clear?"

The hitman affirmed and hung up the phone. The killers knew the score. If the hit couldn't be confirmed, their reputations would be tarnished, and they wouldn't be paid.

After his conversation with Langer, Alex came into the room, and his face was beet red. Although she wasn't privy to their conversation, Cindy could see that something was wrong, but decided that asking was not a good option at this point. Alex made up some excuse about business and went for a walk out in the lower acreage. He was so mad that he took the wood ax and started to chop wood like never before.

Alex felt he would never rid himself of Curt. He knew that Curt was still alive, even though he was the only one who believed Curt could have survived. The only way he could be sure he was dead, was to have his lifeless body in front of him. Even then, he would shoot the body several more times just to be sure. He prayed that day would come soon, because if it didn't, he was sure to go insane.

Chapter 45

It had taken Lloyd Becker a couple of weeks to clean up his affairs before he could head south on his "vacation." He had been in Mexico for more than four weeks and had discovered nothing other than very few people had ever heard of Curt Towers. He had three variations of Curt's picture and carefully selected the right people to show the images. He concentrated his search on bartenders, coffee shop servers, and small-business owners. Lloyd avoided the police and even left his badge and gun at home. Although it was a dangerous thing to do, he wanted to be less visible and to solve this case, once and for all.

He was getting so tired of trying one coffee shop or restaurant after another. It seemed he spent more time in the john than not, after drinking all that coffee. The whole idea seemed a waste of time, but he decided to give it another week.

He was now in Loreto, and working his way south. He already hit two coffee shops, with no luck. They say that the third time is the charm, but he considered it bullshit. Still, being a good detective, he knew the answer could always be just around the next corner.

He sat down at a sidewalk cafe and waited as a pretty waitress approached his table. He ordered coffee with lots of cream and sugar. Before the server could leave, he made one more request.

"Excuse me, Senorita, but have you seen this man?" Lloyd pulled three photos out of his pocket to show her.

She hesitated, smiled, and picked up all three pictures, scanning them slowly. "Why do you want to know? I don't want to get anyone in trouble."

Lloyd's heart pounded. She knew the man. He had to be careful and move slowly.

"I'm just doing a follow-up for a family in the States. We think this man lost his memory and settled down here somewhere. His loved ones are very concerned. I'm just a friend of the family, and you won't get into any trouble."

The waitress set the pictures down, and looked back toward the main kitchen. "Look, I know this man, but I only know his first name. It's Jim. He works in the dive shop down the street. He always comes by every morning for coffee. It's strange though, because this is the first day, he has not shown up. I hope he's all right because he's a very nice man. He's always been very courteous, helpful. He's going to be okay, isn't he?"

Lloyd pulled out money, paid his bill, and thanked the server. His blood was pumping. Hot damn, he had broken the whole case wide open. He was going to play it safe and proceed with caution, because he knew that not everything was as it seemed.

Buck and Henry had been up all night getting everyone they could think of to go look for Curt. The longer they talked, the more they realized they had been set up. The two divers from the States must have been after Curt. The fact that neither the dive boat nor the divers had been found anywhere near the wreck was disturbing.

They put a closed sign on the front of the shop and were in constant communication with the local police, who were not happy that the shop might have had another diving accident. Both Buck and Henry knew the shop's reputation wouldn't survive, even if they found Curt. Therefore, the plan was first to find out what happened to Curt, and then get out of Dodge.

As Buck set the phone down one more time, a loud knock came from the front of the shop. Henry was about to get up and get rid of the visitor, but Buck put up his hand in protest. He would field this one.

"Can't you read the sign? We're closed today," he yelled through the glass. "Whatever you want or are selling; you'll have to come back next week."

Buck waited for the heavyset man to respond or leave. Instead, the man said nothing. He just took out a piece of paper and held it up to the window. Fear instantaneously came across Buck's face. He looked to Henry and then back to the stranger. He read the message again that said, "*I can help you look for Curt Towers.*"

Buck turned back to Henry for a response.

"OK, Henry, what do we do now?"

Henry got up and walked to the door.

"How do you know Curt?"

"Let me in and I can tell you without letting everyone on the street know. You don't have a choice right now because I could easily go down to the police and tell them who your divemaster really is. So what's it going to be?"

Henry finally reached up and unlocked the door, and let the unknown man walk into the shop. Before either Buck or Henry could say anything, Lloyd stuck out his hand.

"Hi, I'm Lloyd Becker from Denver. I've been looking for Curt for almost a month. Now it looks like I just missed him again. Do you have any idea what happened? Before you answer, let me guess. A client with lots of money came into the shop and wanted to make a dive in your beautiful ocean. I'd bet you a month's pay they paid in cash. Am I right so far?"

Buck looked at Henry and then back at Lloyd.

"So, how'd you know all that? And yes, it was two men."

Lloyd said, "They're what you call a cleanup crew. They are highly paid hit men. Curt must have really pissed someone off to bring all this on himself."

Henry was trying to get a read on the stranger, but he couldn't. His gut wasn't giving him a clue, so he reached out and shook Lloyd's hand.

169

"Lloyd, before we go any further, we want to know more about you and why you're here."

Lloyd smiled, and sat down on a chair near the dive compressor.

"I'm a police detective from Denver, and before you panic, I don't believe any of that bullshit the police have on Curt. If you want to save your friend, you need to sit down and listen to what I have to say. It may sound crazy, but I have always been a fan of conspiracy theories."

Curt was so glad he had watched "Survivorman," especially the episode about enduring in the desert. It was going to save his butt right now. He slept the entire night on a sandy berm next to a large tree, and his wetsuit kept him warm.

When he woke, he was unbelievably thirsty, so his foremost task would be finding water. He could not get very far without water, let alone avoid the authorities, but he also had another problem. He could not walk across the local terrain in a wetsuit, so he took off the suit and bundled it up. Although they weren't designed for walking distances, the wetsuit booties would have to do as shoes.

Once he had gathered his wits, he slowly crawled up to the edge of the brush. It formed a perfect fence along the shoreline, so he could get a clear view without being seen. He could hear engines, so he was very careful in his approach. Curt saw several boats working their way up and down the area around the wreck and realized they were searching for his body. If he stood up and called for help, one of two things would happen. Either the police would find out who he was and ship him back to a US prison, or the two men trying to kill him would return to finish the job. His choice would have to be door number three; he was on his own.

He pulled himself back through the brush and worked his way as far from the search area as possible. As he slowly moved through the brush, he started to look for the item highest on his list of survival tools--cactus. He found a sharp rock and started to pound away at the deadly plant. After stabbing himself several times with cacti spines, he finally reached the meat of the plant. He slowly sucked the meat's moisture until there was no more. Gaining water from the succulent plant was not as easy as it looked on TV, but he was becoming experienced at the task.

Frustrated, but refreshed, he picked himself up and started inland. Every sound had to be analyzed for its threat level. By noon, the scorching sun was frying everything in his path. He had to find refuge from the heat, even if he couldn't find water. A small rocky ledge in a shallow dry streambed was all he could find. He stretched the wetsuit up over some branches to create a canopy to block the sun. He realized he would have to travel in the evening and early mornings to avoid the heat. The rest of the time, he would have to hide and rest.

By early afternoon Buck, Henry, and Lloyd had hashed out every possible scenario of what was going on with Curt Towers. Once Lloyd started talking, Henry could tell that he was not a threat and took to him right away. Buck wasn't so sure at first, but when Henry accepted the stranger, Buck relented. Several times during their conversations, they received phone calls updating them on the search progress for the three divers. The police wouldn't let them near the area, and told them to stay in the shop until further notice. They had long run out of coffee, so their meeting transformed into a beer gathering.

Henry had one last question of Lloyd. "So Lloyd, as a detective, why do you think Curt isn't guilty?"

Lloyd polished off his third beer and reached for a fourth.

"Nothing adds up. Everything I've read indicates that Curt is a very educated person. Smart criminals don't make as many mistakes at the crime scene as Curt apparently did. The evidence was flawless and that alone should throw up a red flag. Evidence

171

is never perfect."

He took a huge gulp and said, "Then there was the issue of all the dead bodies showing up that somehow related to Curt. Where he goes, there seems to be collateral damage. There was Brandon's wife and kid, the warden of the prison, the two Mexican policemen, and now the two mysterious divers. If I were to step back and look at this case from a distance, I would say subject A is trying to kill subject B. We know B is Curt, but the problem is that I still can't figure out A."

Henry looked down at the floor and then back to Lloyd.

"We know who your missing link is--Alex Brandon. He was Curt's best friend as a child and a bitter competitor in business. That creates a bad combination, and makes him a perfect candidate for subject A."

Lloyd stared aimlessly at a spider crawling up the wall. His mind was racing, trying to analyze this new opinion.

"Damn, it makes perfect sense. Now that you put a name to subject A, it all fits into place. Alex Brandon has the money and manpower to pull off such a frame. Are you sure about this?"

The two old men facing Lloyd nodded in agreement. The biggest problem now was deciding the next step in the game. How could they fight such a large corporation? They had to find Curt before the bad guys did, assuming he was still alive.

Alex returned to the office to instigate a new direction for the search efforts. Langer met him at the front door, but they spoke few words as they traveled up to Alex's plush office.

Alex waited for Langer to close the door before he spoke.

"I'm disappointed by the way things worked out. With them fumbling the hit, we don't know if Curt is alive or dead. Personally, I'm betting he's still breathing. I just don't know how he keeps resurrecting. I know your men claim there is no way he could have survived, but I'm not so confident."

Alex paced the floor before saying, "So, here's what we're

172

going to do. If he's alive, this hide-and-seek game can go on for years. I'm tired of getting close and then losing him again. If he was working at that dive shop, we have to assume that he wants to stay lost. Put two men down there permanently. You can rotate them every month or so, but I want them to be constantly on the lookout for Curt. When they find him, I want no games. I want them to walk up and shoot him. I don't care if there are witnesses; just make sure he's dead. Pay these men well, because I want them to feel this is the best work they'll ever get. Make sure they keep a low profile, but find him. Kill him dead."

Alex kept spewing words and Langer started to worry. His boss was starting to lose it, constantly repeating himself. He was too focused on killing Curt and it was getting downright scary.

Langer kept nodding until he finally found an opening to leave. He gave a sigh of relief once he was out of the office. If he ran into Curt right now, he personally would shoot him dead and drag his body back into the office. He'd do anything to get Alex off his back.

Cindy Towers was getting worried. Alex was not himself lately. He kept telling her that it was business, but she knew it was more. She sensed it had something to do with her, but she couldn't figure out what.

Her son John seemed unaffected by the tension, because he was heavy into baseball at school. Brenda and Lisa were a different story. Both had come to her in private and asked if everything was all right. It seemed so strange having her kids concerned about her, but it was a nice feeling.

Alex had not been physically close in a week, another sign that something was amiss. She wanted to ask him what was wrong, but she respected his privacy. Discouraged, Cindy fell back into her comfortable chair and proceeded to get lost in another romance novel.

Chapter 46

Curt's feet were getting very sore, and he needed to do something about the dive boots he was wearing. Sadly, that wasn't the worst of his problems. He was between the beach and Highway 1. Although it was a large area, there was a high risk of running into someone who might turn him in. He walked for more than three hours before he heard the cars. He crept low as he approached the old and worn-out asphalt. Several trucks passed by and then it was quiet. He looked north and south and saw nothing, so he decided to take a break.

He ran across the highway, jumped into the brush and scrambled across the sand as fast as he could, swearing under his breath as he brushed through some small cacti. He knew they were getting back at him for eating one of their friends. He started to laugh to himself. He was really losing it, because he was now giving life and feelings to a cactus.

His goal right now was to get as far away from the main highway as possible, and that meant heading west into the lower hills. He knew that someone with a powerful set of binoculars could spot him from a mile away. His solution was to stay close to the ground in low gullies, and near any brush he could find. A few times, he heard a plane and jumped under a rock ledge to hide. Once the sound had diminished, he worked his way west and slightly south. His final direction would be due south, but for now, west would work.

By mid-afternoon, he was exhausted. With no water and searing heat, he realized that he might die out in the Baja desert, and no one would ever know. As he stumbled to the ground, he saw a broken bottle. He looked up from his low vantage point, and saw a few more bottles. It looked as though he had fallen on the edge of a dumping ground. He raised his head once more and could see the roofline of a shack, in the distance. It had to be more than a hundred yards away, but he had to get out of this sun or die for sure. He gathered the last ounce of strength he had and dragged his feet toward this mirage.

As he approached the shack, he looked for signs of life. It looked deserted, but by the time he reached the front door, he really didn't care if it was occupied or not. Curt was ready to give himself up and be happy to go back to jail since this hell was much worse.

The cabin was musty. An old mattress seemed to be the only inhabitant, and it looked very sad. The mattress had been soaked repeatedly, because the roof had more holes in it than not. He looked around for something to eat or drink, but found nothing. No one had been there for years, and the cabin had been stripped clean. Exhausted, he collapsed on the lumpy mattress, and fell into a much-needed deep sleep.

"So, what's the plan," said Buck, as he sipped on his fifth beer. He looked over to Henry and Lloyd who had been kicking around ideas.

Henry had pulled out a map of the Baja peninsula and was looking it over. "Well, Curt and I talked a lot about exit strategies, and I think he'll go south. He knows they're still looking for him to come back to the States. They never would assume he would continue to go south. That would be like backing himself into a corner, but I think that's where he's going."

"Come on, Henry," said Buck. "What the hell can he do going south?" We're on a peninsula."

"Cross over to the mainland by ferry," answered Lloyd. "That's what I'd do. I think we need to go down to the south end and wait near the ferry. We'll spread out and wait for him to show up."

Buck asked sarcastically, "What then?"

"We'll help him any way we can," replied Lloyd with a

voice of authority. "Henry, didn't you tell me that Curt had access to methods for creating fake documents? I don't think we can assume he can do it this time, so we need to find someone local who can help us out. I have plenty of experience with those types of people. Give me a day, and I'll have all he needs to get across on the ferry. Where is your local pawnshop? That will be a good place to start."

As Lloyd stood up, Buck wrote down several addresses for Lloyd to follow up. Before going out the door, Lloyd turned to the two old men still sitting in the middle of the dive shop. "The two of you gather some clean money, and make it small bills. Find him some clothes that will make him look like a local worker. Most important, bring an old worn hat. You know, one like in 'Indiana Jones'. He'll need it to hide his face, and hats are still commonly worn in Mexico. I'll be back tomorrow, and then we head south, so be ready."

The door slammed shut, and there was an eerie silence. The old men looked at each other, and then quickly scrambled to get the tasks done.

Chapter 47

Curt tried to open his eyes, but everything was a blur. He started to sit up, but a small hand pushed him down.

"Mister, you stay down. You hurt bad. Open mouth."

Before Curt could respond, water started to flow between his lips. He began to cough, and then swallowed the wondrous liquid. He opened his eyes and again tried to focus. He was staring at what looked like a ten-year-old Mexican boy, pouring water from a leather pouch. Curt focused his eyes again and saw a woman in the distance, not moving, looking frightened.

The boy realized that Curt saw the woman. "That's mi madre. She OK. She not talks. Drink agua slow."

"Who are you? How did I get here?"

"Mister, I found you last night when I was looking for something we could use at our campsite. You lost?"

"You might say that. Bad men are chasing me. They are trying to kill me. Have you seen any gringos lately?"

"No one, Mister. Just mi madre. Can you walk? Our campsite is mile from here. Mi nombre es Lingo, and mi madre es Maria."

Curt nodded to Maria, and started to stand. He fell and Maria ran to him, grasped him under one arm while Lingo held the other. After an hour's struggle, they reached the campsite. It was higher in the hills and farther from the road, for which Curt was thankful.

They gave Curt more water, and he slowly regained his strength. The trek across the desert hills took its toll. An hour later, Maria cooked up a traditional Mexican meal, which did wonders for his empty stomach. Once Curt had downed more than his fair share, he restfully sat back against a log. He watched as Maria cleaned up the campsite, while carefully maintaining her distance.

Lingo came and plopped himself down by Curt. He glanced over to Lingo's mother as she packed up the old cooking utensils. "So, Lingo, why is it that your mom doesn't speak?"

A tear came to Lingo's eye, and he looked to the ground. "My father drank mucho, and beat us. He hit her in the neck with a bat, and it did something to her voice. But it will never happen again, cuz I fixed."

Wow, here was somebody who had it worse than he did, yet they were helping him. "Lingo, what do you mean, you fixed it?"

"I killed mi padre with a gun he used to shoot animals. We buried his body in the desert, and then we run. We hide in the hills for more than one year. I killed mi padre when I was nine, and I not proud, but had to do it. Not sorry neither, cuz I had to save mi madre."

This poor kid couldn't stop talking. He had been holding everything in forever, and finally let it all out when he found someone he could trust.

Curt put his hand on Lingo's shoulder. "Killing someone is wrong, but in this case, you did it to save your mother. I can understand that. Your secret is safe with me. I owe you at least that for saving my life."

Curt smiled. "Now I have a question. Do you have some pieces of leather I can use to wrap around these wetsuit boots? Do you have any extra clothes?"

Lingo smiled, got up, and ran beyond the tent he and his mother had erected. Ten minutes later, he returned with a large bag over his shoulder. He grabbed the bottom and dumped the contents on the ground. Out fell a half dozen old shoes, a couple of shirts, and an old pair of jeans.

Lingo smiled. "They were mi padre's. He not need anymore."

178

Chapter 48

The sunrise was a colorful palette of pink and magenta, with a pinch of red thrown in for good measure. Curt had regained his strength, and was now helping more around the campsite. He'd been out in the desert collecting firewood, when upon his return; he heard a man's voice. He crouched behind a large bush and watched as the man accepted a cup of coffee from Maria. The boy and his mother seemed to accept this man without fear.

As Curt walked into the camp, the man looked up at him and smiled. Curt's fears washed away with the early-morning colors when he saw the visitor was the local Padre.

The man held out his hand. Hi, my name is Wilton Ramirez. I'm from the local church, and come out here every few days to check up on some of my more distant parishioners. I hear you had a close call with the mother desert. She can be so beautiful, and yet so dangerous."

Curt laughed as he held out his hand to welcome the Padre. "Are you talking about the desert or a woman from your past?"

The Padre took a sip from the cup, and looked at the final remains of the sunrise as it gave way to a darker blue. "When I was younger, I knew a few women like that, but I was really talking about the desert. So, what brings you so far south, Mr. Towers?"

This last bit of information instantly put Curt into a panic mode. He hadn't told the boy or his mother who he was, so, how did the Padre know? Maybe he wasn't a disciple of God after all and was another hitman. Curt was bigger than the man, and he did not see a weapon, so perhaps there was nothing to fear. The worst scenario was that he would be a wanted man on the run again. It confused him, though, because the boy seemed to know the preacher so well. It just didn't make any sense.

"How do you know me, Padre?"

"I like to keep up on current events. My computer network connection is very slow, but fast enough to allow me to keep up with world events. How can I preach about our brothers, if I don't understand them? I also have an excellent memory. You broke out of prison some time ago and everyone now thinks you are dead--something about an explosion in the desert."

He continued, "Now, I pride myself in being able to judge people within minutes, and you aren't the killer the newspapers reported. Because Lingo and his mother trust you, I do too. I guess my question is do you have a next plan?"

"I'm not exactly sure, Padre. I think I'll continue south toward Cabo San Lucas and then cross over to the mainland."

"My friends call me Will. Going south may pose a problem. I realize you are now old news, but a gringo who looks like a famous American murderer can attract some attention. I do offer you another solution. Every month, I send a busload of workers to a sister church at the end of the peninsula. You can work and mix in with them."

Curt was trying to understand why a perfect stranger was being so helpful.

"Will, why are you so willing to help someone you've just met?"

"Curt, your face tells me everything I need to know. I can see that you're an honest man. You would help me if I were in such a spot, wouldn't you?"

Curt bowed his head in embarrassment. "Will, the truth is that a couple of years ago, I wouldn't have helped you. However, I now see the world in a new light. My survival depends on being able to understand people and read them with my heart."

Will smiled. "That's what I do for a living. I try to understand the people in the local area, and help them down the

180

path of righteousness. I now consider you one of those people and know that if you ever get the chance to help a friend, you'll do whatever you can."

His smile became a frown as he said, "One other thing I should mention. A couple of gringos came by yesterday looking for you. They showed me several old pictures from before you went to prison. They said they worked for a lawyer in the US and were trying to find you to award an inheritance. You'd have thought they could have come up with a better story. Anyway, I sent them on their way, but I have a feeling they may come back. It looked like they were down here to stay, and weren't giving up."

Lingo brought Curt a cup of water. He took a sip while studying the Padre. "I have to tell you, Will, a few months ago I wouldn't have trusted anyone. Everyone seemed to be my enemy. Now that I've hit rock bottom, I'm finding friends in the strangest of places. I want to thank you so much for having faith in me."

"Actually, Curt, I had some help from above. I have a feeling that you are not a religious man, yet you appear to embrace the concept well. I have confidence that your life will turn out all right in the end, just differently than you planned. Keep the faith, and know that not everyone is as bad as those chasing you are. I do have one question, though."

"You want to know why I want to get to the mainland."

Will laughed. "So, you can read minds as well, Curt. I read in the newspaper articles that you have a nickname of CAT. I realize that it's your initials, but the articles indicated that there was more to the story."

"Well, the truth is that when I was a kid I had more than a dozen close calls. I almost drowned in a pond when I fell out of a boat. I got hit by a truck, but only received minor scratches. I fell out of a tree trying to get a neighbor's cat. I landed flat on my back, and the cat landed in the middle of my chest. The two neighbors who saw the fall knew about my other accidents, so they nicknamed me CAT. It stuck throughout high school and college. Even my closest friends at my work used to call me by my nickname."

The Padre took all this in for a moment and smiled. "So you are like Bruce Willis in *Unbreakable*?"

"You've got to be kidding," said Curt. "You saw that movie? I didn't like it the first time I saw it, so I watched it a second time to really get into it."

The conversation was disrupted by the sound of an airplane in the distance. Will scanned the sky to see where it was going. As the engine noise faded, he turned back to Curt. "They know you're not unbreakable. I was only making an observation, although you do seem to get yourself out of jams that seem somewhat impossible. I think you're very breakable, but you have an angel watching over you."

"Padre, if I promise to go to one of your services, will you quit the preaching?"

Will just chuckled, but didn't promise anything.

Curt continued, "Regarding my destination, to be perfectly honest, I don't really know why I want to cross over to the mainland. It could be as simple as being backed into a corner and going the only remaining direction. It's just that I have a strong feeling--something seems to be drawing me in that direction. I'm not sure what it is, but the feelings started when I came into Baja. The farther south I travel, the stronger the sensation. It's as if something is pulling me there. You're the first person I've told about these feelings. I have trouble sleeping, because that's when they're the strongest. I've not said anything about this, until now, because everyone would think I was crazy."

Will reached out and clutched Curt's hand. "There's a reason, Curt, but I don't know what it is either. I do know it's the right thing to do, so go with those feelings, and let them guide your way. I think there'll be a pleasant surprise at the end of your journey. Meanwhile, we need to figure out the best way to get you south."

Curt looked over to Lingo, who was helping his mother get breakfast ready. "I hope you're right, Will since I could use a break right now. I may have survived a lot, but it sure has been hell."

Will said, "You know sometimes you have to visit hell to really appreciate the opposite. Let's go get something to eat, before it gets cold."

Chapter 49

Alex had just finished a lunch with two Air Force generals, and things were looking up. He had convinced them that Cindy Towers was on board for the merger combining the two largest suppliers of specialized miniature equipment. Alex was ecstatic because the proposed request for new equipment from the merged companies would yield several billion dollars.

Still Alex felt that he was juggling worlds. Between the generals, his company's board, and Cindy, he felt he was being torn apart. In addition, he didn't hear anything from his men in Mexico. Langer assured him that they had scoured the entire Baja peninsula with no success. No one had seen or heard of Curt since the sinking of the dive boat. Alex was starting to think that Curt might really be dead.

He was about to pay the check when his phone rang. He had told Langer not to contact him unless it was critical. He looked at the call number and saw it was Cindy. He hesitated for a moment and reminded himself that this deal was worth several billion dollars.

He took a deep breath; he could do this. Alex answered the call. "Hi, Cindy, what's up?"

"I just wondered if you would be home on time tonight. Should I leave a place for you at the table, or put it in the refrigerator?"

Alex thought about it for a second. Money meant everything to him, and she represented money. "Actually, Honey, I'm taking the rest of the day off. I just finished a meeting with a couple of clients, and it went very well. I'll see you around three. Is the pool up to temperature? We can go swimming."

Cindy smiled. This was the Alex, who had come to her rescue when Curt was arrested. "Sounds like a great idea. The kids won't be home until late because they all have school activities until five. We'll have a couple of hours to ourselves."

"I'll be there shortly. I'm going back to the office and clean up some things," he lied. He was actually going to make an extra stop on the way home. It was time to move up the schedule. There were billions of dollars to be made--billions.

John Towers was out of breath. He had just finished the mile run and had come in third place. Too bad, there were only four runners. The coach had yelled at him that he wasn't trying enough, which was probably true. It was hard to concentrate because he had so much on his mind lately.

When Alex had first started to help his mother, he detested the man. Over time, he started to like Alex, and began to think of him as a substitute father, but things had changed recently. John could see that much of the Good Samaritan act was for show, and that Alex wasn't the man everyone thought he was.

John started to believe his sisters, who had never liked Alex, and they let him know it loud and clear. They answered whenever spoken to, but left the room as soon as Alex entered. When he started to like Alex, it had driven a wedge between himself and his sisters. Now it was time to make peace and let them know how he felt.

His main concern was that his mother seemed increasingly dependent on Alex. Most certainly, marriage was in their future, but he and his sisters felt that was unacceptable. Unfortunately, he could do nothing about it, so he took a deep breath and started running a lap to cool down. He couldn't wait until he was 18, and out of the house because things weren't looking up for the Towers family.

Curt picked up another bushel of potatoes and shoved them into the back of the truck. The last two weeks were

185

grueling. The Padre had made a deal with him. He would work in the fields in Cabo for a couple of weeks, and then he could pay for his own ticket to the mainland. The farm was miles from any visible civilization and prying eyes, which was fine with him. This was the first time in a long time that he didn't feel he had to look over his shoulder every few minutes.

Most of the workers wouldn't say anything to him for the first few days, but when he kept pulling his weight, they finally accepted him. By the end of the two weeks, they were all laughing and enjoying the outdoor work. He was starting to get a great tan, and his skin was getting very dark. He looked at his arms, and smiled, as he now understood that Will had wanted him to work in the fields for more than just the money. When he looked down at his working clothes, he realized he was starting to look more like one of the locals.

The foreman had given everyone the next day off, so he decided to check out the ferry that crossed from Cabo San Lucas over to the mainland. He would have to be careful that he wasn't recognized, but it was a risk he was willing to take.

Each night the urge to go east was getting stronger. He wasn't sure just where he would go once he was on the other side. Will had told him not to worry, since there would be a sign. He just hoped it would be a <u>big</u> one.

Cindy was still getting ready for Alex to come home, when he caught her by surprise and walked through the door at 2:45. He gave her a big hug and said, "We need to talk," in a very serious tone.

Cindy sat down with fear on her face. Was this the end? Where would she go from here? She looked down at the floor. Alex reached out and put his hand under her chin to raise her head. "Cindy, it looks like it has come down to this."

"What?"

He held out his other hand and opened it up. It contained

a small black box. He opened it, and inside there was a ring with a rock big enough to be a doorstop. Her mind was spinning. This was the last thing she had expected. She knew it might happen someday, but certainly not today. She sat mute for at least thirty seconds.

"I'm sorry, Alex. You caught me off guard. I had no idea you were considering getting married."

Alex took the ring out of the box, confident that she would accept it. "I know the last couple of months have been tough, and I'm very sorry for that. I know it has been much worse for you, and I want that to change. We both need to move on with our lives. I know it's such a short time since we lost our partners, but I don't care. The press will have a field day, but it's the right thing to do. So, what do you say? No...don't say anything, I don't want to rush you; just take your time. Let me know when you're ready."

Cindy reached out and took the ring from Alex. "I'm ready now, Alex. More time isn't going to make any difference. Yes, I'll marry you. To hell with what the press will say; we won't tell them. Let's make it a private wedding, just you, me, and a few friends."

Alex reached over and gave her a long and warm kiss. This was working out perfectly. Today was a great day--a great many billions day.

Chapter 50

Henry took a sip of the oil black coffee. He looked over to Buck and realized that he was faring even worse. Lloyd had warned them that stakeouts could be very boring, but this was worse than they expected. They had been watching everyone come and go from the ferry for the past ten days.

The room that Lloyd had found was perfect. With a good pair of binoculars, they had a clear view of everyone coming and going to the mainland. They decided to rotate every hour, so there was always a set of eyes on the ferry dock. Both Henry and Buck were starting to think that this was a waste of time. Everyone assumed that Curt had survived. Maybe he hadn't endured. Still, they agreed to give Curt the benefit of the doubt, at least for a bit longer.

Buck was about to set the binoculars down, when something caught his eye. A man in a big floppy hat was walking toward the ticket office. The man had a familiar walk. Buck jabbed Henry.

"Wake up, you old fart. I think we have a candidate. Take a look."

Henry opened his sleepy eyes, grabbed Buck's coffee, took a sip, and then snatched the big expensive binoculars. "Naw, that ain't him--Oh shit, it is him! Damn! Lloyd was right. It looks like he's checking the schedule. The way he's carefully looking around confirms it. Damn, he blends in well. What the hell has he been doing?"

Buck picked up the throwaway phone. He punched in numbers before saying, "Lloyd, he's here, just as you said. He's checking the schedule. What? Yeah. Consider it done."

Henry set the cup down. "So, what did he say?"

Buck got up and started to put on his shoes. "One of us

needs to follow him, and the other needs to watch to see if either one of us is followed."

Henry frowned. "Let me guess which one of us gets to go for a walk, while the other stays in this rat hole."

Buck smiled. "I'm sure you've already figured it out," he said as the door slammed shut behind him.

Henry looked out the window. "I guess that would be you." Buck was already long gone and never heard the words. Henry knew that, but just needed to say them anyway.

Buck had to be very careful. Not only did he have to stay out of Curt's sight, but also had to make sure that no one was following him, either. Forty minutes later, Buck stood hidden in some trees at the edge of a farm. The small pair of binoculars allowed him to check out the farm from a distance. There didn't look to be anyone but Curt and a bunch of workers. Boy, Curt sure looked great. This outside work really did him good.

He pulled out the second throwaway phone and dialed Lloyd. "He's at a vegetable farm a few miles out of town. Just follow the main road north and then turn left at the Niles farms. It looks safe, and I'm sure no one followed me. OK, I'll see you then."

Curt sat beside the campfire gazing at the stars. It had been a good day. He now had enough money for the ferry, and a bit more. He found out that the ferry left at 6 a.m. every day, so he decided to go tomorrow. Will had printed up fake ID for him, but it wasn't very good. He hoped that the local police would be blind, or not really care. Either reason was fine with him; he just didn't want any more trouble.

Everyone else had gone to bed, and it was time he did the same. He started to get up when a voice came out of the night.

"Curt, it's me, Buck. Don't run. No one followed me."

As he talked, Buck walked out of the darkness and into the

campfire light. He came over to Curt and held out his hand. "You sly old dog, we knew you weren't dead. How in the hell did you get out of the wreck?"

Curt motioned for Buck to sit down, and then spent the next half hour explaining how he beat the odds once again. When he was done, Buck shook his head. "My God, man, you really do have nine lives. Well, I have another surprise for you. Henry is in town, and we picked up a third fellow whom you are not going to believe. Matter of fact, you will probably start to run when I tell you who it is."

Curt picked up a stick and stirred the fire. "So, you've piqued my interest. Who is it?"

Buck explained the events that had occurred after his supposed diving accident. At the end of the conversation, Buck got ready to call Lloyd, but hesitated.

A voice in the distance said, "I'm right here, Buck. Save the call. We've a lot to talk about tonight. Hi Curt, I'm Lloyd."

Chapter 51

By early-morning, Curt was brought up to date on the events of the past three weeks. Lloyd gave him some more money, better identification, and instructions on how best to cross on the ferry. Buck left at 3 a.m. and was back in town by four. Curt was to follow two hours after Buck, so he arrived with just enough time to buy a ticket and board the ship. Curt had strict instructions to talk to no one. He was to remain on the upper deck where he could see everyone boarding. He was then to go down to the lower deck once the ship was underway.

Henry was awakened by a sharp pounding on the door. He ran over, listened for Buck's voice, and then let him in. The two talked for the next half hour as they reheated the 3-day-old coffee grounds. They were getting very ripe, but then so were Buck and Henry.

Alex was in a deep sleep when his cell started to vibrate. He looked over to Cindy, who was dead to the world. He grabbed his bathrobe and walked out of the bedroom and into the study. "This had better be good to call me this early," he barked into the cell.

Langer didn't make him wait long because this was important. "Sorry, Sir, but it is very important. The two men who worked in the dive shop with Curt have been spotted in Cabo San Lucas. My men just saw the one called Buck return to a hotel across from the ferry dock. They also spotted the other one glancing out the window. Those two are up to something. We think Curt is in the area."

He cleared his dry throat. "We think he's going to try to take the ferry across to the mainland, and the other men are helping him. He may have already gone across, but then the others would have returned home. If they spot him, what do you want my men to do?"

Alex would love his men to walk right up and shoot Curt as he started to board the ferry, but that was unreasonable. There were just too many people around, and the security cameras pointed toward the ferry.

"Langer, here is what you do. Let Curt get on the ferry; just make sure he never makes it to the other side. Make sure your men understand that he has to have a bullet in his head and be dead before he hits the water. Do you understand? I don't want any mistakes this time." Langer responded positively and the conversation abruptly ended.

As Alex crawled back into bed, Cindy opened her eyes. "Who's calling so early in the morning?"

Alex turned to his side away from Cindy. He did not want her to see his face as he lied. "Some idiot on the east coast forgot the time zones. I chewed him out, and he'll call me later today. Sorry to wake you, Honey, go back to sleep."

"Night," she said. She felt sure he was lying, but she wasn't sure why, especially after their wonderful day together. She put it out of her mind, and drifted back into a deep slumber.

Chapter 52

Curt woke with a start. Most of the other workers already left for work. It seemed a little strange that so many were gone. He guessed that some of them saw Curt had company, and that made them nervous.

He gathered his limited traveling supplies and headed east. An hour later, the deep red sunrays came across the horizon, producing long shadows across the barren landscape. The cacti along the road looked like huge sentinels guarding the way.

When he reached the edge of town, he spotted an old beat-up taxi. Henry had given him extra spending money, and now was the time to use a little. The two bartered for a lower price before Curt jumped into the back of the smelly cab and was on his way. His first plan had been to walk up to the ticket booth, but that would leave him exposed as he walked the distance from the edge of town to the ferry. By riding in the cab, he was in contact with only the cab driver. This was a much better plan.

Curt arrived earlier than he had planned, but that also worked in his favor since there were fewer people in the area. He paid the driver, pulled his hat down over his forehead, and slowly walked toward the ticket booth. It had just opened, so he bought a one-way ticket to the mainland, and boarded the ferry. Curt worked his way to the top deck, and found a corner that gave him a good view of everyone approaching the ferry.

He looked across the dock area toward the hotel, where he could see Henry looking out the window on the top floor. As soon as Henry saw that Curt had seen him, he held up a green piece of paper against the glass window. Curt smiled. That was good news. Henry and Buck did not see anyone in the area that might be a threat. He was good to go.

Alex's cell hummed then was quiet. It vibrated again, and he reached over to snatch it before it went into a ring mode. He excused himself to Cindy and walked downstairs to his office. He punched in the security code on the door and entered. He looked back to see if Cindy had followed, and then closed the door. He looked at the calling number and saw that it was Langer.

"Sir, we have a situation here. My men in Cabo have spotted Curt getting onto the ferry. He was alone. They weren't sure it was Curt at first because he has changed his appearance. We can now confirm it's our man, but the problem is that Curt is watching everyone boarding. My men are going to have to board from the other side of the ferry using a service boat. What are their orders?"

Alex waited and listened to the silence. There was not a sound from outside his office. "The order is the same as before. Make sure he never reaches the other side. I want them to understand that they must shoot him before he goes into the water. Curt has a knack of getting out of any situation. We cannot leave anything to chance. Keep me posted on what happens. I will leave for the office right now. I don't feel comfortable talking here."

Alex looked around his office at all of his prized possessions. A signed Babe Ruth home run ball was in a glass case on his desk. A sealed frame on the wall had a number of documents signed by George Washington. His collection consisted of a priceless item from each of several different aspects of collecting. He had one-of-a-kind paintings, stamps, coins, comic books, baseball cards, old computer games, and more. When this was over, he would be able to buy so much more. There would be no limit to what he could collect. His mind drifted for a few seconds, and then he headed out of his office.

When he opened the door, Cindy was walking up to him with a cup of coffee in hand.

"You don't have to go in today do you?"

"Sorry, Honey, but there's a problem with one of the manufacturing divisions, and it needs my direct oversight. I'll try to be back early. We need to celebrate."

He smiled at her and took a sip from the cup. He was a good actor, and it appeared that she had bought it all. He took another sip, gave her a kiss, and ran up the stairs. Twenty-five minutes later, he was out the door and on his way to his ever-expanding empire.

The two men had just finished their last assignment for Langer. They had tracked down their two predecessors who had botched the hit on Curt. Mel and Stan had been spending time in a local bar getting drunk and licking their wounds. They were easy to find, and it was just a matter of time to wait until they left the bar late one night. Early the next morning, the local police found the two in a dumpster, each with a hole in his head. It was labeled a professional hit.

These new hitmen were the best that Langer could find on such short notice. They knew the score; if they failed, they would get the same fate as the two before them. They boarded the service vessel just minutes before the ferry was to leave the dock, making them the last to board.

They enlisted a third member of their team to work as a spotter, to keep an eye on Curt from the dock area. He would let them know if Curt moved to the other side of the ferry. The spotter signaled that the coast was clear, so they made their move and boarded the ferry from the ocean side. They presented their fake credentials to the ferry officer, and then moved to the center of the ship.

They would not move until they were well underway. Their instructions were clear--Curt was not to reach the mainland, even if it meant that the ferry had to go down. They made a call to Langer telling him that it was a picture-perfect day, and they had picked up the gift that he had requested. Langer understood the code. Now all he had to do was to wait.

Curt looked down as one of the dockworkers cast the last line to a ferry crewmember. The twin-screw engines of the ferry were now in full reverse. The 120-foot transport started its journey across the Baja waters.

He headed down to the lower deck and picked up a cup of coffee and a sweet roll from the vendor, and waited for the next step in his journey.

Curt started to relax since he hadn't spotted anyone who looked to be on his trail. He might be safe, but he still felt uncomfortable. This trip was dangerous, but he had to go. Whatever force was pulling him east, was getting even stronger. He couldn't seem to resist the calling. He couldn't put his finger on it yet, but he had the feeling it had something to do with his past, but he had never been in Mexico as a youth. It was very confusing. Maybe when he reached the mainland, the reason would become clearer.

He took the last bite of the pastry and decided he would like another. He bought another cup of coffee and two more pastries. It was going to be a long trip, and he needed the quick energy. Suddenly, he noticed a gringo he hadn't seen board the ship. Then he saw a second man. Oh, shit! He was out of the frying pan and into the fire. He had nowhere to go. He took a big bite out of the pastry and dumped the rest into the trash. The two men were slowly heading his way.

As he navigated toward the back of the ferry where the vehicles were being stored, he noticed a small doorway marked Ninguna entrada – servicio sólo or No Entrance – Service Only. He looked around, saw that no one was watching, and pulled on the door. It was locked, so he pulled even harder. The old lock gave and he quickly went down a small access ladder to the engine room. The workers below were looking the other way, giving Curt enough time to climb down the ladder and hide behind a large generator.

The two workers looked up as they heard a sound from above and saw a well-dressed man who definitely didn't belong in the engine area. Before they could say anything, the man spoke in a loud voice that was easily heard above the engine noise.

"Has anyone come down here in the last couple of minutes?"

The two shook their heads in a negative response. Before they could say anything, the man was gone. They looked at each other, shrugged and went back to work.

For the next hour, Curt endured leg cramps, loud engine noises, and awful smells. When the two men finally left for a break, Curt investigated the area until he found a tiny storage area in the back of the engine room. He grabbed some old work clothes, made himself a small bed, and settled in for the day. His only hope was that the hitmen would not double-check the area and make a more thorough search.

Langer's cell rang just before 10 a.m. His new men were reporting in but the news wasn't good. They switched to their encrypted phone, so that they could be more specific about the situation.

"Sir, we think he spotted us and headed toward the back of the ferry. We looked everywhere and found nothing. He just vanished. There's a chance he jumped ship. If that is the case, he'll be fish food by now. If he is still on the ferry, we'll find him."

Langer knew he couldn't call Alex with this bad news. They still had plenty of time. "You need to keep looking. Go back and recheck everything again. Remember, Curt's a technical guy. My guess is that he's down below deck. Start with the engine room and then work your way up."

The two acknowledged and hung up. They looked at each other and knew they had to find Curt. As they put their phone away, they spotted a new problem. There were two security police on board, and they were making their way through the crowd, profiling the passengers. The hitmen knew that being Americans, would throw up a red flag.

They quickly escaped the view of these security men by heading down toward the engine room. They were about to go through the door when the engineers returned. Langer's two men quickly turned toward the ferry railing to look as though they were enjoying the view.

Once the engineers had disappeared below, the hitmen had a short conversation about their game plan. Collateral damage was always a consideration when the target became difficult, but their orders were absolute. There would be no room for error or failure. Anything goes as long as the target is permanently removed. The payment for this job would set them up for years, so a decision was made.

They opened the door and descended into the belly of the beast. The engineers turned and started to tell them that this was a restricted area. Before another word escaped from the workers, each received a bullet to the chest. The hitmen stood over the two engineers and put a second bullet in each just to be sure they wouldn't give them any more trouble. They dragged the bodies back to the right side of the generator, just out of view.

Curt had heard the shots, and opened the door a crack to see what was going on. Fear ran down his spine as he envisioned the end of his life coming soon. This was it. There was no escaping this time.

When it became obvious that the killers were out of view, Curt decided to make a dash for the stern of the ship behind the engine. He was now hidden from view, but not for long. They would find his nest in the storage room before long and come looking for him.

There had to be another way out of this situation. He looked everywhere, up and down, but saw nothing. Then he saw a small beam of light shining down. It was some kind of access port with a ladder. He only had seconds before they might discover him, so he quickly climbed the ladder and pushed up the access port. It was heavy, but gave way.

As he looked around, all he saw were several car and truck tires, and one pair of short legs. It was a tiny boy standing in front of one of the cars. Curt pulled himself up and closed the access port, hoping the changing of light beams with the open port did not attract the attention of the killers.

He inched his way along the side of the car until he was face-to-face with the crying boy. He was about five years old, and he was rapidly saying something in Spanish that sounded like he was separated from his parents. The little boy smiled when he saw him, but then his smile quickly changed to fear. Curt turned around just in time to see one of the killers exiting the opening, gun in hand. Curt had no time to think. He grabbed the boy and ran around to the front of the car. A bullet whizzed by and hit a support column on the side railing. Curt turned the boy away from the killers, protected behind his own body.

He turned his head to keep track of the killers and heard someone calling out, searching for a lost child. His eyes finally caught those of the boy's mother. The fear on the mother's face turned to smiles as she saw her lost boy, but then her eyes moved elsewhere. Another bullet hit the wall behind Curt. He looked over to the mother and then looked at the car next to him. He opened the car door and threw the boy inside. He closed the door and started to run in the opposite direction. He gave an OK sign to the mother and motioned for her to stay down.

Two more bullets ricocheted off nearby vehicles. As Curt turned the last corner near the stern of the ferry, he saw one of the killers taking aim. He slid to a stop, just in time for the bullet to shoot out into open space. He looked around for an escape, but it looked like he had nowhere to go. He turned again to see his pursuers, and a bullet hit him in the left temple. Curt became dizzy, and reached up to feel blood flowing down his shirt. He had only seconds before they came to finish the job. He was in trouble and realized he had just one option left, so he took it.

When the killers reached the area where Curt had been shot, they found a blood trail that led to the back of the ship. They heard a splash, and ran to the back edge of the ferry, but saw nothing. The water motion from the prop covered the splash immediately.

Before they could turn around, a voice came from behind. "Drop your weapons, and put your hands on your head. Do it now, very slowly."

The hit men looked at each other and smiled. They could take the security people out before they even knew what happened. What they didn't know was that the security officers were retired military police working the ferry for extra money. Guns raised; the hit men started to turn around, but before they completed a half turn, each was hit with a bullet in the chest, killing them instantly.

The mother ran over and opened the car door, grabbing her little boy. One of the officers walked over and started to talk to her. She told the officer how Curt had saved her son just moments before the two men had shot him. They took down some notes and called in the incident to headquarters.

A few minutes later, it was also learned that the two engineers had been killed. A single crewmember was allowed to go below, and then yellow tape was placed around the shooting area, blocking engine-room access.

Cindy was sitting on the couch watching a soap opera, hoping that Alex would come home early today because they had many things to discuss. She was about to change the channel when a special report cut into her show, claiming it was breaking news from Cabo San Lucas. She turned up the volume and watched the report.

"This is Jane Smith reporting breaking news from the Cabo San Lucas ferry dock. We have just learned that Curt Allen Towers, a convicted murderer who escaped from prison several months ago, was allegedly killed today in a gunfire exchange aboard the Cabo San Lucas ferry."

"The two assassins were later shot by ferry security, when they refused to surrender their weapons. Witnesses state that they saw Curt Towers running from the men, but he was shot in the head. He fell off the back of the ferry, and is presumed dead."

"The identities of the other slain men are unknown at this time, but it appears that they were professional killers. We'll have more on this breaking story as it develops. We now return you to our regular scheduled programming."

The soap came back on, and Cindy switched channels. Some of the other stations had picked up the story, but not much more information was known about the incident. Cindy turned off the TV and started to cry. Up to now, she had never been certain that Curt was gone. In the back of her mind, she always wondered if.... Now it was final. Curt used up all his nine lives.

She was about to call Alex, but decided against it. She knew that mentioning Curt always turned Alex sour. It was finally over and time to move on.

Langer was sitting in front of Alex, and they were going over the plans for the next year. There was to be a marriage, and the merger of the two companies. Everything seemed to be working out.

Langer's cell rang. It was from the third member of the Mexican hit team. Langer had been very careful that nothing from this hitman could be traced back to Alex. In fact, this third man would be dead in less than an hour. He would just disappear into the desert, never to be found. Langer listened intently and finally said "OK," and hung up.

Alex looked at Langer for an answer, but Langer simply picked up the remote and turned on the TV. The two sat and watched as the entire story unfolded.

Alex turned off the TV when his phone rang. It was his well-compensated contact in the Mexican police. Alex gave a few short answers, and the man on the other end filled in the rest of the story. Several minutes passed before Alex ended the call.

He walked over, pulled out two glasses, and poured two tall drinks.

"Well, I think we've seen the last of Curt Allen Towers. Now we can move on. That call was from our man inside the Mexican police. It appears that after all the terrorist threats, the ferry company put on a new security camera system. They have the shootout on tape, and it shows the two hitmen shooting Curt in the head before the security team killed them. The blood trail led to the back edge of the ferry. Someone on the upper level heard a splash, and something went into the water. The ferry stopped, and a search of the area was made before the ferry continued, but there was no sign of a body."

"They still don't know who the dead men are. They checked their hotel room, and it was clean. The bottom line is that we are in the clear. Curt and his killers are all gone. We need to pull everyone out, right now. I don't want any loose ends."

"Oh, shit! I bet Cindy is watching TV. I have to go. Clean up any loose ends. Tomorrow we'll turn a new corner. You do this right and you'll get a nice bonus," Alex said as he raced for his car.

John Towers was at a local mall with a couple of his friends when he saw a picture of his father on the news. Once he saw the broadcast about the death of his father, he had to escape and get out of the mall. He jumped on his small motorbike and took off toward the lake, so he could have some privacy.

In the back of his mind, he always knew his father was still alive. Now this made things different. No one survives from being shot in the head. He sat beside the lake, skipping stones, thinking about where his life was going from here. His friends had finally quit asking about his father, but now it was all going to start over again. It was bad for him, but much worse for his sisters. He couldn't count the times he had to defend his sisters from other girls who called themselves "friends." He pulled out his cell phone and made the regretful call to Brenda and Lisa. When he hung up, he jumped on his bike and headed toward their rescue, as his father would have expected.

By nightfall, the ferry was docked and the cars were slowly departing from the ramp. In less than an hour, the transport was empty and ready for the return trip in the morning. The police had finished making the final assessment of the crime scene area and had released the ferry back in service.

Everyone who exited the ferry had been checked and rechecked. They found no evidence of Curt Towers. The case was considered wrapped up. The only thing left to solve was the identity of the two killers.

The two security guards were replaced by the evening shift, which lacked both expertise and physical stature. By 9 p.m., one was already asleep and the other sat watching a Mexican game show in the main lounge. It was time for Curt to make his next move.

When Alex arrived home, the tension in the air was so thick he could cut it with a knife. There was nothing else to do but bring everything out into the open. He and Cindy sat silently across from each other at the dinner table. The kids ate earlier and had gone to their rooms to watch TV or work on their computers.

Alex broke the silence. "Cindy, I know you've heard about Curt. I'm so sorry you had to hear about it on TV. I didn't hear about it for almost an hour after it was announced. You tell me what you want me to do, and I'll do it. I'm here for you. I'll give you whatever you need."

"I don't know what I need right now. I'm so confused. First, he's alive, then dead, then alive, now dead again. I can't handle much more of this. I know you're here for me, and I guess that's all I need for now. I still want to get married, but let's put it on hold for a few weeks. I need to pull myself together again."

Alex had to be as careful as if he were walking on eggs. He needed to get married to complete the merger. The militaries were patient, but they would not wait forever to award their contract. He would have to be supportive and accept a short delay. The tradeoff would be worth it. He smiled and thought about how much he loved the word "billions."

Chapter 53

Curt Allen Towers had been in some real jams before, but nothing like this one. Hours before, he had been shot, and the bullet had glanced along his temple breaking a major blood vessel. It took some time for him to stop the bleeding by applying pressure, but thankfully, it had stopped.

Staggering toward the edge of the ferry, he left a trail of blood. He was about ready to jump off the ferry when he heard the confrontation between the killers and the security guards. In a last desperate move, he grabbed a box of work tools and threw them off the back of the ferry to distract everyone.

He quickly slinked back to the access port in the floor and lowered himself into the engine room. He knew they would eventually check every space on the ferry, including the engine room, so he had to find somewhere they would never look. Then it came to him. He wasn't standing on the bottom floor of the ship. The bilge was below him.

He looked around and found the access plate to the bilge. When he opened it, he saw that it was big enough to crawl into. It smelled terrible, but he had no choice. It was only about three feet tall, so he had to crawl along in the dark, feeling his way through thick oil, and other smelly stuff. He lay in that muck for the next eight hours, praying that no one would offer to check the bilge.

The only thing he could see was the glowing of the numbers on his watch. As time passed, the numbers grew dim. He could see that it was almost midnight, so it was probably time to make his next move.

The ferry had been stopped for hours, and Curt had not heard voices for some time. He gently moved the access panel to the bilge out of the way. He went over to the closet and used some of the rags to remove the oil and grease from his face. He found a pair of gloves that would allow him to crawl up the ladder without leaving any residue on the rungs. He took off his shoes and put them in a bag, and cleaned his feet, so that they wouldn't leave any marks either.

He cautiously crawled up the ladder with the shoe bag hanging around his neck. He looked around the deck and saw that it was empty of cars and people. There were only a few lights visible, but then he saw the camera. The hatch was not in its field of view, but his exit certainly would be. He moved over to the underside of the camera and reached up to cover the lens with oil and grease from his clothes. He then removed the cable from the back of the camera, bent the main pin and re-attached the cable haphazardly so that it looked like sloppy maintenance.

When Curt was sure he was safe, he crawled over the side of the ferry, and swam along the shoreline until he was well away from the ferry dock. Once he was ashore, he donned his shoes and walked the beach for more than a mile before stopping to rest. He used the sand to clean the oil off his body and his clothing. He left his valuables under a log and went for a swim to remove any residual oil and tar.

When he got back from his welcomed swim, he took an inventory of his valuables. He still had some money, his passport with his new identity of Bill Barns, and a Mexican driver's license. He was alive, but he was feeling that it couldn't get much worse than it is right now. Then he realized that he had thought the same thing while in prison and when scuba diving on the shipwreck in Loreto. What he needed now was a new plan. Unfortunately, he had just used up Plan Z.

Henry, Buck, and Lloyd sat in the hotel bar. Lloyd held up his drink.

"Here's to one hell of a guy. We did our best to save him, but in the end, it just wasn't enough."

206

Henry and Buck put their glasses up to toast with Lloyd.

Henry smiled. "You know, they never did find a body. Remember, he was called CAT for a reason. He has survived situations just as bad, or even worse. No, I'll salute him, but only because I haven't given up on him yet. My gut tells me he made it to the other side."

"So, you think he survived all that bullshit that went on the ferry. A shot to the head is hard to survive," said Buck.

"Has everyone you've seen shot in the head died?" asked Henry.

Lloyd took another sip. "You might be right. I've seen a couple of bad guys shot in the head that are still alive and kicking today. So what do you suggest we do?"

Buck said, "Looking for Curt in Mexico, when he'll be doing his best to hide, is close to impossible. No, I think we need to quit looking for him, for the time being."

Lloyd took a sip, and set the drink down. "Let's place a personal ad in as many Mexican newspapers as possible. It should read 'Looking for Digger the Dog,' and then leave a response email address. It may take some time, but Curt is smart enough to know that will be the only safe way we can contact him."

"I'll go back to Denver and see what comes up. I still have many contacts in the department. You two find something to do for the next year down here. I'll send you as much money as I can. Until his body shows up, let's all assume he's alive. Curt must have a guardian angel looking after him. By the way, did Curt tell you any more about his irrepressible need to go east?"

Henry scratched his chin. It had been a very long day. "I'm not sure what all that is about. All I know is that Curt feels driven to go somewhere in Central or East Mexico. He doesn't know what's there; just that he must go there. He said something about his life being turned around once he arrives. I don't have a clue what he was talking 'bout. I think all this runnin' from the law has made him loco. I still believe in him, so I guess we'll just wait and see what turns up with the ad."

They all held their glasses up high in one last salute to Curt Allen Towers.

Chapter 54

More than a month passed as Curt slowly migrated across Mexico. The first few days he cleaned himself up and bought some used clothes at a second-hand store. He had to dry out the money and ID before he could buy anything. His biggest problem was that the wound on his head was a dead giveaway, so he bought some makeup to cover his wound.

When he was sure that he couldn't be identified, he found the local bus terminal. He traveled from town to town, changing buses often and always avoiding a direct route.

Surprisingly, the bullet to his head seemed to make things clearer because he now knew his next destination. It came to him one night in a dream that he had to get to Cozumel. In the back of his mind, he knew that it was not the final destination, just the next step in the journey. Cozumel would point him in the right direction.

He would stay in a small town several days, and then move on to the next. He was increasingly paranoid about people following him, so even a coffee vendor was under suspicion. He was getting stronger daily and back in shape, thanks to the hard labor jobs.

The hours he had spent in the bilge, had taken their toll. He developed a nasty cough that just wouldn't go away. He kept buying drugs to help ward it off, but he suspected that it would take a more serious antibiotic to get it under control. Right now, his only concern was getting to Cozumel and he was just a day away. He wasn't sure what was there, but he knew it was the next step in his new life.

Lloyd returned to his home in Denver and continued to run the ads in several large newspapers in Mexico. No response yet, but he would keep trying.

He also made a few inquiries at the department. As far as everyone was concerned, Curt Towers was old news; he was dead and gone. He checked the society columns and found plenty of tabloid stuff on Alex Brandon and Curt's ex-wife, Cindy. There was a rumor that the two were to be married soon. It seemed everyone was moving on with his or her lives.

Henry and Buck were running a new dive shop out of Loreto with financial help from Lloyd. The locals were leaving them alone, now that Curt Towers was out of the picture. They hired several young college kids to help with the dive operation, but were careful not to mention Curt. Business was good; in fact, they were in the black within the first month of business.

Henry continually checked the police reports to identify bodies that washed up onshore. A few had, but none of them was Curt. With each day that passed, their belief increased that he was indeed alive.

Cindy spent the day with the kids getting ready for a birthday party for a friend of John's. Alex agreed to hold the party at the house and pay for the entire event. Cindy appreciated the gesture because it made everyone happy. She needed all the friends and support she could get, because not everyone had forgotten her husband, the murderer.

She had talked with Alex the night before, and they had decided to get married on July 1 in a private ceremony at the house. The kids weren't very happy with that situation, but realized they didn't really have a choice.

Alex spent a lot of time at the office getting ready for the merger, designed to coincide with their upcoming marriage. The military generals were becoming impatient with the timetable, and told Alex that this was the last delay they would tolerate. He had guaranteed them that it would happen as scheduled. He hadn't heard anything further from Langer about Curt Towers and felt sure that it was finally over. Alex was becoming more relaxed, knowing that billions of dollars were within reach.

Chapter 55

Curt reached Cozumel and found himself a handyman job at a local dive resort straightaway. He was assigned to work on the electrical problems that were common in the old hotel, but would also repair dive gear as needed. He had grown a short beard, and changed his hairstyle. His time in the sun yielded very dark skin. He exercised to strengthen his muscles, but that nasty lung infection he got from the bilge was still haunting him. The hotel doctor had given him antibiotics, but it still wasn't doing any good. He had good days and then some bad ones. Unbeknownst to Curt, today was going to be a dreadful one.

One of the guests had complained about an electrical problem in his room, and requested a repairman. When Curt knocked on the door, an older man answered and showed him the problem.

As Curt moved the TV set to the side for repair, he picked up a newspaper that was lying on top. He froze because on the front page was a picture of Alex Brandon and his wife Cindy. The article stated that they had been married the day before in a small private wedding. The story did a brief background mentioning his murder conviction, and how he had repeatedly evaded death. The story concluded that Curt was finally deceased, and his ex-wife was moving on with her life. The article also mentioned a merger of the two companies. He wasn't sure what pissed him off more, the marriage, or the merger. In truth, it was both equally.

He set the paper down on the dresser, and began to repair the TV set. He was about to leave after making the repair, when the man asked if Curt knew anything about diving in the cenotes. Shivers ran down his spine because this word meant something important to him. It was to be his next destination.

He recomposed himself before answering. "I'm a diver,

but know nothing about diving in a cenote. I'm curious, though, so I'll find out and get back to you later today."

Curt took the generous tip and headed back to his small office in the basement of the hotel. He logged on to the internet to conduct some research. Apparently, the cenotes were part of the Mayan underground cave system that covered a huge area. Dozens of dive shops on the Yucatan peninsula ran basic, intermediate, and advanced dive trips into the hundreds of miles of underwater caves.

He printed out much of this information about the cenotes, and delivered it to the guest who requested the material. When he tried to give Curt a second tip, he refused, telling the guest that he too benefited from researching the materials.

Curt stopped by the hotel manager's office to give his notice, citing health reasons. His cough was enough to convince the manager. One more week of work and then he would be on his way to what he felt was his final destination, wherever that might be.

Alex and Cindy sat on the patio looking out over the sandy beach. They had flown down to Cozumel after the wedding and were spending just a few days before returning to Denver. Alex had promised her a longer honeymoon, once the merger was behind them.

Their room was on the ninth floor of the hotel, and they had a great view of the pool directly below. Cindy was reading a book while Alex sipped a drink, quietly thinking about the billions he was about to control.

He looked down at a maintenance worker who walked from one side of the resort to the other. The man looked familiar, even though it was quite some distance away. The worker was about to turn his face toward Alex, when Cindy asked about dinner plans for the evening. The distraction caused him to pull his eyes away at the same time Curt looked up. The timing was much closer than a photo finish in a horse race. When Alex looked back, the man was gone. The image went through Alex's mind. Something was familiar about the way the man walked, but he couldn't place it.

Chapter 56

Lloyd Becker sat in his dirty brown easy chair, beer in hand, gun on the table, and a medical folder in his lap. He turned the volume down on the news, since TV no longer held his interest. He had things that were more important on his mind.

He had just returned from his doctor's office with some bad news. He had started feeling poorly when he returned to Denver after his vacation. At first, he thought he'd caught something in Mexico, but none of the drugs he tried seemed to help. Finally, he broke down and made a visit to one of the doctors recommended by the police department. They poked and prodded but came up with nothing. He ended up going to different specialists, but then they sent him to see an oncologist. The bottom line was that he had pancreatic cancer. The doctor was very direct and honest, explaining his options. They had caught it too late, and he was told to get his affairs in order. Three to six months was all he had left.

At first, he had started to feel sorry for himself, and had considered using his gun to end it all. The more he thought about it; he realized that he had only one thing left to get in order—Curt Allen Towers. This bad news gave Lloyd a new perspective on Curt. He had been concentrating on helping Curt hide from the police, but the best way he could help him was to clear his name. That was a tall order with a lot of old ground to cover in just a few short months. He decided he had better get right to work.

Next to the TV were several boxes containing papers that covered Curt's trial, and the evidence used to convict him. He had made copies of everything when he was closing Curt's case out for the department. Making copies was against department policy, but he wanted to study the case further, and going back and forth to the evidence locker would arouse suspicion. He had briefly gone through everything, but really didn't have his heart into it the first time. This time was going to be different. Besides, he had nothing else to do but wait to die. There had to be something that the defense attorney had missed. The slam-dunk evidence had to have holes in it, and he was going to find it.

He already started to set his affairs in order. His estate would go to Henry and Buck. He left a dollar to his wife and each of his heirs. They all abandoned him long ago. The truth was that he had been very wise with his money in the stock market. At present, he had just a little more than a million dollars sitting in six different banks. He couldn't take it with him, so he decided that he would buy off everyone he needed to get the information that would clear Curt.

He got up and pulled another beer out of the refrigerator, grasped the first box and started to go through the case folders, one page at a time. This time he read each line of text, and analyzed every bit of evidence that appeared in the reports. He created a timeline for the case on a small eraser board. It sure felt good to be doing detective work again.

Two hours later, he was surprised when he found what he was looking for. He had assumed it would take days, so maybe luck was in his favor. He was reviewing the interview with Wendy Marshall, the murder victim's secretary. She stated that she had worked for Kathy Robinson for eight years. When asked if she knew about certain things going on in Kathy's personal life, Wendy had stated that she knew little of Kathy's private life.

Lloyd stopped at that statement. The detective interviewing Wendy should have dug deeper; a secretary should know everything about her boss, especially after eight years. Wendy's statement that she knew nothing actually meant that she was hiding something. Lloyd knew the detective conducting the interview was new at his job, or he would have pursued that line of questioning. Wendy got off easy. She was hiding something, but Lloyd wasn't sure why.

Now that he had a name, he went through his list of people interviewed in Curt's trial to see what had happened to them after the trial ended. One of his jobs at the end of the trial was to note the address and phone number of each witness, just in case they were needed for an appeal. He found out that Wendy had quit her job on the very day that the guilty verdict had been handed down. She sold her house and moved to an old Victorian house in the south part of Denver. Her phone had been disconnected, and her cell phone had a restricted number. Wendy was trying to hide, and he suspected that Curt was the reason.

Now Lloyd was getting excited. He was onto something. He set the paperwork down, picked up his gun, and put it back in the lockbox. He took a long hot shower, popped a couple of sleeping pills, and was asleep in minutes. Tomorrow was going to be a great day for Lloyd. He could feel it in his bones.

Chapter 57

Lloyd was up at 7 a.m. with a renewed vigor he hadn't felt in years. He now had a new purpose in life. He no longer had to worry about bending the rules; he could do whatever he wanted. He didn't care if he was arrested, because he could always bail himself out. He would never see any jail time because he would be dead long before that could happen. He felt that a huge weight had been lifted from his shoulders.

It took him an hour to find Wendy Marshall's house, because most of the houses in the area looked the same. The street had multiple Victorian houses only ten feet apart, with foliage trying to obscure each other's view.

He walked up the steps to the porch, but it looked as though no one was home. He rang the doorbell, but there was no answer. He thought he heard a small dog barking, but decided that it was a TV set. She was home, but not answering the door. He rang again to no avail, so he tried a new approach.

"Wendy Marshall. This is detective Lloyd Becker of the Denver Police Department. We need to talk. I know you're home, so I'm not going to leave until you come to the door."

There was no response.

"Wendy, this is the last time I'm going to ask nicely. I'll call for backup, and we can do this downtown. Now, open the door."

Lloyd heard the door unlock and Wendy cautiously opened it up.

"What do you want, Detective? I told everything I knew to the other detectives, and the trial is over. Besides, I heard that Curt Towers was dead."

Lloyd looked down at a folder he had in his hands, then back up to Wendy. "What made you think I wanted to talk to you about Curt Towers?"

Wendy hesitated for a second, somewhat flustered. "I don't have to talk to you or anyone else unless you have a warrant," she said as she closed the door.

Lloyd had expected such a response, so he came prepared. After all, he no longer had to play by the rules; he could do anything he wanted. He hated having to talk through the door, but he knew that he would eventually get her to talk. He just had to play his cards right.

"Miss Marshall, we have new evidence in the case. We know about the connection between your boss and Alex Brandon. We know why your boss was killed. It's only a matter of time before Mr. Brandon is arrested. If you stick to your story that you knew nothing, you'll be convicted as an accessory. I'll give you the rest of the day to think about it, but tomorrow, I'll turn my new information over to the DA, and then you can kiss your ass good-bye. I'll leave my card with my phone number inside the storm door. Give me a call, soon. It's your only way out of this mess."

Lloyd set the card in the door and made a hasty retreat to his car. He waited and watched with his high-powered binoculars to see if there was any action. He didn't have to wait long for the door to open, and she snatched the card.

Satisfied his job was done for now, he headed home. He stopped by a video store and picked up every "Dirty Harry" movie ever made. It might be a long wait, so he might as well enjoy watching shows about the detective he wished he could have been.

When he reached home, he checked his cell phone for messages. There were no calls. He opened the refrigerator, pulled out a frozen dinner, snagged a beer, and started the first movie.

Just as the action was coming to a peak, his cell phone buzzed. It was Wendy. She seemed very agitated and wanted to talk with Lloyd right away. She was scared and wondered who else knew about the information that Lloyd mentioned. Lloyd lied and told her that the information was restricted to a small task force inside the DA's office. It was a good lie; he would have believed it. She asked him to come back at eight that night. That gave him just enough time to finish his meal, take a shower, and rig himself with a microphone recording system. He wasn't taking any chances; he needed all the proof he could muster.

Thirty minutes later, he was at the front door of Wendy's house. Before he could ring the doorbell, the door opened, and she motioned him inside. She looked out the crack to see if anyone else was outside, then closed the door and double locked it with two deadbolts.

Lloyd looked around. The house had been restored to look the way it had 50 years earlier. The detail work had been done well, but looked as though it had cost plenty.

"Nice place you have, Wendy. Can I call you Wendy?"

She tried to smile, but instead motioned to Lloyd to follow her into the kitchen.

"Wendy is fine. Do you want something to drink? I have water, lemonade, coffee, or tea."

She pulled the tea kettle off the gas stove that resembled one of the original gas stoves from the 50s. He was gazing around the room admiring the remodel, before his mind snapped him back to this discussion.

"No thanks, Wendy. I just want to talk about the Towers case."

"I really had nothing to do with the frame-up. It was Alex Brandon's idea. He approached Kathy. He never saw me, but I overheard many of the conversations. They set Towers up so that Alex could take over his company. Kathy was going to get very rich from it. Either she got greedy, or Alex thought she was a handicap. That's all I know. When I found out what was going on, I stayed as far away from the situation as possible. I played dumb when the police asked questions. I feel relieved that it's out in the open now."

Wendy was about to continue when a red laser dot appeared on her dress. Seconds later, a "thump" sound came from behind Lloyd, and blood appeared on Wendy's front as she dropped to the floor, dead.

Lloyd turned to see who had fired the kill shot and found Ross Langer standing in front of him.

"Well, if isn't Lloyd Becker. What are you doing nosing into something that doesn't concern you? What did she tell you? Tell me everything, or you'll get the same as she did."

Lloyd knew that was a lie. Langer had shown his face, so he wasn't about to let Lloyd live. His only chance was to buy some time to come up with a plan.

"She was about to show me something about the Towers case, but the information was in the bedroom down the hall. She kept it in the closet on the upper shelf. Just take the information and go."

Langer smiled and pulled the trigger on his silenced weapon. It hit Lloyd in the chest, and he crumpled to the floor. Langer was about to put a bullet in Lloyd's head when he heard someone outside calling for Wendy. It was only a matter of time before he was discovered. He looked down at Lloyd and decided he would bleed out in minutes. Killing a cop was so easy that he began thinking about going back into his old assassin profession.

When he got to the bedroom, he found the closet, but discovered nothing. Why had Lloyd lied to him? He ran back to the kitchen to find Lloyd leaning up against the stove, a big smile on his face, and a cigarette lighter in his hand. The bullet that struck Lloyd had hit the recording device attached to his chest. That had slowed down the bullet's impact, so he was alive, but the wound was still very severe.

Lloyd didn't give Langer any time to process the events unfolding. He pulled his thumb down against the flint of the lighter. Langer saw the hand movement, and out of instinct, he pulled the trigger. He instantly realized his mistake, but it was too late. When the fatal bullet hit Lloyd, he fell like a sack of potatoes, with the flame dropping close behind. As the lighter approached the floor, it was exposed to the stream of gas venting from the broken gas line. Lloyd's last gallant action was to break the gas line. He knew his life was over, but he wanted it to count for something more than another unexplained death.

The explosion was devastating. The entire back of the house blew out with such a force that the load-bearing walls in the house collapsed, crushing anyone who might have survived the explosion. Langer had only moved a few feet before the force of the blast ripped his arms and legs from his body. Death was more merciful than he had deserved.

Chapter 58

Susan Bishop sat in her spacious new office overlooking downtown Denver. She still couldn't get used to the feel of the place. It took a lot of hard work for her to move up to the top position in the DA's office. She knew that if it had been left to the voters, the good old boy politicians probably would have never allowed it. She wasn't a team player, and they all knew it.

The only reason she was sitting here was a big favor she had done for the present governor of Colorado. He wasn't able to get critical support from the working-class voters in the southern part of the state. She had stepped in and convinced them that he was the best man for the job. He asked her what she wanted in return for her help, and she had refused anything, stating that someday she might need a favor.

The current district attorney was forced to step down because of bribes he had taken from some of the local mobsters. The governor knew that as soon as he asked for the DA's resignation, he would get a call from Susan. She gave him one day. He hated to assign her the spot, but he was afraid that she might have collected too much dirt on him. Thankfully, she was now off his back and would happily stay that way because she had the job she had coveted for the past ten years.

One of her negotiating terms was that she could select her own personal task force. She summoned all three to her office for a meeting about the explosion that had just occurred. While waiting for their arrival, she thought about what a strange mix they were.

Thirty-seven-year-old Victor Kemples was originally part of the Denver CSI team and a young hot-dog detective. He was strong as an ox, and looked like a professional model. The women loved him, but he loved his job more. That's why Susan liked him so much. He was like her personal pit bull.

Forty-one-year-old Lynda Sanders was the best background researcher around. If someone was trying to hide information from the police, she could find it. As a black policewoman, she had a tough time working her way up through the police department. Her solution was to be the best there was at her job. Susan had known Lynda ever since she had graduated from the Police Academy, and knew she eventually wanted this woman to work for her.

If there was ever a person destined to characterize a computer geek, then forty-six-year-old Ken Maples fit the bill. He was overweight, out of shape, and poorly dressed, making him the least desirable member of most police investigations— that is until they needed someone to hack, decipher, or trace a web connection. He was the best hacker around, and Susan had found him in the basement of a police department on the south side of the city.

Once the three had been seated, Susan closed the blinds and locked the door to her office. The members of the task force seemed unaffected by this unusual action.

Susan sat down at her desk. "I want to welcome the three of you to my special task force. Here's how the task force works. We work only one case at a time, and I select the case. The rest of the cases are handled by other departments. I was nominated by the governor for this job and do not have to report to anyone in the department.

"I have several rules by which you must abide. Break any of them and you are out. The first rule is that nothing leaves this task force. You talk to no one but each other and me. I don't care what anyone says, you only report to me.

"The second rule is that everything we do must be aboveboard. There will be no bending the legal boundaries.

"The third rule is that there are no set working hours. You work when you want; I just demand that you get the job done."

"The fourth and most important rule is that at no time will you ever lie to me. Break that rule, and I will make sure you never work in any police department again. Before I get into the case, are there any questions?"

Victor seemed about to say something, but then he just took another sip of coffee. A groan escaped from Ken and Susan smiled. They were going to be a perfect team.

"This is a very high-profile case with plenty of political connections, so I need to lay down some ground rules. We have to be extremely paranoid and protective about what we are doing. This means that we will use throwaway phones, new email addresses outside the police department, and encryption software for all our electronic reports. We cannot trust anyone except those of us in this room."

Susan stole a glance at her team before continuing. "Ken, are you able to set us all up with encryption software that has a personal security key that will fit on a thumb drive? I want it set up with a password that when incorrectly entered will destroy the data on the thumb drive."

Ken had not expected to be called upon and almost spilled his cup of coffee. "Not a problem. I'll have it set up by late this afternoon."

"Good, now to the case. Yesterday afternoon there was a gas explosion on the south side of town. Three people were killed in the blast. Now that may not sound like a big deal, but there's more. The woman who owned the house was Wendy Marshall. If that name doesn't sound familiar, she was the secretary to Kathy Robinson, who was the woman whom Curt Towers supposedly murdered. She wasn't directly killed by the blast because a bullet passed through her heart before the explosion took place."

Continuing on she said, "The second victim was one of our own, a police detective by the name of Lloyd Becker. The last case he worked on was about Curt Towers. He was shot by the same gun, but the gas explosion was what finished him off."

She paused before saying, "Now I get to the good part. The third victim was Ross Langer, Alex Brandon's right-hand man. We have information that many of the activities he supervised may have been illegal."

There was brief mumbling among the team members.

Susan raised a hand to quiet the group. "For those of you not familiar with the Curt Towers case, he was convicted of killing an employee. Alex Brandon was a direct competitor to Curt Towers and recently married Curt's wife, Cindy. The bottom line is that everyone killed in that explosion had a first-hand link to Curt Towers."

She glanced around to see their reactions. "Now, I really never believed there was such a thing as a perfect case. Everyone claimed the Towers case was a slam-dunk; a DA's dream comes true. The problem was that Curt Towers was a very smart man, and yet all the evidence pointed to a very stupid criminal. I think it was a frame, and that maybe everything came to a head in that house explosion."

She paused to let her comments be absorbed. "So, from this day forward the three of you will live, eat, and breathe Curt Allen Towers. I don't care if he is dead; I want an end to this case. There are too many loose ends, especially with yesterday's events. Over in the corner is everything I could find on Curt's case. Go through it with a fine-toothed comb, then go back out on the streets and do what you three do best. Find me the truth, and I don't care how it plays out. Close this case once and for all."

The three got up and introduced themselves to each other. Lynda told them she would look through all the boxes, and the other two should start working the case from the start. Victor looked at the list of people still working at Curt's company, wrote down a few names, and left. Ken made a few calls to electronic shops and was out the door. Fifteen minutes later Lynda moved all the boxes into her office.

Susan was now alone, and she wanted to scream with excitement. This was one of the best days of her life.

Today was one of the worst days in Alex Brandon's life. He felt he had lost a member of his family. He wasn't informed about Ross Langer's death until early in the morning. He had turned off his phone last night so that he could take a few hours off at his country home.

He didn't realize just how much he depended on Langer. He had been his confidant, and now there was no one he could really trust. He was so lost, and it scared the hell out of him.

Cindy had called him several times at the office, and his secretary made up excuses for him since he just couldn't talk to her right now.

He wasn't even sure who was second in command under Langer. He would have to hope that whoever replaced him was someone equally evil. He sat back in his chair and put a call into Langer's office.

Chapter 59

Curt turned off the valve to the two tanks against the wall. He had already filled a dozen tanks from dives on the previous day, and he still had four to go. They were pretty beat up, but then so was most of the equipment in the store. He had to admit that he'd never seen a worse dive shop.

When he first hit the mainland, he found that most of the dive shops along the Cancun coast ran thorough background checks on new employees. He knew he would never pass. He asked around and found several shops inland that specialized in diving the cenotes. The cenotes were a vast system of freshwater caves that went for miles underground, many of them connecting to the ocean.

He found a shop where the owner, Greg Wong, never checked his employees' backgrounds. He told people all he needed was his gut to determine if a person was good or not. At first, Bill, as Curt was now known, filled tanks and swept floors, but when Greg found out that he could fix almost everything, he started piling up dive gear to repair.

It wasn't long before Greg started training Curt to lead scuba diving groups into the cenotes. Normally, the training period took a lot longer, but Wong desperately needed help, and Curt's previous experience was enough to convince Wong that he was capable.

The two main caves that Wong's dive shop used were less than two miles from the shop. They were located on private land and required a payment for each dive made inside the caves. The top hole surrounding each cave was too high to jump from for most beginner divers. Wong had found a much smaller entrance that approached each large cave from the side. A small ladder and pulley system for the equipment was rigged to make cave entry easier. A platform at the base of the ladder allowed enough space for two divers to put on their gear and jump into the water.

The caves had more than a dozen underwater outlets. Three were suitable for beginners, five for average divers, and a couple for advanced cave divers. Wong told Curt that under no circumstances should he take any customers into the advanced section of the cave. Two divers had been lost in them the year before, and Wong didn't want a repeat of that event.

The shop was particularly busy this morning. Three college jocks stopped by to schedule an afternoon dive. Wong decided that Bill would be the one to lead this excited group on a tour of the cenotes.

The trip to the underground caves took about twenty minutes, and then another thirty transporting the gear to the cave entrance access. The fellows were antsy to get diving and kept pushing Curt to hurry. He knew this wasn't going to be a good day.

The three argued who was going down the ladder first, and finally, Curt took the lead. He geared up, jumped into the water, inflated his BC, and waited as the next two geared up. Neither of the two divers did a safety check of each other's gear; instead, they were suited and in the water in minutes. The first started to choke and tried to reach back to the tank's valve and turn on his air. Curt swam over and turned it on for him. The third member turned on his air supply, then put on the rest of his gear, and joined the group in the water.

The largest fellow in the group was about to descend when Curt got their attention. "I know the three of you are anxious to get underwater, but we have to go over the rules one more time. There are signs at the three entrances we're allowed to enter. You fellows have never been cave diving before, so you will be restricted to those three rated as level one. Do not enter any other level cave and make sure we all stay together. Remember to watch your fin movement because it's easy to kick

229

up sediment, which reduces our visibility. We also turn around when the first person's air supply registers 1500psi. Is everyone ready?"

Two nodded, and the third yelled, "No problem, Bill," but Curt knew that they couldn't care less about what he had to say. At first, they stayed behind him as he started through the first cave. When they reached the end of the cave, one of them handed him an underwater camera. He wrote on his slate that they wanted a picture together. Curt took the camera and took several shots. He started to relax. Maybe they weren't going to be a problem after all.

As they approached the second cave entrance, Curt looked back to check and found only two were in view. He held up three fingers to the other two and gave them a "where is he" look. They both pointed to a level three cave entrance. Curt cussed to himself, motioned for them to stay, and took off as fast as he could. A few minutes later, he found the group leader in a panic, lost in a cave off the main entrance. The kid raced toward him and used the hand signal for exit. Curt motioned for him to calm down, and the two slowly swam back out of the cave.

Before long, all four divers surfaced. The other two stripped down their gear, tied it off to a rope, and climbed up the ladder. As Curt and the wayward diver sat on the platform taking off their gear, the jock kept yelling at him.

"This is one of the worst dives I've ever had. I can't believe you charge money to dive in that hole. I would never recommend it to anyone."

Curt knew that he was walking a fine line, since Wong was one of those people who believed that the customer was always right. "I'm sorry you didn't like the dive. I told you not to go into the level three caves. They are reserved for more advanced divers."

The jock said nothing, and jerked his way up the ladder. They loaded the gear into the truck, and not a single word was uttered on the ride back. Back at the shop, the three jumped out of the truck and headed toward the front door of the shop. Curt schlepped the gear to the back of the shop and waited for them to leave.

Ten minutes later, Wong came to see what had really happened. "Well, Bill, that was a total bust. What a bunch of jerks. I had to refund their money. Two of them would have paid, but it seems the gigantic one has a father who's a big-time lawyer. I just couldn't take a chance on a lawsuit. I don't have any qualms with you, because I could tell by the looks on their faces that you did your best."

Wong thought for a moment and then continued. "In a way, I understand why they were upset. The two caves we dive are some of the worst dives in the area. Before there were any regulations for scuba diving in a cenote, divers did plenty of damage to the formations."

He reached over, put his hand on Bill's shoulder, and said, "I've a new plan I've been putting off for more than a year, but now it's time. I have a relative who lives about thirty miles from here who told me about a cenote that no one ever dives. Take a few tanks and go check it out. If it's as good as I heard, we could sell this place and set up a new shop close by. I'll handle the customers here for the next few days. Take a week or even more if you need, just find me a new cave. Even if it doesn't pan out, I think I'll sell anyway and go find something else to do with the rest of my life."

Curt started to fill the four used tanks. "I'm sorry it didn't work out today. I could have killed that kid, but he almost killed himself in that cave. I would be glad to go search for a new cave. I'll pack up this afternoon and leave tomorrow. I'll take that old beat up truck, if you don't mind. It took a bit for me to get it working again, but it should get me there and back. I'll try to call in from the local market or gas station every other day. Does that sound all right?"

Wong nodded and headed into the office.

Even though the noisy air compressor was running, Curt's mind was lost in thought. He missed his friends, his kids, and even his wife, although she had married the man who framed him. He pushed those thoughts aside and concentrated on the fact that he was heading off on a new adventure.

Chapter 60

Alex paced back and forth in his office. He'd called Langer's office several times and always got a secretary who said that the second-in-command was in the field. He finally got a response from Deric Osterland, who said he was Langer's right-hand man. The message was short, but it indicated that Osterland would be there by 11 a.m.

At 10:59, Alex's secretary beeped him that Osterland had arrived. The door opened and a very tall, muscular man walked into the room. Osterland had to be at least six to eight inches taller than Alex, which he found very intimidating. Alex deduced from Osterland's firm grip that this was a man not to be crossed.

Osterland set his briefcase on the floor and sat in the chair opposite Alex. "I apologize for not getting back to you earlier, but I was investigating Langer's death. I wanted to make sure there were no leaks in our organization. Langer knew there was always the possibility of not returning from an assignment. We devised a contingency plan, and now it's in place."

He looked Alex directly in the eye and continued. "Langer kept a personal encrypted file that didn't come into play until his death. He kept it with a very well paid lawyer. I have reviewed the file, and I'm up to speed on the Curt Towers thing. It looks like we may not be done with Towers, even though it appears he's dead."

"So you know everything that Langer knew?"

"Yes, he was like a brother. You can trust me completely, Sir. Just tell me what you want me to do."

Alex seemed relieved. This man appeared to be as ruthless as Langer was. Maybe he could get to like this fellow.

Alex knew that if Osterland was on the payroll, he had been checked out and approved by his private security firm.

Nevertheless, he hesitated and his intuition told him to hold back. The problem was that Alex was desperate; he needed to trust someone. He reached down and opened a safe on the floor. He pulled out a stack of folders and handed them over to Osterland.

"Here is everything I have on the Curt Towers case. Make sure this is for your eyes only. Keep it in a safe place. Once you have read everything, bring it back to me. I will then destroy it all, and we can get past this Towers business."

Osterland surprised Alex with the next statement. "How is the merger going between your company and Xtreme Machines?"

Alex was starting to get a pain in his gut again. This fellow seemed more intelligent than Langer did. He just wasn't sure if that was a good thing or not. "The merger will be completed by the weekend. We will be the largest supplier of miniature weapon devices to the military. Stock has already gone up 50% in the past few days."

Osterland smiled for the first time. "I know. I bought over 5,000 shares last week. Langer told me it would be a nice retirement. So, you can see I have a lot to gain by making sure everything runs smoothly from now on."

A call came into Alex's private phone. It was Cindy. He couldn't put her off anymore. He waved Osterland off, and then took the call. Cindy was asking too many questions that could spoil the merger. He needed to go home and settle her down. He told her that he was going to be home for the rest of the week, so they could spend some time together. He sensed her mood change, and Alex smiled as he hung up. He whispered to himself a single word repeatedly - Billions.

Chapter 61

Denver's new district attorney, Susan Bishop, sat at her desk reviewing the decrypted files from Lynda. It was amazing how much that woman had put together in just a few days. Lynda had organized everything in chronological order from the day that the murder occurred up to the day of the explosion. Sure, there were a few holes with gaps, but they were filling in quickly. The evidence was starting to point to a corporate conspiracy, with Alex Brandon heading the list. The problem was that they had no concrete proof, at least so far.

Ken had presented her a brief report saying that he was working through some of the phone and computer records of the three killed in the blast.

Susan had not seen Victor since the first meeting, and thought that quite strange. There was one encrypted message stating that he was following a strong lead, but nothing since. She would give him a few more days before applying pressure for results. Susan had learned that good help was hard to find, so you don't screw with those you trust.

Several thousand miles to the south, Curt was using a machete to hack his way through some very thick brush. Wong's cousin had given him approximate directions to the new underground cave, so he had taken his backpack and survival gear deep into the jungle. So far, he did not see anything remotely resembling a cenote.

His chest cough had returned with a vengeance, and he found himself stopping every fifteen minutes to catch his breath and drink some water. If he didn't improve, he was going to have to return to Wong's cousin because he was getting weaker by the moment.

Earlier, that morning he passed a small Mexican village in the jungle. When he heard the children playing, he veered around the edge of the village. He didn't need any more trouble than he'd seen over the last few months. Besides, he was really starting to feel very ill and didn't want to infect anyone.

By early evening, Curt made camp in a small clearing. He set up a tent with netting and rolled out a sleeping bag. In less than ten minutes, he was out from pure exhaustion and from fighting the chest cough, which was now tearing him apart. He decided that the next morning he would head back to the truck because he was too sick to continue.

During the night, Curt's fever increased and he alternated between chills and fever. He woke to find his shirt soaked with sweat and he felt just miserable. He started to consider the possibility that he might not make it back to the truck.

Chapter 62

Curt Allen Towers was in big trouble. The time he had spent in the ferry bilge was catching up with him. He spent the night fading in and out of consciousness. His dreams were intense. At first light, he attempted to get up, but collapsed on his sleeping bag each time. He knew he might die here if he didn't make an effort to get back to civilization.

After several tries using a large branch that had been meant for firewood, he was finally able to get on his feet. He tried to pick up his backpack, but knew that if he fell down, he might not get back up. Instead, he grabbed the one bottle of water he had left and started to drag himself toward the truck.

A hundred feet later, fever and chills returned and down he went. He waited for thirty minutes, and then inched his way up the trunk of a tree to stand again. He took a sip of water and instantly threw it up. His throat was very raw, and his head was burning up. He stumbled another twenty-five feet, and gave in to the microscopic virus that had invaded his body. He looked down at his watch and saw it was 11 a.m. He was still in sight of his own camp. He wasn't going to make it.

Late in the evening, Curt woke to find swarms of insects trying to get a free meal from his skin. He tried to swat them, but it didn't help. He thought he heard a dog howl, but suspected he was hallucinating. This was the end of Curt Allen Towers, and no one would ever know what had happened to him. He rolled over on his back, looked up at the sky, and watched the bright stars twinkle.

"God, what have I done to deserve all this? I tried to live a good life. Why is this happening to me? If you are truly merciful, please take me now and end my misery. I beg you to

237

please watch over my family."

Then a strange feeling came over him. It was the same sensation that had drawn him to this God-awful place, but why did he come? His eyes closed, and the stars disappeared. Curt's destiny was now in other hands.

Chapter 63

Curt slowly opened his eyes and tried to focus on the room around him. He was on a narrow military cot next to a table that held several books. He tried to read the book titles, but his eyes blurred. His clothes were soaked with his perspiration, and a wet towel drooped over his forehead.

He could hear children laughing and dogs barking in the distance. His throat was raw from coughing his guts out. His head was pounding with the headache of the century. His vision started to clear, and he could read the titles on the book bindings. They were veterinary books on goats, sheep, horses, dogs, and just about every other animal.

He rolled over on his back and looked up at the ceiling. The room was primitive, with cracks in the ceiling and an old lamp cord hanging down to provide light. That strange feeling that had drawn him to the cenotes was back again.

Out of the corner of his eye, he spotted a group of pictures on the wall next to the bed. They were of a white woman with several villagers. There were other pictures of the same woman with a horse, a goat, and other animals. She looked a bit familiar, but he must be imagining things.

Then he saw an edge of an older picture stuck behind the new ones. He reached up and pulled it out. The shock was almost more than he could handle. Tears sprang to his eyes, and he could no longer see. The picture was of five baby squirrels sitting in Bonnie Sellers' lap. His life had come full circle. He now understood what force was drawing him here – it was Bonnie. For the first time in weeks, he felt at ease. He knew he was safe, and he fell back into a peaceful sleep.

Three hours later, sounds brought Curt back to the land of the living. This time when he opened his eyes, Bonnie Sellers smiled down at him. "You gave us a hell of a scare, but I think you're through the worst of it. I'm not sure what you had, but it was the worst bug I've seen. I tried every type of drug I could find, and finally, a new super dose of penicillin seemed to work. Do me a favor - your throat is very raw, don't talk, and just relax."

He nodded and then she continued. "No one here knows who you are except me. I trust everyone in the village, so rest assured you are safe. By the way, you still owe me for taking care of those squirrels."

Curt was about to say something, but Bonnie put a finger to his lips. She reached down and handed Curt a pad of paper and a pencil. He took them both and set them on his lap. He sat back and took a prolonged look at Bonnie. She was the best-looking woman he had seen in a very long time, even with the rubber boots, dirty jeans, torn shirt, and unkempt hair. She was gorgeous. He wrote his first message: *Thank you.*

"You're very welcome, Curt. I couldn't believe it when the kids told me that one of the dogs found you in the jungle. At first, I just thought a local drunk had lost his way home, but when I saw you, I was in shock, just as you are now."

She stared in his eyes and said, "All the years we've been apart haven't changed the way I feel about you. I never believed you killed that woman. You couldn't even stand to see a squirrel killed. I know you were framed. I heard you died several times, but you keep showing up again."

Bonnie picked up a cup of water and handed it to Curt. "Curt, I have to tell you that you told some bizarre stories when you were delirious. I'm assuming that Buck and Henry were good friends of yours. I checked the internet in town and located their dive shop. They're still in business, and they sound like folks who should know that you're alive and well. Should I contact them?"

Curt took the pad and wrote another message. *"We can in a few days. I need to make sure it's safe."*

"I understand, Curt. Get some rest and we'll talk more

tonight. Make sure you remain quiet. You talked so much while you were delirious that you made your throat even worse. Just use the pad and paper for a few days."

The smile on her face was wondrous. He wondered if he was in heaven, and she was an angel. He took a sip of water, and fell back on the pillow. In seconds, he was in dreamland again.

Alex Brandon was starting to get nervous again. He had heard nothing from Osterland and was about to call his office. As he picked up the phone, his secretary buzzed and told him that Osterland was in the outer office. He sat back in his chair, trying to look as though the whole thing with Curt wasn't bothering him.

Osterland entered with a briefcase in hand and sat down. "Sorry I didn't get back to you sooner, but I was tracking down several leads on the gas explosion, and I ran into a snag."

Osterland opened his briefcase and took out a stack of folders. "Here are your papers back," he said. He then took out an additional folder and opened it to share with Alex.

"While I was snooping around on the gas explosion, I contacted one of my associates in the police department. He told me that a special task force had formed to investigate the explosion and to review the Curt Towers case. You're the number-one subject in their case. They've put together quite a bit of material that connects you to the murder and the frame job. It doesn't look good. I would expect they'll be knocking on your door soon."

Alex sucked in a short breath. This was not what he had expected. He had been on the offensive and now all of a sudden he was on the defensive. He had to do something to change things.

"So, how many people are in this task force and who knows what they're doing?"

Osterland looked down at his report, and then back up to

Alex. "Well, that's the good news. They wanted to keep the investigation restricted to the task force. My person inside the force only found out by overhearing a conversation. Including the DA, there are four team members. So far, they seem to be the only people putting together the pieces. The rest of the department is wrapped up in a dozen other investigations."

Osterland hesitated before continuing. "If I might suggest, I can fix the problem by cutting off the head, so to speak. The DA can have a fatal accident, and the rest of the team will probably be reassigned. The Towers case is old business, so with the DA gone, so should the problem."

Alex was impressed. He was going to make a similar suggestion, but Osterland had already beaten him to the draw. He was beginning to like this new fellow better by the minute.

"All right, I agree, but make sure that it doesn't smell like a hit. You know, make it an auto accident, or an interrupted home invasion. You can be creative, just make sure it doesn't look like an out-and-out hit."

"Not a problem, Mr. Brandon. It may take a few days to set up, but she isn't going to be a problem for you much longer."

Osterland closed his briefcase, shook Alex's hand, and left as quickly as he came in. Alex looked out the window. He was getting really tired of this Towers problem. Maybe Osterland could put the final nail in Curt's coffin.

Chapter 64

Curt woke with a start. His throat was still raw. He looked over to the side of his cot. There holding his hand was Bonnie. She smiled and put her finger up to her lips.

"Remember, no talking. Your throat is doing much better. Maybe tomorrow you can talk. Right now, you need a lot of rest. Is there anything I can get you?"

Curt picked up the pad of paper and started to write. "*How long have I been here?*"

Bonnie took the paper and read the short message. "We found you almost a week ago. It's been touch and go. I swear; you almost died a couple of times. You know you really do have nine lives. Either that or you're like a computer game, where you die and then come back to play again."

He grinned and then she smiled and said, "It's so good to see you feeling better. I don't know what I would have done if you'd died. You put a real scare in me."

Curt looked puzzled.

Bonnie blushed. "You still don't get it, do you? I've always had a thing for you. It tore me apart when you didn't have the same feelings for me. I got over it, but I still care very much about you. There, it's all out now. I've been holding that inside me all these years. Now just forget I said anything."

Bonnie got up with tears in her eyes and started to leave. Curt took her hand and pulled her back to her chair. He started to write another note, and handed it to her. "*Bonnie, I'm so sorry. When I get well, maybe we can start over. I would like to get to know you better. Please don't leave me. I feel so good with you here.*"

Bonnie smiled, leaned over, and kissed Curt on the cheek.

"I'll be back later this morning. I have a few four-legged

patients that need my attention. I'll bring you some lunch, but until then you can read the newspapers that are on the floor next to your bed. You may find them quite interesting."

Curt took a deep breath. He still felt bad physically, but his mental status had picked up when he found Bonnie. He picked up the newspaper dated a few days ago and started reading. The headline was about a new problem with Congress, but a story at the bottom of the page struck him like a hot iron. Three people had died in an explosion in a Denver house, and Lloyd Becker was one of them. The second name he knew right away was Kathy's secretary. The third he also knew from his dealings with Alex. All three people were connected in one way or another to him. The strangest part of the article was that the writer hadn't made the connection. Either Alex was controlling the situation, or he had bought someone off.

Bonnie returned with lunch, but she was covered in blood and some kind of slime. Curt started to get a worried look on his face, but Bonnie stopped him from talking.

"It's not my blood. I had to deliver a calf this morning, and it didn't go well. Now do me a favor and turn your head. I have to change and take a shower. No peeking."

Curt smiled and put the newspaper in front of his face and then quickly pulled it down again. Without saying a word, Bonnie stared at Curt as a mother would stare at a misbehaving child. He finally got the message and rolled over to the wall.

A few minutes later Bonnie said, "Okay, you can roll over. I'm decent now."

Curt grinned, wrote a note and handed it to her. *"I'm sure you looked more than decent a few minutes ago."*

Bonnie blushed and wadded up the paper. Before she could say any more, Curt picked up several sheets he had written while Bonnie was delivering the calf.

She took the sheets and started to read. *"I read the newspapers while you were gone. The article on the front page about the gas explosion relates to me. Lloyd Becker was a good friend of mine. He, Henry, and Buck helped me in Baja. I owe the three of them; they saved my life, just as you have. I really need to contact Buck and Henry. They need to know I'm alive and that Lloyd isn't. They may still be monitored by those who tried to kill me, so we have to be very careful."*

She glanced up at him before continuing to read. *"We devised a backup plan for contacting each other. Buck and I set up an email drop at Hotmail. If we needed to contact each other, we would send a one-word message. If I was OK, the one word would be 'Digger'. If it was safe to respond, they would send a second message: 'Digger is a Dog'. I would then send a coded message with Longitude, and Latitude coordinates."*

Bonnie read the message twice before she gave it back to Curt.

"Who is trying to kill you?"

Curt looked down at the newspapers on the bed. He knew she would ask that question, and he really wasn't ready to answer. He looked up at her.

"I really need to know who's trying to kill you."

He painstakingly picked up the tablet, wrote one word, and handed the paper to her.

She looked in his eyes, and saw the anguish. What could be so terrible? She found out when she opened the paper, and it read *"Alex."*

"Alex. No, it can't be. Are you sure?"

Curt already started to write a new note.

She picked it up and read. *"Yes, I'm sure. So were Lloyd, Henry, and Buck. I think that's why Lloyd was killed. That's why you must send the email."*

Tears began to form in her eyes again. She got up and left the room without saying another word. Curt hated having to tell her. She didn't know the whole story between himself and Alex, but that was a long story for another day.

Susan Bishop had a busy day working with Lynda, going over her research on the Curt Towers case. It was starting to come together, but one thing still bothered her. She hadn't heard back from Victor, and she was getting worried. This wasn't like him.

She packed up her briefcase, locked her office door, and headed down to the parking garage. She was one of the last to leave from the day shift, and the garage was almost empty. It was a bit eerie, but she had her gun, and was a proficient shot. She set her briefcase down, took out her keys, and started to open the car door. Before she knew what had happened, a hand covered her mouth, and she was pulled back into the darkness.

Chapter 65

Curt woke with a start. Several kids were looking in the door to his room, giggling and pointing at him. Then suddenly they took off running, as Bonnie came through the door with a smile on her face.

"Curt, I'm sorry I left so abruptly yesterday. It was such a shock hearing about Alex in that way. It took me some time to wrap my head around the whole idea. It's so hard for me to believe that he's trying to kill you. I know he married your wife; does that have any bearing?"

Curt started to write and then stopped. He could talk if it was in a whisper, and he took breaks in between.

"It took me a long time to believe it was possible, but all the evidence points that way. The problem is he has everything and everyone on his side. That is, except you and the three musketeers with me in Baja. Sadly, there are now just two. We need to discuss some things. Henry and Buck are first on the agenda, and then I'll tell you about Alex."

Bonnie handed Curt a drink before she answered. "You need to take it easy talking. I know you're feeling a lot better, and that's great, but don't overdo it. Go slowly; we have all the time in the world. I did as you said and sent the email and got a response right away, and decoded it as you explained. They're closing the shop as we speak and will be here tomorrow. So, now tell me about Alex."

Curt pushed himself up against the wall and took a deep breath. "Okay, here goes. After high school, Alex and I went our separate ways. He went to MIT, and I went to Cal Tech. He had lots of family money and was handed a company as soon as he graduated. I had to work my way up the hard way, but had the support of several large corporations who encouraged me to form my own company."

He took a sip of the water and rested a second before telling her more. "Unfortunately, Alex and I ended up going after the same clients, many of them military contracts. The bottom line is that Alex would do anything to get a new client. On the other hand, I was very naïve about business, and told my clients the truth. I paid dearly for it for the first few years of business, but slowly gained the respect of some of Alex's clients. Several dumped Alex and moved their business to me. I never asked them to move over; they did it on their own."

He gathered his courage to continue. "The last customer Alex lost to me put us into an industrial war. The client had doubts about the specifications Alex had quoted, so they came to see one of my engineers. Now keep in mind that my honesty philosophy is passed down to my employees. The truth is how we do business; no bullshit."

Without even taking a breath he said, "I would have never approved my engineer talking to Alex's client, but the engineer was trying to make an impression. He said the specs were bogus, and then proceeded to prove it beyond a doubt. The client canceled his contract with Alex and moved a seventy-five-million-dollar contract over to us."

He gave her a minute to realize the scope of the problem. "Since then it has been an out-and-out war. Alex would do anything to discredit me. I just had no idea that he would go this far."

Bonnie looked toward the door and saw the faces of the kids poking in. She got up, said something, and closed the door.

As she walked back, she said, "I admit I really never knew what happened to Alex after high school. However, I kept track of you. My heart was broken when I heard you got married. I was happy for you and yet angry at the same time, but that's water under the bridge."

She sat back down in the chair. "I'm so sorry about you

and Alex, but you're safe now in Mexico. No one ever comes near this village, because we're so isolated. Besides, from what you tell me, you covered your tracks well. Sorry to hear about Lloyd, but I'm looking forward to meeting your friends Buck and Henry. They sound like a couple of really nice old guys."

Curt looked up at Bonnie and then down. He was having trouble getting to the next part. He looked back up at her puzzled face. "Bonnie, I'm so sorry about the way I ignored you. I was young and stupid; you know how boys are at that age. You've always been such a good friend. So...uh...are you married?" He was nervous about what her answer would be.

"I married another vet, but he found something younger and richer a few years later. It just never took. Since then I put my heart and soul into helping animals. A few years ago, I started to come down here a few weeks at a time to help the locals with their animals. Eventually, it became months at a time, and then two years ago, I moved here permanently. I have to renew my work visa every few months, but the local authorities are happy to help keep me here."

She hesitated shortly before continuing. "They need so much help, and there is very little money inland. Most of the wealth is along the coast, where the rich and famous go to get away from it all. I love it here, and now it just got a whole lot better."

She smiled as she got up to leave the room. "Curt, you rest and we'll talk later. We still have a lot more catching up to do."

Chapter 66

Lynda arrived at the office early wanting to update her boss. Susan hadn't come in the day before and that worried her. There wasn't any scheduled meeting or any known reasons to explain her absence.

She walked by Ken's office and saw he was working on some new computer encryption. She was about to talk with him, when her phone rang. It was Victor.

"Lynda, listen carefully. We have a big problem. I'm down here in the morgue. I don't know how to tell you this, but they found Susan's body dumped in the brush a few miles from here. It looks like she was abducted from the parking garage and killed nearby. We don't know who did it yet, but I have my suspicions. Pack up everything you and Ken have on the case. We need to move to a safe house. I think we're all in danger. Move fast and don't say a word to anyone."

The look on Lynda's face was pure fear. She had never been close to the violent part of her job. The closest she would get was always on paper, but now she might be in danger. First, there was the gas explosion killing three people connected to Curt, and now her boss. This was very bad. She walked over to Ken's office, whispered a few words, and headed back to her office, panic-stricken.

Alex sat in his office watching the local news report that said the new DA had been murdered. He had told Osterland it was supposed to look like an accident, but this looked like a hit. He was nervous and on edge. He broke a pencil in half when his office intercom rang. It was Osterland. Alex started to go to the door, but instead Osterland hurried in, this time without his trusty briefcase.

"I know what you're going to say, Mr. Brandon, but it couldn't be helped. She put up a fight, and there was no way I could make it look like an accident. She isn't the biggest problem we have right now. Her task force disappeared this morning with all the case information. I'm assuming that they're holed up in a safe house, but I have several men looking for them. When they find them, they'll become missing persons. The bottom line is that I have it covered. You have nothing to worry about. I'll get back to you, as soon as I hear something."

Alex was impressed, even though he still wasn't happy about the hit on the DA. Osterland seemed very good at his job, fixing any problems that arose. "I understand about the DA, even though I'm disappointed. Those other three must never be found. They need a trip to the bottom of a very deep lake or ocean, with plenty of ankle weight. Do I make myself clear?"

"Not a problem, Mr. Brandon. Consider it done."

Buck and Henry spent most of the previous day winding things down at the shop. They hired a young Mexican named Joel, who seemed to have good business sense. They put him in command of the dive shop saying they were going on a much-needed vacation to visit friends in Santa Barbara for a few weeks. They purchased a throwaway phone and gave him the number, but told him not to tell anyone else.

When they were sure that Joel had everything straight, they headed north in a rental car. A hundred miles later, they traded the car in for a second and then doubled back. They took several side roads and kept checking to see if anyone was following them, but couldn't see anyone. It looked as though they were in the clear.

It was mid-afternoon when Bonnie finally returned from her rounds. She had to take care of sick goats several miles away, but had one of the village women make sure Curt had food and water while she was gone. Curt was about to re-read the same newspaper for the tenth time when Bonnie opened the door. He could tell it had been a difficult day for her. She looked as if she'd been rolling around in a barnyard. She smiled and started to take off her shoes.

"You know the drill. These quarters are very small, so privacy is difficult. I need a shower, and would appreciate your looking at the pictures on the wall again."

Curt laughed and put the newspaper down. "Hey, you might look a little rough on the edges right now, but you still look pretty good to me. Besides, I've seen you naked before."

Bonnie took a second to scan her memories to recollect what he was talking about, and then it came to her in a flashback -- the swimming hole. "Hey, Curt, we were kids. It wasn't my idea to go skinny-dipping, and if you remember, you didn't want to either. It took Alex calling us chickens to get us to strip down and jump in. Besides, at that age there wasn't much to look at."

Curt knew she had opened the door for a little fun. She needed some cheering up. "So who are you saying had nothing worth looking at? I saw plenty when you stripped down, so you must have meant me."

Bonnie was blushing again. "No, I didn't mean you. I was talking about myself. I was so concerned about how I looked, that I don't really remember looking at you."

"Really, you didn't look at all?"

"Well, uh, maybe some. You're changing the subject. Turn around so that I can undress and shower. No peeking."

Lynda and Ken safely reached the new headquarters set up by Victor. He told them that the normal safe houses might not be secure anymore, so this was a rental from a real estate agent friend.

The two sat watching the TV news coverage of the murder of their boss, and waited for Victor to return. Two hours later, they started to get concerned. Lynda was about to call Victor on the burn phone, when a car drove up. Ken carefully looked out the window to see that it was Victor. Victor took a large cardboard box from the car, and they met him at the front door.

"Well, guys, this is it. You were sure you weren't followed?"

Both answered with a defiant, "We're sure."

Victor said, "We have an additional directive from our new boss who'll be here later tonight. I can't tell you who it is yet, but that doesn't matter right now. Ken, I want you to set up here and begin working your computer magic. There are still a few projects to work on before our new boss arrives. I know you both liked Susan and so did I, but she would want us to find her killer, and that's what we're going to do. In addition, we're still on task with the Towers case, so we have a lot of work to do."

Bonnie left right after her shower and spent the rest of the afternoon taking care of chores around the village. By 7 p.m. Curt was wondering where she'd gone and was missing her. When the door finally did open, two local men were with her. One had a handmade crutch and the other carried a basket. The men set their loads down and walked over to Curt. Bonnie directed them to help Curt out of bed.

"Curt, it's time for you to take a trip outside. It's still light, and I want to show you something. That is, if you can support yourself using this crutch."

Curt grabbed the crutch and found it was perfect in length. He was sure it had been made especially for him. When he first got up, he almost fell back on the bed. Bonnie reached out and grasped him around the chest to break his fall. Curt leaned forward and whispered in her ear. "I'll start falling over more often if you are going to be the one to catch me."

"Don't push your luck, Curt."

"Are you telling me that you won't catch me next time?"

253

"Hey, you don't have to fake a fall to hold me."

He gave her a questioning look.

Bonnie answered his look, saying, "But not right now. Can you stand on your own?"

Curt nodded, and started to walk using the crutch for stability. The two men left and Bonnie picked up the basket.

"Time we went for a walk. You need to get some fresh air, and your bed needs a change. While we're gone, the women will wash your sheets and make up the bed. We, on the other hand, will enjoy a nice evening meal."

Bonnie walked beside Curt to make sure he didn't fall again. He was doing really well with the handcrafted crutch. Fifteen minutes later, they came to the edge of a simple village carved out of the jungle. It was built using old wood, concrete blocks, or whatever else they could find as building materials. It was small, but clean, and had friendly folks, youngsters, and animals running about.

A small trail exited the village to the east. Curt was about to start down the trail when Bonnie stopped him.

"Before we go down this trail, you have to promise me that you'll never tell anyone about what I'm going to show you. Normally, this trail entrance is hidden, but I asked that it be opened for us for this evening. The villagers have trusted me with this secret, now you must do the same."

Curt looked into her serious face. "I promise. Besides, I owe you for saving my life. So what's the big secret?"

Bonnie started down the long winding trail. It was cut with a machete, but not well maintained, and looked as though no one had been down it in months. Curt struggled, but after several stops to rest, they eventually came to a large clearing. There were tall trees with long vines hanging down around the edge of a big cenote. Bonnie helped Curt go the last few feet, so he could look down into the crystal-clear water. It was one of the most pristine entrances to a cenote he had ever seen.

Once Curt was settled on a log, Bonnie opened the basket and took out a small blanket. She set down several containers of food, two plates, and silverware. The biggest surprise was when she presented a bottle of wine and two glasses.

Curt looked at her and smiled. His life completely came full circle and was good again.

"Wow, this was totally unexpected. If I didn't know any better, I would say you were trying to seduce me."

"It's just a meal. Men try to read so much into even the simplest event. I just thought you needed a change from my cramped quarters, but maybe the wine was too much."

Curt reached out his hand and held hers. "No, it's perfect, and you're a fantastic dinner companion. Thank you for this. The cenote is gorgeous and so are you."

Bonnie blushed and then looked at him seriously. "You promised not to say a word, and I'm going to hold you to it. I like you very much, but if you say anything about this place, all bets are off."

"You just like me?"

"Okay, smart guy, I love you. Are you happy now?"

"I couldn't be better. What's there to eat?"

Bonnie rolled her head in disgust. "Men, all you think about is food first, then everything else."

They both laughed and spent the next hour devouring the wonderful meal that the village women had prepared for them. Curt tried to help put everything back in the basket, but Bonnie told him to sit down and rest. Once she finished the job, she joined him on the blanket. "So, Curt, where do we go from here?"

"Are you asking for a hug?"

"Well, that would be a good start."

Curt passed on the hug and went for what he really wanted. He pulled her into his arms and kissed her so ardently that they almost rolled down the hill. When the kiss was over, they looked like teenagers who had been caught by their mothers.

Bonnie took a deep breath. "That's much better, but I have to broach a subject you may not want to talk about. If we want this relationship to continue, I have to ask you some personal questions. I know this may not be the time, but I don't want to be hurt again, and you could easily do that."

"You want to know about my ex-wife, Cindy?"

"Sorry, Curt, but yes I do. I love you. I always have, but I won't compete with anyone else for your love."

Curt caught her hand, "I knew it might be bothering you, because it bothers me, too. I loved Cindy very much and thought she loved me. I guess I didn't know her as well as I thought. I was confident that she would stick by me throughout the trial, but as it progressed, we became more distant. I was even in denial when she started to question my innocence. When the evidence started to pile up, she totally abandoned me."

He paused before continuing. "When I think about it now, I don't blame her, but I sure did then. I understand now that she was just cutting her losses, so she could save the kids. As much as I want to see my children, I know I can't. My status as a felon means that I must stay as far away from them as possible."

He stared into her face. "I guess the real knife to my heart was when I heard she had married the man who framed me. I'm sure she's in the dark about all that and was just swayed by his charm. You need to know that my marriage to Cindy was over the day she married Alex. I didn't realize how much so until I saw you again. If I could go back and do it over, things might have been different for us. I will always have good feelings for Cindy, but I know that we can never go back, so you have no worries about Cindy."

He smiled broadly and said, "Let's make a deal and start with a clean slate. We just met for the first time a few days ago and discovered we liked each other. Let's just let the cards fall where fate has planned."

Bonnie kissed him with a passion Curt had never experienced before. "One last thing," she said, "don't take any offense at what I'm going to say, but you need a shower."

He pulled back from her, as though he had the plague. "You mean I stink? Why didn't you say something earlier? I could've showered before we came."

She laughed, "I planned this picnic all day, and I really didn't want to wait. To be perfectly honest, I wanted to know your intentions before we got you into the shower. You might need some help, and I wasn't quite ready for that confrontation. Now, I think I can deal with seeing you naked again. That is, unless you think you don't need any help taking a shower."

Curt grinned. "Oh, I'm going to need help, lots of help."

"I figured that would be your answer."

When they arrived at Bonnie's cabin, she helped him with his shower and a whole lot more. The two lost souls were now joined together on a new path in life, but they were still far from being safe.

Late that night, Victor, Ken, and Lynda were busily putting together a plan for the new task that had been added to their list of duties. Victor seemed quite nervous and the other two asked him several times if everything was all right. He assured them things were okay, but they weren't confident.

There was a knock at the door, and Lynda pulled out a gun she had hidden. Victor told her to relax and put it down. He went to the door and escorted the new group leader into the room.

Ken and Lynda's jaws both dropped at the same time. Lynda was the first to recover and say what both were thinking. "My God, you have to be kidding!"

Chapter 67

A knock at Bonnie's door made her realize she overslept. She looked over to Curt and saw he was still asleep. She tried to remove the blanket on her side so that she could exit and get dressed. As she did, Curt's hand cupped and gently caressed her breast.

"Do you have to go?" he asked.

She leaned over, kissed him on the lips, and then reached under the blanket to reciprocate with a gentle squeeze. "Yes I do. I'm sure the villagers have already taken over my chores when I didn't show up this morning. They'll all be talking because you can't hide much of anything around here."

"Let them talk. I don't want to hide the fact that I'm falling in love with you."

"So, you're finally catching up with me, huh?"

She dressed quickly, and gave Curt a kiss before she hurried out the door. Outside, several of the women she knew were in a group whispering about her. This just proved that nothing is a secret around here. She didn't care what they whispered about her, because she was in love.

By mid-afternoon, Henry and Buck arrived in the village. They had taken great efforts to zigzag back and forth and backtrack, even though they were sure no one was following. They had been waiting for an hour when Bonnie showed up escorted by several strong village men. She wasn't taking any chances, which impressed the two.

As they introduced each other, Buck's burn phone rang. It was a number he hadn't seen before, with a Denver area code. Alex was in Denver. Buck was about to throw the phone away, but something in the back of his mind told him to take the call.

He clicked the talk button, and waited while Bonnie and Henry tried to figure out who was on the other end. "Am I talking to Buck or Henry?"

"Buck. Who are you?"

"Does it really matter? All you need to know is that I'm one of those who believe that Curt was framed, and we now have the proof. We know that you were friends with him and if anyone would know if he is dead or alive, we thought it might be you."

Buck hesitated. Damn, they knew who he was. Hanging up would do no good, because with all the fancy trace technology today, they probably already knew his location. He might as well find out what this person knew and why they had called. "Okay, before I continue any further, who are you, and why are you asking about Curt Towers?"

When Bonnie heard that part of the conversation, she tried to grab the phone from Buck and destroy it. He stopped her and gave her an OK sign, even though he wasn't certain that was really the case.

Buck continued, "Okay, you have my attention. Answer my questions or I'll destroy the phone, and we'll all disappear."

"My name is Victor Kemples. I work for a special task force in Denver that is investigating the Curt Towers case. We now have sufficient evidence to prove that he was framed by Alex Brandon. There is ample evidence to clear all charges. Curt no longer needs to run or hide."

Victor continued, "We also know that Alex's men have been trying to kill Curt, and the only way that is going to stop is if we can put Alex Brandon away. Many people have died by Alex's hand to protect his conspiracy. If Curt is alive, we need his help. If he isn't, we would still like to clear his name for his family and friends. We know you wouldn't readily admit it, so we need to come up with an equitable solution so you can trust us."

Buck was trying to make sense of it all. "Why should I believe you? You could be working for Alex Brandon."

"If I was working for Alex Brandon, I wouldn't bother calling you. I would just send down more hitmen to remove you all. However, I'm working for a task force that is trying to clear Curt's name and undo this injustice. Now what can we do to convince you we're the good guys?"

"Let me get back to you on that one," Buck said.

Buck turned the phone off and removed the battery. He looked over at Bonnie and Henry. "Boy, have we got a lot to talk about. It looks like we fell out of the frying pan and into the fire."

Bonnie didn't like the sound of that statement. She was just getting used to Curt being around, and now this. She was beginning to regret sending for Buck and Henry.

When the three arrived at her abode, Curt was outside on his crutch. Buck and Henry ran over and gave him a hug.

Buck was the first to question Curt. "Okay, how in the hell do you keep getting out of so many life-threatening situations? We were sure you died on the ferry crossing. There wasn't a word from you to tell us otherwise. We're your friends. Sorry, I'm doing all the talking."

Bonnie held up her hand as a teacher might do in class and took the lead.

"Before we start bringing ourselves up to date, we need to address a new problem that Buck and Henry seem to have brought with them. Buck got a call from someone in Denver. Buck, tell Curt about the conversation, and leave nothing out. We may need to make a hasty exit out of here because I'm not about to endanger this village because of my association with Curt."

Curt lost his happy face and put back on his fugitive face. This wasn't good. He listened as Buck went through the call word by word as best he could remember. When he was done, there was silence in the group.

Bonnie, who seemed to be the most rational, said, "We need to brainstorm all the facts we have so far, and then make a plan. It's obvious that someone with good information-gathering abilities has our number. As I see it, there are only two options. If this Victor is telling the truth, then it's very good news for us all. If he's lying, we're in big trouble. We first need to decide if the call was real or bogus. Once we decide, then we formulate a plan."

Curt was impressed at how Bonnie attacked the situation. She wasn't the kind of person who stood aside and let other people make decisions. He liked that. "I agree with Bonnie. We need to come up with a way to confirm the call was real. Unfortunately, I don't have a clue how, but I don't think we have a lot of time to think about it. If it is bogus, we may only have hours before we're compromised."

The four sat around and ran through scenario after scenario. After an hour of arguing over different concepts, Bonnie came up with the best solution. She would call this Victor and have him lay all his cards on the table. If she was satisfied with his answers, then they would consider whatever this task force wanted.

They grabbed a quick bite to eat and headed back to the area where the cell phone worked best. Before she could call, the phone rang, and it was Victor.

"So, have you decided to help us?"

"Not yet. We have a few more questions."

"Go ahead, Bonnie."

"How do you know who this is?"

"Bonnie, I have one of the world's best computer geeks, and an unbelievable researcher on staff. With their help, I know everything about the four of you. So, what do you want to know?"

"It's simple. I want to know exactly what you know about the Curt Towers case. How do you know who framed Curt, and how was he framed? Until we have that information, I couldn't care less about how much you think you know about us."

Then Bonnie froze. Victor said the four of them. My God, Victor has to have access to a satellite.

"Okay, Victor. You said four. Buck, Henry, and I only make three."

"I would assume that the fourth person is Curt."

With an unsure voice she said, "How are you doing this?"

"You may think Alex Brandon has all the connections. Well, it's true that he has lots of political powers, but not all of them. Curt had many friends in the military. They couldn't help him when he was on trial, but they can help now. One of them has loaned me one of their satellites. If one of you waves, then I will tell you which one."

Several seconds passed, and Victor came back on the line.

"I know it wasn't you, Bonnie, and I already know what Buck and Henry were wearing when they arrived, and so it has to be Curt."

Bonnie pulled the phone away from her ear, and covered the receiver. This was spooky and way out of her league.

"Okay, you've impressed me with all your high-tech toys. Now tell me how Curt was framed."

Bonnie handed the phone to Curt and put her fingers up to silence him, indicating that he should just listen. She wasn't ready for him to confirm he was alive yet. A few seconds went by before Victor came back on.

"Hello, Mr. Towers. It's nice to talk with you. You don't have to respond, but I can see that Bonnie handed you the phone. She seems like a nice lady. You're a lucky man that she's looking out for you."

Curt looked over to Bonnie and smiled. Victor said, "Now I hope your battery, and minutes are charged because this might take some time. Here goes. Kathy Robinson made a deal with Alex to set you up. She was paid a lot of money, but she didn't know the entire plan. If she had, she would have turned the plot in to the police and run for the hills."

He continued, "Alex had several military contacts that remained loyal to his company. One general worked on hallucinogenic drugs for military operations. He gave a small dose to Alex, who in turn gave it to Kathy to use on you. The drug is totally undetectable and while under its influence, you will unquestioningly do whatever you are told."

He gave him a minute to digest this information. "When you went to her rescue that night, she injected you using a ring with a special needle – just like in a *James Bond* movie. In minutes, you were no longer in the real world. Once you were under, Kathy undressed both of you and had the agent, posing as a photographer, take pictures of you both in compromising positions. What she didn't know was that she too was then given the same drug. The agent told you that Kathy was your wife, Cindy, and you were told to make love to your wife. Thanks to the effect of the drug, you were obliging."

"Kathy was supposed to make a police report that she was raped, and the semen samples would implicate you. Alex wasn't happy with this original plan and had the agent stab Kathy instead. The agent helped you up and put the knife in your hands. His last task was to call 911, and you know the rest."

Victor paused briefly. "You don't remember a thing because of the drug, and the police had an iron-clad case against you. Alex's conspiracy plan was to remove you, marry your wife, and take over your company. He's accomplished all that, and as far as he is concerned, he's getting away with it."

"Oh," he said, "there's one last thing before responding. There is a downside to all of this. Only Alex, his people, and my team, knows the information I have given you. Alex is trying to locate our task force as we speak. If he finds us, everything I have told you is irrelevant."

Curt was in shock. Now he knew everything. It really didn't make him feel any better, but at least some of it now made sense. It was obvious that he could no longer stay silent, but he needed to know where to go from here. He decided to speak to Victor.

"Assume I believe everything you have said. Where do we go from here?"

"It's nice to hear your real voice Curt since I have listened to all the court tapes. I'm so sorry you got into this mess, but we're going to help fix it. The problem is that it requires a giant leap of faith on your part. If we bring all this information to the new DA, they'll want you in the courtroom. There's probably no way around it. I wish there was another way, but I don't see one."

Victor hesitated, "Now we have to get you back here without anyone finding out. I've contacted a friend in the U.S. Marshals Service. They're willing to loan us a plane that will fly down there and pick you up. We'll set it up with a military flight plan, which is the norm for transporting witnesses who are big targets."

He let that last comment sink in. "We can land you at a private airport, and bring you to a safe house where you would stay until the grand jury trial against Brandon starts. We have restricted the fact that you exist to inside our task force and to the new DA. Even the U.S. Marshal doesn't know who we are transporting."

"Here's the next problem. The longer we sit on this information, the more time Alex has to find us and kill the whole process. Be assured that Alex Brandon is very powerful. We are literally in a David and Goliath battle. Do you have any questions?"

Curt was shaking. The information flying at him for the last ten minutes had been overwhelming.

"Do I come alone or can someone come with me?"

"Normally, the U.S. Marshals' office likes to restrict the travel to just the witness, but in this case, I would recommend one of your friends, either Buck or Henry, come with you. I think

264

having Bonnie next to you in court might confuse the grand jury."

"Victor, let me think about it. How do I get back to you? What's your number?"

"There is no need. Just come back to the same location. We can see you, and will track your cell phone."

"I'm trying to trust you, but I've done that before, and look where it got me."

"I understand," said Victor as he ended the conversation.

Curt turned off the phone and took out the battery.

"Let's go back and get a stiff drink and talk this over," said Curt.

Bonnie stopped Curt. "The village does not allow drinking. We've had too much trouble with alcohol. I do, however, have a few beers hidden away, but we need to take them to the cenote."

Both Henry and Buck looked at each other. What she said had made no sense. She ran into her cabin and came out carrying a small backpack. She pointed the way to the cenote, and they all followed.

Bonnie went through the same spiel about the secrecy of the area, and Buck, and Henry easily agreed. They both really liked Bonnie and thought she was perfect for Curt. When they all had settled down on the two logs near the cenote, Bonnie handed out the warm beers.

"You guys have a choice. You can drink warm beer, or we can tie them to a rope and drop them down below to cool them off. What do you say?"

The men popped the caps simultaneously in answer to her question.

She opened her own beer and took a sip. She hadn't had a beer in weeks and warm or not, it tasted great. She looked at Curt, as did the other two.

"Okay, Curt. We could only guess what was being said, and you listened for a long time. What gives? Do we need to run away fast, or can we rest for a while?"

Curt took a long sip on his beer and gave them a complete rundown of the phone conversation. When he finished, he had three speechless friends.

Henry was the first to break the ice.

"I don't think you should do it. You're fine right where you are. I don't trust those government fellas and never will. I vote no."

"I don't agree," said Buck, as he took another sip of an already half-empty beer. "I do trust the U.S. Marshals Service. As for Victor, if he worked for Alex, why would he show his hand? If he wanted all of us to return, that might be a different story. Splitting us up when we all have the same information would be stupid, and I don't think Alex is that stupid."

Bonnie had been half-listening to Buck and Henry as she was thinking about losing Curt for a second time. As much as she wanted him to stay, she realized that it was Curt's life that hung in the balance. The decision had to be his and his alone. She set her empty beer down and looked into the cenote before responding.

"I think the decision is totally up to Curt. I want him to stay, but I also know he has unresolved issues. Sticking his head in the sand won't make them go away. I know there's a part of him that wants to end all this. As much as I want him to stay, I'm on the fence."

Curt squeezed her hand.

"Thanks, Bonnie. I already knew how you felt, and I feel likewise. You other two scoundrels have saved my life more than once, and I can't thank you enough. I'm tired of running, so I think I need to go and take my chances."

"I want to stay with you, Bonnie, but not with my murder conviction constantly hanging over my head. I'll always be looking for someone behind me."

Bonnie looked over to Buck and Henry. She reached into her pack and pulled out two more beers.

"Here's the deal. Take these two beers and hide them until you get to my room. Close the door, so no one in the village sees you. We'll be along soon, but Curt and I have some things to work out."

Once the two had left, Bonnie moved closer to Curt.

"Curt, don't say anything right now because enough has been said. We all know what has to happen. Just hold me and don't let me go."

Chapter 68

Back at the cabin, the four continued to discuss what Curt should do. Henry started to waver toward Bonnie's position, but still let everyone know that he hated government folks. By late afternoon, Curt decided to go back to the States with Buck.

Curt and Bonnie spent several hours at the cenote holding each other, talking about her work, painfully avoiding Curt's departure. They decided to make the call later that day, as there was no sense in delaying the inevitable. Besides, the longer they waited, the greater the risk that Alex could win. Bonnie asked Buck and Henry to stay behind while they went to make the call.

As soon as they arrived at the spot, the phone rang. Curt pressed the talk button and waited.

"Curt, welcome back. Have you made a decision?"

"Against my better judgment, I agree to your plan. What do I have to do?"

"It's easy. There's a private airstrip about 30 miles south of you. I'll send the plane down tonight and pick you up at 9 a.m. Turn your phone on at 7:30. I will call you and guide you to the airstrip. Bring just the clothes on your back."

He paused before saying, "I assume that Buck will be your companion choice because I know Henry doesn't trust us. We have a passport for both of you that will pass any undue scrutiny. The trip back will take about five hours. You'll then stay in a safe house for a few days while we arrange for your appearance before the grand jury."

With defined confidence, he continued. "The DA has guaranteed you a free pass, and you'll not be arrested again, even if you were proven guilty. This case isn't about you; it's about Alex Brandon. We want to bring him down. See you tomorrow."

The phone cut off at the end of the last sentence. Curt

took out the battery again, put his arm around Bonnie, and headed back to her cabin. Villagers who were worried about Bonnie's safety stopped them several times. She assured them that all was well.

Once they entered the cabin, neither said a word. They made love the rest of the night, desperately holding each other as if it were their last time together. Bonnie wanted to tell him to stay with her, but in her heart, she knew that would never work. He had unfinished business.

Chapter 69

Curt and Bonnie were up early to say their good-byes privately. Curt felt that he might be making a big mistake, but knew that as much as he loved Bonnie, he had to do this if he was ever going to regain his life.

When Curt left the cabin, Buck was waiting outside. The two said nothing to each other as they headed toward the old village truck, a mile away. Once they were in the truck, the phone rang. Victor was like a very sophisticated GPS. The satellite delay forced Victor to give instructions up to thirty seconds ahead of time, but he was still able to help them maintain their course.

An hour later, they reached the airstrip. The well-dressed pilot, copilot, and a man in black were waiting next to a very sleek Learjet. As Curt and Buck drove up, they looked around and saw a couple of sheepherders, an airplane mechanic working on an old biplane, and several kids playing catch. It looked safe enough. As they approached the plane, the pilot, and co-pilot got into the plane and waited. Buck slowly went up the steps and looked inside. He motioned for Curt to follow. When he was on board, the man in black entered and closed the door.

The interior looked like a plane reserved for the rich and famous. There were plush seats, personal TV monitors, and cup holders next to each seat. Buck commented on the plane's luxury items, but Curt was worrying that it might be a wolf in sheep's clothing.

The man in black motioned for Curt to sit down and fasten his seat belt. Buck had already turned on his TV set, and was searching through the channels. Curt looked out the window and saw the airplane mechanic was no longer working on his biplane. He had come out of the hangar and was looking directly at the jet.   Curt hoped it was just aeronautical envy.   The engines increased in power, and in minutes Curt was on his way back into the States.

Alex Brandon had been trying to contact Osterland, without success. Osterland's secretary told him that her boss was out on assignment, and wouldn't be back until late in the day. This worried Alex; he heard nothing from his sources in the police department about a special task force. He was about to make a call to his mole in the police department when he was buzzed by his secretary.

"Yes, what is it?"

"Mr. Brandon, there's a call from Mexico for you. He said he was the airplane mechanic who works on your plane when you go down to Cancun."

"Tell him to talk to my travel assistant.   I have more pressing problems to deal with right now."

"But Sir; he said it was about Curt Towers, although I thought he was dead."

Alex froze. It didn't matter what the mechanic had to say. If it was about Curt, he wanted to know everything.

"Put him on."

"Mr. Brandon, this is Pedro. I'm sorry to call you, but I thought you should know. I worked on your plane in Cancun. I made a trip north to work on a friend's biplane that is located on a private airfield.   An hour ago, a very fancy Learjet landed and picked up two passengers. The men who got off the plane looked like police officials. The two men who got on the plane are the reason why I'm calling. One I did not recognize, but the other I have seen in the newspapers many times. He looked exactly like Curt Towers, that guy who killed one of his employees. I thought he died in the Mexican desert or on the ferry."

"Are you sure it was Curt Towers?"

"Sir, I have a very good memory. It was Towers. What

271

do you want me to do?"

"Nothing, just go back to work. I appreciate being notified. I'll be sending you a handsome bonus for your loyalty."

"Thank you, Mr. Brandon."

Alex hung up the phone and looked out the window. Damn that Towers. How could he still be alive? His return must have something to do with that task force. If this happened an hour ago, that meant he had only two or three hours to figure out a plan.

He pressed the intercom to his secretary and told her he wouldn't take any more calls. He had to come up with a plan-- and fast. Ten minutes later, he had a desperate one, but he was running out of options.

A few years back he'd been down in southern Colorado hunting and met up with a group of survivalists. He hit it off with Zeke, the group leader. Alex supplied them with weapons now and then in exchange for favors that often required less than legal tactics. Right now, the group owed him a big favor, and he was going to call it in. After he hung up the phone with Zeke, he made a second call to an Air Force general, who also had a warm spot in his back pocket.

Bill Decker had been a U.S. Marshal pilot for more than five years and loved his job. Before that, he had worked for the airlines, flying large commercial jets, and fighter jets in the military. One of the reasons he loved this job was that each trip was different, a bit like his military days. Most of his flights were with dangerous criminals or people requiring witness protection.

One of the passengers he picked up today looked familiar, but he tried to put it out of his mind. When he had first started flying, his superiors had warned him to stay focused on flying the aircraft and forget about whom he was transporting. Easy to say, but difficult to do, especially when someone looked familiar.

This trip was definitely not the norm. It had been put

together in a few short hours and crossed inter agencies. Everyone involved was told that everything was on a need-to-know basis. His guess was that his passengers were witnesses against some big politician, or the mob. All he cared about was that so far the trip had gone smoothly. Soon he would be home to see his wife and teenage son.

Curt got up from his seat and looked through some of the magazines in the rack. One of the covers featured Alex as the upcoming techno giant of the decade. Curt showed it to Buck, who dropped it on the floor and pushed it under the seat. U.S. Marshal Bart Franco looked up at Curt.

"Is there a problem?"

Curt sat down across from Bart. This was not a man to cross. He was young and built like a bull, with the physique of a bodybuilder.

"I'm concerned about the safety of this flight. The man who is trying to kill me is very powerful, and has plenty of influential contacts. I'm concerned that he could sabotage this plane."

Bart set the paper he was reading on the small table next to him.

"Sir, I really don't want to know who you are, or why you are on the plane. It's better that way. It's just my job to get you to Denver safely. Regarding the safety of this flight, I can tell you that we use military flight plans and change it every trip we make. Only a few people know about our flight. We fly at a lower altitude than most planes, and over unpopulated areas. We avoid all normal flyways. We even change our transponder codes every flight, so no one can track us. You have nothing to cause nervousness. We'll get you to Denver without a scratch."

Curt nodded as if his answer had settled him down, but it didn't. He was starting to think he should have taken a bus or car back to Denver. He was getting a bad feeling about the flight.

273

Spike Wilcom slipped and cut his leg on the sharp rock. He cussed at himself for being so clumsy. The leader of his group would have his head if he failed in this mission. The Stinger missile he carried on his back had several sharp parts sticking out of his pack, and it was very heavy.

The plan came up so fast. One minute he was playing cards, and the next he was getting set up for the long uphill climb. On the ride to the drop-off spot, Zeke warned him that he must not fail because their weapon's benefactor was depending on him.

He had been elected because he was the only man who had ever fired a Stinger missile. A dishonorable discharge for hitting an officer had shortened his stay with the Army, but it was long enough to get him through missile school. When in the Army, his first target was a drone, but it was a flying object no less. He had done well with his shot, and if he hadn't crossed the officer, he would still be in the Army.

Now he was climbing up this steep mountain trying to get into position for his shot. He wasn't sure where the tracking equipment came from, or how Zeke knew where the plane was flying, but that wasn't his job. He was just supposed to get to the top of the mountain, wait for the correct transponder code, and then fire the missile at the sender of the code. It was that simple.

After crossing the Gulf of Mexico, pilot Bill Decker turned the Learjet northwest to cross Texas, and then turned again to head straight north into Denver.

Curt looked over Buck's shoulder to see what movie he was watching. The movie looked familiar. Actor Tommy Lee Jones was sitting on a plane, looking back at the prisoners in the back of the 727. Curt had seen the movie several times and remembered it was called *U.S. Marshals*. The movie now took on a completely new ironic meaning. He couldn't bear to watch it.

He fidgeted in his seat and glanced out the window. The

jet has started to make a slow descent, as it was getting closer to Denver. Below him were some of the roughest mountains he had ever seen. The mountain range was not as high as the snow-covered Rockies, but it was thick with tree cover. He spotted several small winding roads, but saw no buildings or towns.

He put his hands together and popped his knuckles. Buck kept looking up wondering what was bothering Curt. He took several deep breaths, and that seemed to help. He started to pick up a magazine to read, when an alarm went off in the cockpit.

"Missile warning," was a loud cry from Bill Decker.

"Buckle up, everyone," was the call from Pat Kipson, the copilot.

The jet dropped five hundred feet in seconds. Everything in the plane became weightless as the plane dropped like a rock. Pencils and magazines seemed to float in midair. There was a quick jerk to the right, and they went down at an even steeper angle. The way the pilot was handling the plane, Curt knew he had to be an ex-fighter jock. He hoped he was a good one.

The plane rolled to the left, and started to level off. Just as the right wing came level, a bright explosion appeared off the opposite side to Curt. Although the explosion had missed the engines and the plane, it was close enough to damage all the control systems. The plane started to drop fast as both engines started to fail. Curt looked to the front cockpit as the copilot turned around to yell out his last commands.

"We're going in. We have very little power, and almost no control. Put the pillows in your laps and your faces in the pillows. Brace for impact because it's going to be bad. Good luck, guys."

The copilot turned around and the two pilots were yelling commands back and forth, trying to come up with a landing solution, but there was none. The engines were losing power fast and in seconds, they would quit. There was no open area to land because there were trees as far as they could see.

The pilot pointed to an area slightly to the left of their

glide path. It had been harvested forty or fifty years before and then replanted. The veteran pilot had been thrown every possible problem in the flight simulator, but nothing like this. In one last desperate effort, he pulled up the flaps, which raised the nose and stalled the plane. The idea was the craziest he could come up with, but maybe it would work.

The tops of the trees were level and very close together, because man had planted them. His hope was that he could use the treetops as a landing pad and soften the impact. The tricky part was that when the plane stalled, it would probably fall like a rock through the trees. This wasn't a very good plan, but it might be better than crashing at a higher speed.

The plan worked for a while, but then a slightly taller tree in the pathway caught the left wing and spun the plane around in a circle as it crashed through the trees. Afterwards all went silent.

Alex had paced in his office so much that it was starting to create marks in the carpet. It was late in the afternoon, and he had heard nothing from his contact. Then his computer beeped and there was a new email from the compound with only two words on the screen. *It's done.*

He breathed a sigh of relief. He should go home and try to appease Cindy, because she was getting more difficult to handle. She was always on his case about spending less time in the office and more with her and the kids. Truth be told, he hated the kids, and they hated him. The merger of the two companies had gone through smoothly, so his next steps would be to send the kids off to boarding school, and then keep Cindy busy with volunteer projects.

Somewhere down the line, he would plan to remove her and the kids permanently from his life. Eventually, he would be the rich bachelor he had always wanted to be. He could then select his women, use them, and throw them away when he tired of them.

The one thing that still bothered him was Curt. He had been in some narrow escapes in the last few months, and seemed to get out of all of them. Curt had supposedly died multiple times, but always returned to taunt Alex.

He was certain that Curt couldn't get out of this one. The Air Force general assured him that if the Stinger hit the plane, there would be no survivors. He wanted to call and find out if there had been a crash, but that would directly point back to him. No, he had to be patient.

He turned on the news to see if there were any breaking news reports. As he was surfing through the channels, he found one. A small private jet crashed in southern Colorado. Rescue attempts were being hampered by a storm that had moved in after the crash, and by the fact that the area of the crash was a dense forest. Ground searchers would take at least a day to reach the site.

The newscaster went on to say the station would keep them updated on the progress as they received news from the crash site, and there would be a full story on the late-night news. Alex leaned back in his chair. It looked as though he would have to wait another day before this was over.

Lynda Sanders was in shock. All the work that had gone into getting Curt Towers back to Colorado had just gone down the toilet. The whole thing with Alex Brandon was like a chess game. Each time they made a move; Alex would block or counter their move with a better one. The task force was running out of options.

When the news came on, Victor watched the broadcast, made some calls, and then left for an hour. When he returned, he looked as though his world had ended. Lynda was about to ask if there was a problem when Victor told her, and Ken that the U.S. Marshal had been a close friend. They had gone through the police academy together, and then drifted in different directions.

They kept in close contact, and often had family barbecues. Now there was a good chance that his friend Bart Franco was dead. He didn't look forward to telling Franco's wife that her husband had made his last trip. The rest of the evening, the three stayed glued to the TV set, and awaiting calls providing updates on the plane crash.

Curt's arm and leg felt like hell. His vision was blurred and he was hanging upside down from his seat by his seatbelt. As his vision cleared, he saw Buck lying below him, his leg at an awkward position, obviously broken. He yelled down to Buck, but there was no answer.

He looked toward the front of the plane, but it wasn't even there. The plane had been torn in half just forward of the wings. There was only a large jagged opening where the cockpit used to be. Curt yelled as loud as he could for the U.S. Marshal and the pilots, but received no response.

His seat belt was really starting to cut into his waist. He held the armrest with one hand while he released the seat belt with the other. As soon as he did, he fell to the floor right next to Buck. He cautiously reached over to see if Buck was still alive. As he touched Buck's shoulder, a voice whispered.

"I'm alive, but I feel like shit. I think something is wrong with my leg. I can't seem to move it."

Curt got up on his knees and found his own leg was either broken or sprained. He started to turn Buck over, but realized that he had broken his own arm in the fall from his seat. He carefully used his other arm to roll Buck over. Buck's face was bloody, but Curt realized that it was from a broken nose. Curt helped Buck sit up against one of the damaged seats and looked down at Buck's leg.

"I told you this was a bad idea," said Curt, as he tried to sit down beside Buck. "I don't know what happened, but I think we were hit by a missile. I looked up front, but there are no signs of anyone else. I think we need to first assess our damage, and then see if we can find the other three."

Buck winced in pain. "You were right about the flight, but right now we need to fix our broken bones. If you can wrap my leg with splints, I can do the same for your arm. Then you can help me out of the plane, and we can see if we can find the others."

Curt looked around and started to put together a splint kit for Buck. He located a first-aid kit and gave Buck as many painkillers as he thought he could stand. He then yanked Buck's leg straight before applying the splint made from bits and pieces he found in the cabin. Buck screamed during the process, but when Curt had finished, he was no longer feeling any pain.

Curt located a second set of smaller splints and wrap for his arm. He took the remainder of the painkillers and waited as Buck repeated the process to his arm. When they had finished, Curt located four bottles of water and a half-dozen bags of pretzels. The two wolfed down some pretzels, and doused them with a bit of water.

For the next hour, they helped each other pull themselves to the front edge of the plane. Then they were presented with a new problem. That section of the plane was about fifteen feet off the ground.

Curt braided the wire that was overly abundant in the broken edge of the plane and attached it to a seat belt that was still firmly attached to the plane. He wrapped the new braided line around Buck's waist and helped lower Buck to the ground below. Once Buck was on the ground, he removed the line and Curt pulled it back up.

Curt looked around for anything else they could use to survive. He found more water, another first-aid kit, a whole box of snacks, and several blankets. He stuffed all the goodies in a pillowcase and lowered it to the ground. When he was sure that he had everything they could use, he started to lower himself to

279

the ground by wrapping the line around his waist, one leg, and his arm. He gradually released the tension on the braid and slid down the makeshift line.

When he reached the ground, he looked around for the front of the plane, but it was nowhere in sight, so they had to assume the worst. The U.S. Marshal and the pilots were in the area of the plane's first impact. Chances were that it was crushed and dropped off long before the other section stopped. If they were alive, it meant they were probably in the opposite direction of the final crash.

Curt realized he could walk with a sprained ankle and a broken arm, but Buck was going nowhere. After surveying the area, he looked back at Buck's leg.

"Buck, your leg looks bad. You're not going anywhere, and that's a big problem."

"I know, Curt. Whoever shot us down will be coming to see if they completed the job. If they find you alive, they'll finish the job. I wouldn't count on the rescue teams beating them here. I understand that you have to leave now. I'll tell the rescue team that you were up with the pilot when the plane crashed. That should give you some time. Don't worry I'll be fine. Just leave me some of the food, water, and the blankets. I'll wait for the rescue teams. You need to go, now."

Curt continued to look around to get his bearings.

"Are you sure? I can wait and take my chances."

"What and die? If I'm going to go through all this and get a broken leg for my efforts, then you damn well better make it worth it. Now get out of here."

"I'll go, but I want to make sure you're all right."

"I'm fine, Curt, just get the hell out of here, or I'll cut you out of my will."

"I'm in your will?"

Buck just shook his head and waved his hand. Curt got the message. They shook hands, and Curt started out in a direction toward Denver but away from the crash scene where he suspected the other three had been pulverized into the ground.

The slope angled downward at about thirty degrees. Curt looked around, and then started down the incline. He would eventually hit a road, a stream, or maybe both. He did his best not to leave evidence of his trail, but it was hard with a limp. He fell down several times, but picked himself up and continued down.

His recovery under Bonnie's care had been a big help, but he still wasn't over whatever ailed him. That, combined with a broken arm and a sprained ankle, was making travel slow. Eventually, the slope evened out, and he was on flat land. The trees were still dense, and he could hear a stream, in the distance.

Another thirty minutes of walking and it started to get dark. One of the items he found on the plane was a small flashlight and two sets of batteries. It was one of the new LED flashlights, which could last days or even weeks on a single set of batteries, or so they claimed. He knew he had to put as much distance as possible between himself and the plane before dawn. The search teams would expand their search pattern once they located the plane. He had to be outside that area in the next five to eight hours, or he might be discovered.

He could hide and sleep in the day, and travel by night, using the flashlight sparingly. He finally reached the stream, but it was about fifteen feet across and several feet deep. The water was fast flowing and ice cold, so he knew he couldn't wade across. He would have to follow along the banks and see where it led.

Chapter 70

Buck woke to the sound of a helicopter overhead. He looked up to see several rescuers rappelling down on long ropes. The first came over to check Buck and called back for additional medical help. It was then that Buck realized their mistake. Curt had helped him fix his leg. It was going to be difficult for a medical technician to believe he had set his own leg. The medic came over, looked at his leg, and asked him who set it. He told him that he had, but with great pain. He lied and said he had previous emergency medical experience, so he knew what to do. The urgency of the rescue was on Buck's side, and the medic didn't take time to question his response any further.

The two rescuers asked if there was anyone else from the crash. Buck told them he was the only one in the rear of the plane and that the other two passengers and two pilots were in the front. Buck knew that if he fibbed about the number of passengers, he would be caught in a lie. It was better to tell a partial truth, to give Curt more time to get away. Buck agreed with Curt; they should have driven, but everyone always says flying is safer. "That may be true, unless you fly with Curt Towers," he thought to himself.

As the stretcher was being lowered from the chopper, Buck thought about Curt and wished him well.

Over the last ten hours, Curt had traveled almost nine miles from the crash. That seemed like a safe distance, so now it was time to rest. He found a large tree with a rotted out base and collected as many leaves as possible to create a cave. He nestled in among the leaves and was soon out of sight. He lay back against the soft leaves, and in seconds, he was in a deep sleep.

Bonnie was in a panic. She had just heard that a plane had crashed south of Denver, and was worried that it was Curt's airplane. Henry went into town to check the local newspapers and log on to the internet. When he found the article about the crash, he discovered the bad news. It talked about the crash of a U.S. Marshals' Learjet that was transporting an unknown witness. There was no doubt in his mind that it was Curt's plane.

When he reached the camp, Bonnie could read his face like a book. Seconds later, she turned and ran down the path to the cenote. Henry knew he should follow, but not right now, because she needed some time alone.

He knew Curt was good at getting out of jams, but this one seemed close to impossible. Then again, they were talking about Curt Allen Towers.

Alex spent the entire night and most of the day in his office. His secretary thought he was crazy, but kept bringing him food and drink. Finally, he went down to the company gym to take a shower and change into fresh clothes he always kept in a locker.

When he returned, he received a call from the general who had supplied him with the plane's locator frequency. The rescuers found one man, named Buck, in the rear section of the plane with a broken leg. The front of the plane had burrowed into the ground so deep that it was taking some time to identify the bodies. Reports were that the four other people on the plane were in this section. So far, the rescuers made an identification of the pilot and the U.S. Marshal. They would continue digging, but it might be another day before the last two people could be identified.

Alex was so pissed. Five people on the plane and three were identified. Curt was not one of them. Damn. Damn. Damn. This was never going to end with Curt. Alex was starting to think that Curt had magical powers. There was no way that someone could survive all the things that Alex had thrown at him, and yet he did. Alex sat down, pulled a liquor bottle from the desk drawer, and decided this was the time to get drunk. "To hell with Cindy," he thought. "She can fend for herself for a couple of days."

It was late in the day, and the sunbeams were poking through the leafy bed that Curt had created. His back and arms felt like hell. It certainly wasn't the most comfortable bed he'd ever slept in. He pushed the leaves away, took a sip of water from the bottle, and got up to check his bearings. He finished off a few more snack packs and headed downstream.

It was a real struggle for the next three miles. When he was about to give up, he realized he was standing in the middle of a fire road. It hadn't been used for a while, but it had been used this year. He looked in both directions, and decided that heading downhill was the best option.

As it started to get dark, Curt looked up to see a full moon. Fate was shining on him. He could now travel without using a flashlight. He could also make good time on the smooth fire road. In the next four hours, he covered what he guessed to be almost eight miles.

He was about ready to stop again when he hit a narrow, level gravel road. He determined which direction was west from the moon, and then headed off to the north. It appeared that the logging road had been used recently, so he needed to be careful. As much as he would like to be rescued, he decided he would be selective about his helpers and let his gut serve as his guide.

Chapter 71

Walter Pence was awakened from a deep sleep by his faithful hunting dog. The dog was restless and kept scratching at the back door of the cabin. Walter knew that something was wrong because he had taken the dog out earlier to do his business.

He got up and grabbed his gun, motioning for the dog to be quiet. The dog obeyed his owner. Minutes later, Walter and his dog were prowling along the road that led to his small market. He had owned it for five years, and loved running it. Walter had built his cabin behind the store, so that he didn't have to drive far to work. Only locals came down to buy supplies and gas, and they always stayed for a while to chew the fat with Walter.

He financially didn't need the store because his parents had left him more than two square miles of land loaded with trees ripe for harvesting. He was worth millions, but he still enjoyed running the market because it was his way of staying in contact with the real world. Sadly, someone had invaded his space.

When Curt first saw the building, he was tempted to veer around and get closer to civilization. Since it was so early in the morning, the odds were good that it wasn't even open yet. If he could find more food and water, he would try to break in and stock up. He was taking a big chance, but knew he would need the supplies later.

Glancing through the store's back window, he could see just about everything he needed. He was about to move around to the side window, when a loud voice came from behind.

"Raise both hands in the air very slowly, and then turn around. I have a shotgun pointed at your back, and I'm not afraid to use it."

Curt was pissed. He had been so careful up to this point. Now some local yokel had caught him. As he turned, he came face to face with a white-bearded fifty to sixty-year-old man with a large hunting dog that seemed ready to attack. Curt thought he should take a stab at bullshitting this guy.

"Hey, man, you can lower the gun. I'm just lost and looking for some food and water. I mean no harm."

Walter held the gun steady as he walked toward Curt. He looked at Curt's broken arm, and then at his dirty shirt and muddy shoes.

"Are you from the plane crash?"

Curt was caught completely off guard by this question. His mind was racing, trying to figure out what had given him away so quickly.

"What plane? I'm just a hiker who got lost in the woods."

Walter motioned with his gun for Curt to move to the front of the market.

"You must think I fell off the turnip truck. I know you're one of the survivors everyone is looking for. The broken arm, the wrong clothes, and the direction you came from tell me all I need to know. Oh yeah, that and the two fellows in suits who showed up last night was another indicator. I hate government officials and the police, so at least you have that going in your favor. Who are you and why are you running?"

"Can I please sit down and get a drink?"

Walter threw him a set of keys and Curt quickly opened the front door. As soon as they were inside, Walter motioned for him to sit down in one of the chairs arranged in the front of the store. Curt took a cold drink from the old Coke machine, and guzzled it. He took a minute to look around the market. On one wall was a picture of Walter in a military uniform with a group of soldiers in a jungle. One of the names under the picture matched the man sitting in front of him.

"Okay, Walter. Even if I told you the truth, you probably

286

wouldn't believe me."

"Let me be the judge. I've always believed the truth is the best way to go. Now spill it or I'll have to call the local sheriff, and he hates outsiders as much as I do."

Curt took another sip of the Coke and spent the next fifteen minutes telling Walter everything, from his murder conviction to the plane crash. When he had finished, Walter was shaking his head.

"I have to tell you, Curt; either you're one of the biggest storytellers, or you've had the worst run of luck I've ever heard. Normally, I would've called the sheriff, but after those two guys came by last night, I knew something wasn't right."

Walter scratched his beard. "As crazy as your story sounds, I do believe you. Here's what I'm going to do. I have a cabin about two miles up in the hills, and I'll take you there. It's stocked with enough supplies to last a few weeks. You need to hide up there until I give you the all-clear signal to come down. If you go to Denver right now, the roadblocks and the extra police will find you in hours. I hope I'm doing right by hiding you, but something in my gut tells me it's the right thing to do."

When Walter put his gun down, the dog started to wag his tail and then went over to lick Curt's hand. They packed up any supplies that might be missing in the cabin, and jumped into an old beat-up truck. In fifteen minutes, they were a couple hundred yards from a well-hidden hilltop cabin. Walter gave Curt a quick tour, and told him that the sheriff would come up to check on him if he wasn't down running the market. He always played a game of checkers with the sheriff, and it was getting close to game time.

After Walter left, Curt looked around to see how to occupy his time. The cabin was small, but it had a functional stove, a bookcase, a small eating table, and a comfortable-looking bed. He lay down in the bed, slowly closed his eyes, and was asleep in minutes.

287

Chapter 72

Curt sat across from the checkers' board contemplating his next move. Walter had been playing this game so long that he beat Curt every time. Even so, Curt enjoyed playing a challenge match with Walter every evening since he had provided him refuge in the cabin.

More than a week had passed, and the majority of the people associated with the crash had left the scene, including the police and the FBI. Only the investigators from the NTSB were still hanging around. The local sheriff was around a few times asking Walter if he'd seen anyone. He hated lying to the sheriff, especially since he was a good friend.

Curt took a sip from the oil slick coffee and set it back on the table.

"Walter, we haven't really talked much about why you're helping me. I honestly didn't want to pry, since you were going way beyond the call of duty, but I have to ask. Most people would have turned me in right away. You even lied to the sheriff, and he's your friend."

Walter removed two more of Curt's checkers before he responded.

"You know, I haven't talked about this for a very long time." Walter reached over to a small table, pulled out a picture, and put it upside down on the table.

"I had a son, who could have been your identical twin. When I first saw you, I thought you were he, only older. If he had survived the second Gulf War, he could have looked just like you. The resemblance is uncanny."

He gave a sad sigh. "I felt there was a special reason you showed up on my doorstep. The odds of your finding someone with a dead son who looked exactly like you seem astronomical.

Besides, having you around is like giving me my son back for a week. You even talk like him. If I didn't know any better, I'd say you are him. I don't mean to scare you, and I'm not planning to keep you hostage; helping you was just something I felt I had to do."

Curt found it hard to look at Walter. He could see Walter was still in pain, even though many years had passed.

"I'm so sorry about your son. Was he married?"

"Yes, and he had one kid. She moved into Denver after he died. It was too hard for her to stay out here because it reminded her so much of my son."

Walter reached out and turned the picture over.

"This is my son Allen."

Curt looked at the image. It looked like a picture of him a few years back. He now understood and wished there was something more he could do for the man.

"You know my middle name is Allen. I know that doesn't help, but it does seem strange that I look like him and have his first name as my middle. Maybe we are kindred spirits."

They finished their game and put together their last evening meal. As they sat down to the table, Walter briefed Curt on the most-recent information about the plane crash.

"The sheriff was by today and told me they had removed the last of the plane crash. They were still concerned about the fifth person in the plane, which I assume was you. Anyway, everyone still thinks you're part of the human remains dug out of the hole. For some reason, and I don't understand this. They have DNA from the fifth person. How is that possible?"

Curt held up his arm, which was starting to mend after some help from Walter. "If you remember, when you rewrapped my arm, there was a large cut from the accident. They must have found that blood."

Walter processed what Curt had presented. It made sense except for one thing.

289

"So they found your blood. Wouldn't they have matched it to you? After all, you were in the system."

"That's true; I was in the system, but not the active system, since I was deceased. They may have narrowed the search to those alive, which makes the most sense. Eventually, someone will expand the search when nothing shows up. This means my time is limited before the manhunt is back on again. I need to get to someone in that task force, but first I have something else I need to do."

"Curt, you mentioned going to see your ex-wife. I'm not sure that's a good idea. Alex probably has high security around his summer home. What if you run into him at home?"

"I know it's probably a stupid thing to do, but I have to talk to her. I need to know if she's part of the conspiracy with Alex. I know in my heart that she's not, but I have to hear it directly from her. When I go to the task force, I need to know if I want to implicate Cindy too."

Curt took a bite of his steak before he presented his plan.

"As far as security goes, Alex likes simple codes, and everything I remember about him tells me he's a workaholic. I'll monitor the house for some time before I go in. I really don't want to be caught again, so I'll be careful. Finding the members of the task force is going to be the difficult part."

Walter picked up the empty plates and put them in the sink.

"After you leave, I'll give you a few days to see your wife. Then I'll talk to the sheriff. He has some connections in the Denver police department. I know he'll be pissed at me for lying to him, but we go back a long way. If there's anyone who can find out about your task force, he can."

"Well now" he said, "we need a plan to get you into Denver. Even though things have settled down, riding in the truck with me would be taking too much of a chance. So I have this harebrained idea."

Curt listened as Walter described his new underground railroad that very closely resembled the back of his truck.

Alex had been patient for the past few days while the investigators did their job. He had heard that they found DNA from the fifth person, but had no identification match. He really wanted to call and tell the investigators that they should look in the deceased files, but that could lead them directly back to him. No, he had to remain quiet.

He hated to go home, too. He and Cindy continually fought about his extended office time. Her kids wouldn't have anything to do with him either, but that was fine with him. Alex told Cindy that the company was going through some difficult times after the merger, and that it would be better by Thanksgiving. She wasn't buying it, and Alex was running out of ideas to satisfy her. They rarely slept in the same bed, and sex was no longer an option. He knew he still needed her to maintain the merger, but he was starting to regret marrying her. She would always be Curt's wife, and he would forever be second fiddle.

He was determined never to be in second place again when it came to Curt. Alex wasn't going to tolerate it any longer. He made a call to his mole within the police department. He would make sure the DNA matched.

Cindy sat on the couch reading a Fern Michaels book about the Sisterhood. She had read the entire series up to the eleventh book, and found the distraction necessary to offset her confrontations with Alex. She wished she were as strong a woman as the women in the Sisterhood.

She had hoped for more from their marriage, but Alex had changed so much over the last few weeks. He was always on edge, constantly yelling at her and the kids. She was even considering divorce. The marriage seemed like a good idea at the start, but now it resembled a lost cause.

The only reason she had held on was for the kids, but as time went on, she realized how much the kids missed Curt and hated Alex. No matter what he bought them, they wouldn't warm up to him. Curt always said that money could never buy love. Now she was really starting to understand that philosophy.

She wished that she understood what was sending Alex into the tantrums he was having lately. She knew it was work-related, but he was secretive, never sharing information.

Alex had called saying he would be late tonight. "What else was new?" she thought. She told him there would be dinner in the refrigerator that he could reheat. She decided she would sit in front of the fireplace and finish her book before she headed off to bed. She wasn't about to wait up for Alex. They would have to talk in the morning.

Chapter 73

Walter and Curt stood at the back of the old pickup truck and looked at their woodworking handiwork. They had built a solid container large enough to house a man, and buried it inside the woodpile. Once Curt crawled inside the blanket-lined container, Walter filled the back of the truck with adequate wood so that the center container was invisible. Curt had food, water, a flashlight, and a walkie-talkie to communicate with Walter.

Once everything was set, Walter called the sheriff, told him that he was going on a trip for a couple of days, and asked if he could keep an eye on the market. The sheriff agreed, never asking about Walter's destination. That was the way of life in this small valley. Everyone minded their own business, but still watched out for each other.

By the time the sun rose above the trees, they were on the road. He had instructions from Curt on how to find Alex's country house, and headed off in that direction. As Walter approached the first highway intersection, he saw a highway patrol car blocking the road up ahead. It appeared they had dogs. This didn't look good. He picked up the walkie-talkie.

"Curt, we may have a problem. Turn off your walkie-talkie until I start up again. We have a roadblock."

Walter turned his unit off, and hoped Curt had done the same. He slowed the truck as one of the police officers put up his hand. Walter had never seen either man before. One man held a clipboard and the other controlled a dog. The police dog started to pull at his leash toward the truck. Walter swatted his dog in the butt, and it jumped up to the open window. The patrolman backed off.

"Sir, can you restrain your dog. We have several questions."

Walter gripped his dog by the collar and told him to sit down. The second man did the same. When the dogs had settled down, the first police officer came over to Walter.

"Where you headed?"

"I'm going to Denver, delivering some wood."

"Who are you delivering it to?"

"An old army buddy. What's the problem here?"

The officer stood back and looked at the truck, not answering his question. "Have you seen any strangers in your area?"

"Nope, just a few deer, couple skunks, but not really anything else."

The officer walked around the truck, and Walter's dog started to growl. The officer took a quick look and then backed off toward the second officer. He made a motion to Walter that he could go, so he moved up the road. He waited for a few miles to make sure his walkie-talkie wouldn't alert anybody listening. He clicked it a couple of times before speaking. "How are you doing back there? That was close."

Curt shifted his position and clicked his mike. "Fine, how does it look from here?"

"Fine, I think we're in the clear. Get some rest if you can. I'll check on you every half hour. It should take two to three hours to get there."

By early afternoon, Walter reached the edge of Alex Brandon's property. The two men had gone over several maps of the area. Walter even had a satellite internet connection, so they could use Google Earth to get a clearer idea of what lay ahead. The back of the property was going to be the best bet for his invasion.

Walter pulled off onto a fire road, out of sight of the main road. Once he was sure that no one had followed or could see him from the road, he started to unload the wood. When he finally got to the box, he helped cramped Curt out of his small hiding place. Curt sat on the edge of the truck, trying to get the blood circulating back into his legs.

The two men removed the box, hid it in the brush, and restacked the unloaded wood into the truck. When the task was completed, Walter got back into the truck and rolled down the window. "You know, Curt; you don't have to do this. I can call about the task force, and you can do this later. It's awfully risky."

Curt leaned against the truck because his legs were still cramped. "I know what you're saying, but I have to know her answer before I go any further. It's a risk that I have to take because I still care about her."

They shook hands, and Walter backed down the fire road and left. One of the last things they did was to say good-bye on the walkie-talkies. Each threw their communication devices into the woods, as agreed. They would now communicate by phone and only at predetermined times.

Curt moved into the brush and found a place to wait. It was too early to make his move. He would have to wait until dusk. He pulled out his maps and looked for the culvert that crossed onto Alex's property.

Alex went back to business as usual, buying people the same way you buy merchandise. The Curt Towers issue was shifting to the back of his mind because he had problems that were more important. Several of Curt's clients, inherited in the merger, were unhappy with the way they were being treated. Many had commented that Curt never did business that way. Alex smugly replied that they could take their business elsewhere if they wanted, knowing there was nowhere else for them to go.

Alex had just finished sealing the deal on a new military contract when his secretary called; indicating Osterland was in the outer office. Osterland entered and Alex closed the door, telling his secretary that he didn't want to be disturbed.

Alex sat down at his desk waiting for the updates on the

crash.

Osterland pulled out a manila folder and looked it over before saying one word.

"It appears that the police department has finally matched the DNA in the crash to Towers. They never announced it in the press because it would open many old wounds. They preferred to bury the information, and had several hearings in private. The case is closed, as far as the police are concerned. They are positive that Towers was in the crash. The last two bodies were so badly burned that there was almost nothing left. It was a bit strange about the fire, considering that most of the fuel was in the rear of the plane. Something else in the front of the plane must have caused it to burn so hot. I guess we'll never know."

He paused and waited for a reaction from Alex before continuing. "I've been checking around with the police, and as far as anyone knows, the task force no longer exists. It looks like the three members have dropped off the face of the earth. The department has listed them on a permanent leave of absence, a bit like military AWOL. The bottom line is that it looks like your troubles with Curt Towers no longer exist. I think you can relax for a while."

They talked about tidying up any other loose ends, and the meeting ended in less than fifteen minutes. Osterland headed out the door and Alex pressed the button to his secretary. "I think I'll take the rest of the week off. Cancel all my meetings. If anything critical comes up, you can get me at my home in the country."

He headed down to the gym to work out, shower, and then head home. He was not looking forward to talking to Cindy, but he was still concerned that the company could be in trouble if she put up a stink. Therefore, he would have to continue to play her game. God, he loved playing God.

Curt was ready to make his move to the culvert. There originally had been a security gate across it, but storms had eliminated that problem for him. Once he was on the other side, he hiked through the forest until he was at the edge of a clearing. The country house was still more than a half-mile away. He took out a small pair of binoculars Walter had given him and scanned the backyard to the house. There was no one outside.

He made his move slowly working his way along a tree line, so he would approach the house from the right rear. He was now less than fifty yards from the back and there was still no one around. Then he saw someone cross in front of a window. It looked like Cindy, so he moved in closer to be sure, but she had disappeared.

It was almost dark as he approached the back windows to check for security. As expected, all the windows were wired. He went around to the right front and saw one small compact car that had to be Cindy's vehicle. Alex would never drive anything that wimpy.

He had to get her attention. He rattled the back door, and then hid, but nothing happened. He tried again but with more force. This time he heard someone come to the back door, disarm the alarm, and open the door. Cindy walked out and looked around to see what had made the sound.

As she was about to head back in, Curt took a chance. "Cindy, it's me, Curt."

Cindy froze. She turned to see Curt looking out from behind the bushes. Her face was white with fear. "It can't be. You're dead. Curt, is that really you?"

"Yes, it's me. Obviously, I'm not dead. Who's in the house?"

"It's just me here because the kids are at your sister's, and Alex is still at work. The police think you're dead, but if they find out you're alive, they'll put you back in jail. This was a bad idea for you to come here."

"Cindy, did you help Alex frame me? I'll leave peacefully once I hear your answer."

"What the hell are you talking about, Curt? Alex helped me after you were convicted. If it hadn't been for him, the press would have made the kids' and my life miserable. He protected us from all the bad press that you brought down on our family. I don't know if you really killed that woman, but I had to get away from you to protect the kids. Alex was there for me and helped me get through it all."

"And now I'm ready to finish what I started," said Alex, as he pointed the pistol at Curt.

"Get your hands up, Curt, and get inside the house. I don't want any nosey neighbors with binoculars seeing you."

Cindy was in shock. She didn't expect Alex home so early. "Alex, let him go. No one has to know he's alive. If you turn him in, our family will have to go through hell again."

Alex smiled. "Who said anything about turning him in? Get in the house, Curt, and you too, Cindy. I'm sick and tired of your constant complaining."

Fear came across Cindy's face. Something was not right. She hesitated, but Alex shoved the barrel of the gun into her chest. "Move, bitch, or I'll do you right here."

Curt and Cindy slowly moved down the hall and into the living room. Alex yelled, "This is perfect. The kids are gone, and it's just the two of you for this friendly reunion. The way I see it, Curt returned to my house and killed Cindy because she had married me. I came home a few minutes later and discovered that Curt had killed my wife. We struggled and you tried to kill me, but I got the upper hand. I framed you once, and I can frame you again, or maybe I'll just kill you instead."

Tears were running down Cindy's face. "Alex, how could you frame Curt? You were boyhood friends. I thought you were trying to help our family."

Alex motioned for Cindy to move closer to Curt. "The only thing I wanted from you was Curt's money. Now I have all of it and even a perfect solution for getting rid of you and your ex-

298

husband. Things change, Cindy. Sure, we were boyhood friends, but that friendship ended when Curt tried to undermine my business."

Before she could respond, Alex pulled the trigger and the slug hit Cindy in the chest. She crumpled onto the fireplace hearth. Curt ran toward him, but Alex had expected his move, and hit Curt on the side of the face with the gun. Curt fell backwards to the right of the fireplace. He reached up to feel the blood streaming down his neck.

Alex moved closer, took out a second smaller gun, and pointed it at him. "Curt, you traitor; you're not going to get out of this one. I've thought of everything. There's one gun for you to shoot my wife, and another for me to shoot you. It will be a closed case in a matter of days. You lose, and I win. It looks like you have no more lives left."

Alex pulled back the hammer on the small pistol and was about to put an end to all his problems, but he unexpectedly had an odd feeling in his chest. He looked down to see the sharp end of a fireplace poker sticking out the front of his shirt.

"Die, you son of a bitch," said Cindy, as she fell back and let go of the poker she'd just rammed through Alex's back. He turned to look at Cindy with a questioning face. Then Alex Brandon died without really understanding what had happened.

Curt got up and ran over to Cindy, but he could see she was moments away from death. He pulled her onto his lap and wiped the blood from her mouth. She looked up at Curt and smiled. "I'm so glad you're all right. Please forgive me for not believing you. I'm so sorry, Curt. The kids...."

Before she could say another word, he lost her. Curt sat next to the hearth, holding her and rocking, crying like never before. It was over, but it didn't end the way he wanted. It had all happened so fast, there was no time to react.

He saw her phone lying on the floor. He dialed 911 and just sat and waited, as the sirens got louder and louder. This wasn't how it was supposed to end.

As the cars arrived, several police officers jumped out and headed into the house. When they reached the living room, they pointed their guns at Curt.

"Put your hands up. Don't move."

A few seconds later, more than six cops surrounded Curt and pulled him to his feet. One pulled out his cuffs and was ready to put them on when a detective entered the room.

It was Osterland. "There's no need for cuffs. I'll take Mr. Towers with me and accept full responsibility. Everyone get out of here now. Give the man some space. Be respectful since his wife was just killed."

Curt looked up at his rescuer, who moved aside to let his boss pass. Susan Bishop reached out to shake Curt's hand. "You're a hard man to find, Mr. Towers. I'm the head of the task force that will clear your name. Victor here is my right-hand-man, and has been working undercover in Alex's company to help prove your innocence. We have proof beyond a shadow of doubt, but we'll still need to take you down to the police station. I know you need to make a call to Bonnie, so we have a satellite phone available when you are ready."

Curt swallowed hard and looked over to Cindy. She saved him with her final dying breath. Susan grasped a blanket from the couch and gently covered her body.

"Don't worry, Mr. Towers. She won't be listed as part of the investigation. She's been through enough, and your family will be protected by my task force. I guarantee it. We'll be making some announcements in the next few days that I think you'll really like."

Victor dialed the number to Bonnie and then handed the phone to Curt. Victor motioned for everyone to leave Curt alone so he could talk privately. When Curt put the phone to his ear, the voice on the other end was like a sound from heaven.

"Hello," said Bonnie, with some hesitation.

"It's over," said Curt holding back his emotion. "Cindy died saving me. Um...the...uh... task force is clearing my name. I miss you so much, and ...I'll come back to you...as soon as I can."

There was silence from Bonnie before she yelled, "I'm so glad you're alive. I'm truly sorry about Cindy. I want you back here, but I know you need to take care of your family first. Just know that I'll be here waiting, for as long as you need. I'll be fine, as long as I know you're coming back."

"Thank you for standing behind me. I'll be home, as soon as I can. I love you, Bonnie."

Chapter 74

The rain was coming down in buckets as the small group stood under umbrellas at the cemetery. The police surrounded the area to protect Curt and his children from the press. The ceremony was simple. The minister told everyone about better times and how fine a mother she had been. Henry, Buck, and several members of Xtreme Machines were at the funeral to pay their respects to Curt.

Curt held the kids close to him as the words from the minister went by in a blur. Everything had happened so fast, but he still couldn't believe she was dead. His sister and her husband stood behind Curt, ready to take over for him. He told the kids he had to make a statement to the press. Their aunt would take them back to her house, and he would meet them there.

After the ceremony was over, Curt thanked the minister, shook everyone's hand, and then patiently waited for everyone to leave. When his family and friends had gone, Susan Bishop came to him and asked him if he was ready to tackle the press. He nodded and they headed to the area police had taped off for the press interview.

When he arrived, everyone started to ask questions at once. Susan held up her hand. "Okay, here's the deal. Mr. Towers is going to make a statement and there will be no questions. I know you all have your own spin on this trial, but keep in mind that Mr. Towers chose to talk with you. He didn't have to agree to do it, so just listen to what he has to say. I guarantee it will make a good story. If anyone interrupts, I'll have you removed."

The press was quiet. Curt looked down at his notes. Bonnie and Cindy would both be proud about what he was going to do.

"Tomorrow I will return to my company that was forcefully taken over by Alex Brandon, and I will take back full control as CEO. One of my first acts will be to undo the merger that Alex Brandon instigated between his company and mine. My lawyers tell me that I now own both parts of the merger. Once I have separated them, I will dismantle Alex's company and sell off all his assets. The proceeds will be used to try to rectify some of the wrongs that have been inflicted upon various people and companies.

"Anyone who loses their job due to this dismantling of companies is welcome to re-apply to my company. Those who choose not to apply will still be compensated. This has been a dark period for my company, and I plan to mend it, at any cost.

"There is one last thing. Please leave my family alone. They have been through more than anyone should have to bear. Some of you may think it is your God-given right to invade my family's privacy when they are grieving, but I would recommend you don't even try. You won't like the results. Thank you for your time."

Susan motioned for several police officers to block the press, so Curt could make his exit.

Chapter 75

Mary Pense, Walter's daughter-in-law, watched the news coverage. It reported about Curt Towers and how a local man, Walter Pense, had helped him. She was so proud of what her father-in-law had done; she even called to tell him so.

Before her husband, Allen had gone off to the second Gulf War, he'd taken care of all the household repair chores. He was gone now, and she was on her own. Mary wasn't very handy at fixing things, but a neighbor had been coming over occasionally to help her. Her father-in-law had even offered money to hire help, but she wouldn't take it. She was stubborn and determined to do it on her own.

The newscaster was about to review the same story again, when her doorbell rang. She opened it to find her father-in-law standing in the middle of nine men dressed in Army uniforms. They all smiled and saluted her.

Her father-in-law came forward to explain. "Mary, I know you don't want to go through this again, but this group was in Iraq with Allen. They all knew him well, and wanted to share some stories with you. Then tomorrow, they'll be back in work clothes with tools to repair things in the house that Allen would have done for you. These men are tough and won't take no for an answer."

By this time, she was in tears, and tried to say something in response. Before she could regain her composure, each soldier came up, shook her hand, and marched into the house. When the last one had passed through the door, she turned to her father-in-law. "I love you, Dad. Thank you so much for bringing them."

Henry and Buck deplaned in Loreto and were now standing

in front of their dive shop. They were about to go in, when a large Humvee drove up with four men inside. The driver got out and looked at them. "Are you Buck and Henry?" They were almost afraid to answer, but they nodded.

"My team is here to help you with the preparations for sinking your second shipwreck. The destroyer will arrive in a week, and my team will sink it and make it safe for diving. While we're waiting for it to arrive, our orders are to finish making the other wreck safe for scuba divers."

The man continued. "A second truck is following behind us, carrying fifty sets of brand new Oceanic dive gear for your rental department. Curt asked that you destroy everything else in your shop, because most of it is unsafe."

The man turned to go, but then did an about face. "There's just one other thing. A generous donation in your behalf has been made to the local police station. I think they'll be very helpful to you in the future."

Buck and Henry looked at each other and just laughed, saying, "Curt strikes again."

The young blonde watched the TV news report on Curt Towers. She couldn't believe what she was seeing. He was the man who had saved her in the desert. She remembered his mentioning that she and his wife had the same name. It was so sad, hearing about her dying like that.

Cindy had just finished ironing the last shirt, when the doorbell rang. It was a salesman, but before she could tell him to get lost, he held up a set of car keys.

"Ma'am, these are for you. The car is paid in full, including insurance and all taxes. Curt says to enjoy."

She looked out at the car. It was a fancy red sports car worth at least sixty thousand dollars. A second car drove up and the man who had dropped off the keys got inside. She looked at the new car in a bit of a daze and said aloud, "Well; I'll be damned. Thank you, Curt."

Wilton Ramirez ambled toward the front of his church, busily cleaning each pew. He'd heard about Curt Towers and felt proud that he had been instrumental in helping him escape from Alex's hit men.

One of his last chores was to count the change in the offering box and take it to the bank. There had been times when he could go for weeks before there was even enough worth depositing. Today didn't look any better, except, there was a white envelope with his name on it. He tore it open and gawked at the contents. He had to sit down and take a deep breath. Inside were two checks, each made out to the church for one million dollars. The typed instructions indicated that one million was for an abuse center, which came complete with lawyers and counselors. The second check was a slush fund for the church, for whatever Will deemed necessary. He looked up to the ceiling and prayed aloud, "Thank you, God, for pointing him my way."

Curt and his sister Kendra had set aside this evening to talk to his children. Kendra agreed to cook everyone's favorite food and then leave them alone. The three kids had already figured out that something was up. After dinner was finished, he asked them to come and sit quietly with him in the living room. Curt realized that this was going to be difficult.

"First of all," he said, "I know the three of you have had a very tough time of it all, and I wish things could have been different. Your mother loved you very much. She's one of the bravest people I have ever known. She saved my life and yours. We can never forget her or what she did for her family."

He paused to gather his wits. "Now I need a big favor from you. My company is in a mess right now, and I have to do many things to fix it. Kendra has agreed to keep you here until we can find a new house. I've already scheduled a moving company to transport all your things tomorrow.

"I need you all to be brave," he said. "When I get things worked out with my company, I'm going to make Peter Harden president. You remember him; he's the one who worked on the subs. He is going to run the company for now, because I'm turning the company over to each of you on your twenty-first birthdays."

Curt swallowed for a second and took a deep breath. "I've also decided to do something different with my life. I'm going down to Mexico to visit a friend I knew when I was growing up."

"You mean Bonnie?" said John.

This was going to be harder than he thought. "How do you know about Bonnie?"

Lisa, the oldest piped up before John could blurt out the answer. "Dad, we may be kids, but we do understand some things. Aunt Kendra told us about your friend Bonnie. She saved your life, just like Mom did."

"Yes, Bonnie was a good friend when I was growing up, and she did save my life in Mexico. We have renewed our friendship again. So, how do I say this without upsetting you kids?"

"Do you really like her, Dad?" said Lisa.

"Yes, I do. I know that no one can replace your mother, but I need new friends. So all I ask is that you keep an open mind when you meet her. It won't be right away, because I still have problems to fix here, but I want you all to come to Mexico. Is that a deal?"

All three agreed, jumped up and acted as though there was nothing special about this family meeting. Curt was sure they were just too young to truly understand what he was trying to say.

Chapter 76

Bonnie got up early because she had a full day ahead. She had two sick cows and a goat that refused to eat anything. By noon, she was exhausted. As she was about to go into her cabin, she spotted one of the children running down the path that led to the cenote. The children all knew the rules that the cenote was off limits, so she followed him.

The boy stopped at the trails' entrance and looked back at her. As soon as their eyes met, he sped off again. She panicked thinking he could fall in and drown. She dropped her medical supplies and ran, following the winding pathway until she arrived at the cenote. She heard a rustling sound from behind her and saw the child returning to the village. Somehow, he circled back and gotten around her.

She looked back at the cenote. There was a pink rope tied to a small tree at the edge, and it trailed off into the deep water. She was curious as to what shenanigans these kids had been up to, so she reached down and tugged on the long rope. She pulled it up until a small bag tied to the end appeared at the edge of the rocks. She bent down, untied the pouch, and found a black case inside. It contained a shiny wedding ring with a note that read, *Would you marry me?*

Bonnie excitedly turned around to face Curt. He took her eagerly into his arms and kissed her, showing her the measure of his love. When the kiss ended, she simply said, "Yes, of course I will, but what took you so long?"

The two sat down together on the log, and he kissed her again. He held her hand and lightly slipped the ring on her finger. "Bonnie, I'm sorry, but I had a lot of unfinished business. No worries now because I have just one thing left to do, and it's going to take me the rest of my ninth life."

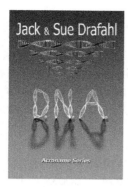

Next book in the Acroname Series

D.N.A.
By Jack and Sue Drafahl

Fifty-five-year-old police detective Frank Ridge has hit a slump in his career. A recent homicide case is botched, and Frank is blamed for not keeping up with crime scene technology. To rectify the situation, he enlists the help of Dennis Andrews, a young CSI military scientist who is fascinated with all the latest technologies. Dennis has created a new device that quickly analyzes DNA samples at the molecular level, without damaging or even touching the samples.

The two crimefighters initially start working together solving virtually impossible cold cases. Everything seems to be going well, but eventually the two are under fire from government officials who would like to see the DNA device disappear, along with the dynamic duo. To further complicate matters, a cold-blooded killer in a botched murder scheme has decided that Frank is to blame for all his legal problems, and is hell-bent to make him pay. Frank and Dennis become moving targets as they continue their insatiable quest to solve cold cases.

Other books by Jack & Sue Drafahl

Jack and Sue Drafahl are a husband and wife writing team. For almost fifty years, they have written over 800 articles in sixteen national publications from *Petersen's Photographic* to *Skin Diver Magazine*.

They have also authored seven non-fiction technical books for Amherst Media on various aspects of photography, both topside and underwater.

In 2006, they changed the course of their writing to include fiction. They have written three book series; (the *Acroname* series, the *Ship* series, and the *Time & Space* series) that currently include seventeen novels that span the gamut of genres from Action/Adventure to Science Fiction.

They both received their scuba diving certification in the early '70s, and have logged over ten thousand dives in almost every ocean on earth. Jack and Sue were awarded Divers of the Year from Beneath the Sea in 1996, and were given the Accolade Award for their conservation efforts. Sue is an inaugural member of the Women Divers Hall of Fame (2000) and is an Honorary Trustee. They are members of the Pacific Northwest Writers Association.

Jack and Sue make their home on the Oregon coast. In addition to their book-writing, they enjoy leading underwater photo expeditions around the globe. Send any comments or errors you may find to: novels@jackandsue.com.

http://www.JackandSueDrafahl.com
http://www.EarthSeaPublishing.com

Made in the USA
Middletown, DE
21 February 2022